Roguish. Reckless. Unreliable.

Raff Pineda has a certain reputation among the Animari. He's the one to call if there's a party starting, not the man to rely on when all hell breaks loose. Though he's nominally the leader of the Pine Ridge pack, he defers to his second on the tough calls. Raff prefers to live fast and hard and keep his heart hidden, but a certain Eldritch princess won't fall for his usual tricks, and their contract political marriage may be anything but convenient.

Ambitious. Elegant. Isolated.

Princess Thalia Talfayen may not have been raised by a witch in a tower, but she's spent the last few decades locked up for a failed insurrection. Plotting and scheming come naturally to her; personal connections do not. Since she's come this far in her unstoppable quest to claim the silver throne, she won't hesitate to do whatever it takes to unite her people, even if that means giving herself to the big bad wolf...

THE WOLF LORD

Ann Aguirre

For Suleikha Snyder
Who writes beautiful books
And still finds time to read mine.

Acknowledgments

I wish I could download books directly from my brain, but alas, making words takes time. Thanks so much for waiting eagerly to receive Raff and Thalia's story.

First, thanks to Karen Alderman, Fedora Chen, and Pamela Webb-Elliot for sticking with me through so many books. I also appreciate Rachel Caine, Bree Bridges, Melissa Blue, Kate Elliott, Suleikha Snyder, and Charlotte Stein for offering moral support, kindness, and humor during one devil of a year. Thank you to all my readers and anyone who's enthusiastically recommended these books to others, such as Patrick Weekes.

Kanaxa also merits special mention as the artist who packages my books so beautifully, even when the ask seems impossible. My editor, Victoria West, needs a thank-you, as well, since she polishes my prose so well. Thanks to Lillie for the fantastic proofreading. I couldn't do this without the whole team.

Finally, thanks to my family, who are only a little jealous that I have a special office mini-fridge stocked with juice boxes, string cheese, and pudding. My son, Alek, helped me a lot in working out the plot for this book; he's a fantastic listener and he always comes up with great solutions. The action scenes often contain his ideas!

Please enjoy this story and look forward to the rest. We're halfway there; thanks for sticking with me. If you're wondering whether there will be more books—more couples—after the planned six-book series ends, that depends on you, dear reader. Keep talking about these stories and let it be so!

The Story So Far...

In *The Leopard King*, Latent shifter Pru Bristow went after the pride leader, Dominic Asher, who had holed up at the seer's retreat after the death of his wife, also Pru's best friend. With the conclave approaching, Ash Valley couldn't afford to let Dom's second, Slay, run the show. It was rocky going, and they were attacked by Eldritch assassins. In the furious fight that followed, Pru finally shifted and saved Dom's life.

In time, she convinced Dom to come back to Ash Valley because the fate of the pride rested on completing the conclave and renewing the Pax Protocols (a peace treaty between supernatural communities). Her success didn't come without a cost, however. She agreed to become Dom's mate and lead the pride alongside him.

Their return startled a lot of people, Slay most of all, because he'd always thought that Pru would wait for him forever. Since he didn't want her when she couldn't shift, she didn't want him once she could, and Pru devoted herself to working with Dom to make the conclave go smoothly.

That wasn't in the cards. Though the attendants all arrived safely, the Pine Ridge wolf pack and the Burnt Amber bear clan hated Lord Talfayen of the Eldritch, and nobody knew what to make of Prince Alastor of the Golgoth. Everything that could go wrong, did, including the murder of an Eldritch envoy. Talks broke down, culminating in treachery, but the Eldritch Lord's plot went awry, as the bombs he'd set detonated too soon, catching his own people in the trap. King Tycho of the Golgoth attacked thereafter and it was all Ash Valley could do to hold.

Meanwhile, Dom and Pru tried to keep things together while falling in love. They did battle with their enemies and each other, before eventually admitting their true feelings. Slay vanished mysteriously and the leading couple finally had a wedding party, once Ash Valley was safe. Soon after, the visiting dignitaries departed, and the Numina prepared for war.

In *The Demon Prince*, Dr. Sheyla Halek reluctantly agreed to take charge of Prince Alastor Vega and work on synthesizing the medicine he needed for his rare illness. Since she preferred research to treating actual patients anyway, she didn't hate the idea, but she was quite annoyed to be saddled with someone she considered an enemy. For his part, Prince Alastor liked the prickly doctor at once and spent a good deal of his time trying to charm her.

They left Ash Valley together—with her ostensibly in the role of company medic—and became closer through an arduous journey to Tycho's likely next target: the unprotected city of Hallowell. Alastor tried his best to woo Sheyla, and while she wasn't susceptible to his brand of charm, she did admire his determination to do the right thing for his people. Slowly, they drew together, because he understood her, and she—without realizing it—quietly partook of Golgoth courtship rites.

Eventually, they decided to embark upon a wartime romance because their passion could no longer be denied. They'd only stay together until Hallowell was safe. Afterward, they'd go their separate ways, because Sheyla belonged in Ash Valley, and Alastor had heavy responsibilities to his people. Since she couldn't have a relationship, even a brief one, with a patient in her care, Sheyla turned treatment over to a colleague and focused on researching Alastor's medicine.

Neither one cared to admit how deeply they'd fallen for one another, and the risky romance only intensified, set against the backdrop of impending doom. When Tycho's forces invaded, it seemed like all might be lost, but Alastor eventually won against incredible odds, mounting a successful defense of a critical foothold in the war effort, though not without painful loss and sacrifice. He also secured the allegiance of Tycho's surviving forces, which was when Sheyla left him, as per their original agreement.

Realizing he couldn't live without her, Alastor chased her down and officially proposed in front of her family, offering to make her his queen once he liberated Golgerra. Though her relatives were skeptical at first, eventually they agreed, and the demon prince was set to live happily ever after with his physician-queen. This decision meant rejecting other marital offers, however, which would have a fascinating impact on the war effort elsewhere...

1.

PRINCESS THALIA TALFAYEN loathed scoundrels, but she might marry one. She stared at the dossier before her and then glanced up at her aide. "Is there truly no hope for an alliance elsewhere?"

Lileth had been with her since birth, sharing her incarceration when Thalia proved resistant to her father's agenda, and now, sharing her rise to power in the rebellion as well. She was a slight woman with fair hair and green eyes, average appearance matched with superior intellect and near infinite patience. Therefore, she didn't even sigh over the repetition of the question.

"Prince Alastor has declined your offer and chosen a low-ranking female from the Ash Valley pride. She's also a doctor so this may be a more politic maneuver than it first seems, as our agents inform me that he has an incurable illness."

The important part of that report was the firm rejection. She didn't *want* to marry into a dynasty of demon-kin, but she was prepared to do whatever she must to consolidate her hold on Eldritch leadership. There hadn't been a true king or queen in eons, only petty backbiting between the

four houses. Her family had the strongest claim to the
succession, however, and she meant to bring back the days
when each house pledged to a single ruler or die trying.

Accomplishing that goal wouldn't be easy without the
Golgoth playing the enforcer's role, and in the centuries her
people had remained so insular, they'd also lost the
technological edge to the Animari. Thalia had no access to
heavy weapons such as the rest of the Numina could mount,
which meant that if it came to a siege, her people would be
slaughtered. *I can't let that happen.*

"Understood. Then what about Burnt Amber?" On the
surface, the bears were no different than the wolf pack, but
the bear clan heir seemed far more serious, a better match
for her in terms of temperament.

"Shall I read the official response?" By the twitch of
Lileth's mouth, she found the verbiage amusing.

"Please," Thalia invited.

"'Tell the woman that I'm a sodding *monk*. Then ask if
she knows what that means. My cousin is my heir, and he's
married with five cubs. My line is secure, and I don't have
time for this shit.'"

She didn't laugh, though it was a near thing. "Has he
never heard of a marriage of convenience? I don't remember
demanding bedsport in my offer."

"St. Casimir is a...bachelor order. They forswear *all*
worldly pleasures, all bonds save those of brotherhood."

"I see. That does, indeed, leave only Raff Pineda."

"Or his second," Lileth said.

Thalia considered for a few seconds. From what she
knew of Korin, the woman would likely be a better fit in
terms of personality. Then, regretfully, she weighed the rest
of the factors and shook her head. "If I'm undertaking this

endeavor, I will acquire all possible leverage from the alliance."

"Yes, yes, you're far too important to waste yourself on a mere lieutenant."

There was no doubt that Lileth was mocking her, but Thalia ignored the provocation. A lifetime of such gibes had rendered her composure nearly inviolable through mere words. She hadn't even wept when Noxblades carried word that her father was dead, a mercy killing on the cat king's sword, and her eyes remained dry when she heard that it was her father's agents who had set timed charges in Ash Valley to destroy eons of peace in a fiery cataclysm.

That is my legacy.

Unless she could unite the Eldritch, she would be remembered as a traitor's daughter, and already, the other three houses were moving against her. To secure her hold and take the throne as none had managed to do in centuries, she would need outside help. Unlike other aspirants, she was willing to do whatever was required.

Even barter herself in marriage to a complete reprobate.

Thalia squared her shoulders. "Send a message to the wolf lord. Use the formal stationery and invite him to our holdings."

"I assume you'd like calligraphy as well," Lileth said.

"Of course. If the realm wasn't so dangerous, I'd dispatch a messenger in livery for full impact, but we can't risk our personnel recklessly. Write the message and then take a picture and send it. He'll grasp the gravitas."

"Are you sure?"

Even if Pineda understood the long tradition behind this choice of approach, he'd probably be amused rather than moved to reply in kind. "Perhaps not."

Skimming the data file, she saw that Raff Pineda was just shy of sixty, young middle age for an Animari. *Hardly more than a baby, here.* Those under fifty were children among her people, so it was novel to entertain the idea of offering for someone so young, but then, the Golgoth prince was a fetus in comparison.

She had questions, logistical ones, primarily. *If he accepts, will I be expected to bear him an heir? If that's even possible?* Ultimately, there was no point in wondering about theoretical issues when she had so many problems already demanding attention.

Thalia closed the dossier. "Has Gavriel returned from Hallowell yet?"

"Early this morning. His casualties were grievous."

"How many did we lose?"

"All but three."

"Gavriel, and who else survived?"

"Tirael and Ferith."

Her heart sank when Zan wasn't named. Like Gavriel, he had been a close friend and her strongest supporter, even when she was too young to understand the sort of choices she would be forced to make for greater good. Thalia didn't show grief; perforce, her features had become a placid lake over long years of training. To show her emotions was to offer a weakness that could be exploited. It didn't matter that she was alone with Lileth or appeared to be. Nowhere was safe if *any* of her father's loyalists remained at large.

"Did they see to the final rites?" she asked quietly.

"In Hallowell, yes. Apparently, the service for our fallen was well-attended."

"Noted."

Thalia rose and would've liked to stretch her shoulders

and pop her neck, but revealing physical discomfort qualified as weakness too. The furniture in Daruvar wasn't modern or comfortable, but she had moved her forces to this fortress for a reason. Bare stone walls couldn't be camouflaged with a few tapestries here and there, and the floors were just as cold. While it was ancient and dilapidated, it was also the most defensible of her holdings. When the other houses challenged—and they would—she had sufficient numbers to bide unconquered here, even without factoring in any forces she might acquire from Pine Ridge. With proprietary wolf-tech drones, she might even go on the offensive. It was paramount to unite the Eldritch before Tycho completed his death march through Animari territory.

"Lord Pineda is known to be a man of...particular appetites," Lileth said. "Are you certain you only wish to send the written invitation and nothing more?"

That was Lil's way of correcting her when she felt Thalia was about to make a tactical error. "You make a good point. Please summon Madu and her team. I should record a personal message as well and give the wolf lord a sense of what I'm offering."

It took two hours before the stylist was satisfied with Thalia's cascade of platinum curls, pinned with fresh flowers and precious gemstones, longer for the artfully applied cosmetics, then, at last, she was laced into the ice and silver gown that befitted her status as a descendant from the lost line of Eldritch queens. Thalia studied herself in the mirror, noting the blush at cheek and lips, the shadow deftly emphasizing the curve of her breasts, before nodding briskly.

"Thank you. This should suffice as enticement."

Once the equipment was set up, she spoke directly to the camera, as if she was addressing Raff Pineda himself. "I extend my personal invitation to you and your retinue to visit Daruvar to commence talks for a marital alliance. I offer myself as potential consort to Pine Ridge, though I will not accept full title as pack mistress. In return, I extend to you all rights and privileges pursuant to consort of the Eldritch. Though you will not be a king in our lands, none but me will hold higher status. All other terms and conditions may be discussed…at your pleasure."

Lileth switched off the feed. "Well, that was…something. Should I send this?"

"Without delay," Thalia replied. "We have no time to waste."

RAFF LAUGHED SOFTLY, switching off the screen.

The would-be Eldritch queen was alluring, no doubt, and she knew it, but she possessed the icy and terrible beauty of an avalanche burying a village. He'd seen her relentlessly gunning down the enemy atop the walls in Ash Valley, as comfortable with combat as she was difficult to read. She would not make a congenial partner, and her ambitions might cost his pack more than they could afford. On the other hand, the alliance would boost Pine Ridge to undeniable strength among the Animari. If an opportunity to renegotiate the Pax Protocols came again, the talks would be held at Pine Ridge this time, not Ash Valley.

The cats had their chance. Time for this dog to have his day.

"What do you think?" he asked Korin. She had seen some hard fighting in Hallowell and his second wasn't the same. It took two tries to capture her attention and he had to repeat the question before she engaged.

"If you can stomach it, we should move forward. Our losses will be incalculable if we have no one we can rely on for reinforcements, if the worst comes to pass."

No invaders had set foot in Pine Ridge for...well, he didn't even know how long. He'd have to delve into the archives, but he guessed it would've been during the territorial wars after the humans ceded the north. It seemed unlikely that the cats or bears would go on the offensive and use the chaos to gain more ground, but without treaties in place, he couldn't risk the rest of his pack on accumulated goodwill.

"Must I put on my good pants and record a reply?"

"It would be polite, especially if you want to impress the princess with your attention to detail."

He grinned. "We both know that's not my style."

Now he had Korin's full attention. "You're going to make my life worse, aren't you?"

"That's not my intention, but it *may* be the result."

"Just tell me what you're planning," she demanded.

Raff uncoiled from his chair without answering. As he'd known she would, Korin followed him as he strode through the complex toward his personal quarters. Purposely, he quickened his pace so Korin had to chase him, which she hated. This provocation was purposeful, meant to shake her out of the depression that had gripped her since Hallowell. She'd taken the loss of their people hard; Raff did as well, but Korin saw it as a personal failure. Talking wouldn't help her. Only time could.

"Raff!" she called, as he closed the door in her face.

Magda was lounging in his favorite chair when he stepped into the sitting room. Few people saw his inner sanctum, and many would be surprised at how shabby it was: worn sofa and chairs, the brown fabric pilled and unraveling at the seams. The paintings on the wall were terrible, all originals by his grandfather, who had styled himself as an artist, usually to lure potential lovers to his bedchamber.

Raff came from a long line of rogues.

"You're leaving," Magda said.

She was the chief of security at Ash Valley, and she'd chosen to come with him to Pine Ridge—he'd hoped it meant the start of a wondrously entertaining liaison—but the woman was formidable and intrinsically gifted at shutting him down. Instead, she spent most of her time digging through his video files, searching his drone records for a clue related to their second's disappearance. Mags had been friends with Slay for a long time, so she wouldn't give up on him easily, though Raff privately thought the bastard had absconded the minute his backdoor deal with Talfayen went south. He wasn't dumb enough to say it out loud. His stomach still remembered the impact of Magda's fist from the last time he pissed her off.

"You can tell that from the way I'm putting clothes in a bag? Marvelous. I see why they put you in charge of security."

"You're such an ass," she said without rancor.

"Guilty. I suspect you already have your own sources inside Pine Ridge, however, and are merely testing whether I'll be honest. I *will* be that, my dear Magda, even if other promises are unwise."

Magda merely growled.

"Right. Well, I'm taking an honor guard to Daruvar to discuss the possibility of a marital alliance with Princess

Thalia."

"Why is she a princess when her father's title was 'Lord'?" Magda asked.

That was unexpected curiosity, but Raff answered anyway. "She means to be queen, to resurrect the defunct royal line."

"Then it's a self-assigned title," Magda said, curling her lip.

"I suspect that's the case with any monarch. They start calling themselves king or queen, and then they defend against all opposition. If they're strong enough to defeat all challengers, the claim becomes the truth."

She shot him an unreadable look. "I'm glad the Animari did away with such antiquated bullshit. It's asinine to believe that competent leadership is a quality that runs through bloodlines."

"But…once a family takes power, it's still rare for it to shift, even in our culture," Raff said gently. "A Pineda has led Pine Ridge since my great grandfather's day, and I believe it's much the same for the Ashers who lead—"

"I got it, shut up already," Mags muttered.

His point made, it seemed wise to change the subject. "You haven't told me what you've found, if anything, but it's time to make a choice. You can stay here with my blessing, accompany me to Daruvar, or return to Ash Valley."

"That's convenient. The trail points toward the El-dritch, and I'd like to dig around in their ranks, if they'll let me."

"Then I'll appoint you as my personal bodyguard, an attaché sent courtesy of Ash Valley. There should be no problem."

"Does this mean you won't be pursuing me any longer?" It was impossible to tell how she felt about that, but Raff suspected her chief emotion was relief.

Magda had proven to be a mountain he couldn't climb, not with wit, barbs, or charm. As far as he could tell, she hadn't responded to anyone's overtures in Pine Ridge, which rendered her an intriguing question mark. What would the person be like who could get through her iron walls? Raff reckoned they'd need to be either a barbarian or a thief, capable of knocking down defenses or scaling them swiftly.

"Are you disappointed?" he teased.

She almost smiled; he glimpsed the spark of it in her dark eyes, but her mouth didn't move. "Tough shit, you'll never know."

He laughed as he fastened his travel bag. "In all seriousness, I doubt the good princess and I will have the sort of relationship that requires fidelity."

With a grim sort of resignation, he could picture the formality and the endless talking, culminating in agreements and provisions, rights and responsibilities, ending in a tepid night of consummation, whereupon they would largely live their own lives apart from occasions of state. Most probably, this marriage was a good fit for him, as he'd always been easily...distracted, prone to chasing one person while another slept peacefully in his bed. Not that he ever promised anything more.

Ruefully, he touched the scar that skated over his cheekbone down into his beard. The woman had used a specially treated blade, or the wound would have healed too fast to leave a mark, a perk of Animari accelerated metabolism. As it was, it took doctors two weeks to figure out why the wound was infected and why it wouldn't close. By the time they solved the mystery, Raff had a permanent souvenir that resulted from his reputation. Ironic, since he hadn't even been guilty *that* time.

"That seems…sad," Mags said finally.

"What does?"

"That you'll never know what it's like to have a true mate. Won't you be lonely?'

He already was. It was why he was always searching for the next warm body, because nobody ever touched his heart. Raff was starting to doubt he even had one.

He forced a smile. "Going soft on me, Mags? I'll meet you out front. We're moving in an hour."

2.

"STILL NO RESPONSE from the wolves?" Thalia demanded.

Lileth shook her head. "Not yet."

Slamming her palm against the door would've been extremely satisfying, but Thalia controlled her temper. One did not acquire a reputation as an ice queen without swallowing a lot of indignation. She paced the length of the strategy room—a large chamber with gray stone walls, a cavernous hearth and rugged wood furniture—largely unchanged since her grandfather's day, except the hostile pieces on the table, told a far more disturbing story than in his time. While Tycho the Pretender's forces might be temporarily in check after the unexpected turnabout at Hallowell, she had three enemy groups moving on Daruvar. Intel indicated that the first would reach the hold in four days.

She did *not* wish to begin her rise to power besieged in her own fortress.

"This is beyond discourteous," she said softly. "We got an insulting reply from the Golgoth Prince and a terse one from the bears. But the wolf lord cannot be bothered to send a single word?"

"I'm certain he has his own challenges," Lileth answered.

It was easy for her to be placid. If Thalia failed, Lil wouldn't be beheaded for her father's treachery, her skull impaled on a pike as an example to others. Though it had been a long time since the last such barbarous display, these were brutal times. She controlled a shiver, but before she could reply, two brisk raps sounded and Gavriel let himself in.

He slid a significant look at Lileth and Thalia nodded. "Please leave us."

Considering his last report, whatever he had to say probably wouldn't brighten her day, but he had served too long and too loyally for her to dismiss a rare request for a private audience. Once Lileth had gone, the door closed behind her, Thalia gestured at the grouping of ornate crimson armchairs. "Make yourself comfortable, then talk."

Gavriel waited for her to arrange herself first and then took the seat opposite. His red eyes burned with the intensity of white-hot embers as he gazed at her. She had learned to pretend she didn't notice his unbridled fervor, so different from his customary impassivity. Thalia couldn't ask for a more reliable agent, but his adoration wouldn't help her consolidate her hold on Eldritch lands.

"You've borne enough disrespect," Gavriel said, his hands tightly laced. "Send word to House Gilbraith. They're the next strongest and can help you fight off challengers."

"Ah. You're concerned about my pride?"

To some degree, it stung being treated with such a profound lack of deference, but outside of official diplomatic events, she couldn't expect the Animari or the Golgoth to care about her rank. The cats had offered sufficient courtesy, considering the devastation in Ash Valley at the time. If her ego was so fragile that she couldn't accept that war brought additional friction, then she had no business trying to lead the Eldritch.

Gavriel bit his lip, visibly choking back some other response. "Not as such."

Not my pride. My feelings. He's worried I'll be hurt.

"It's not time to contact House Gilbraith." If Thalia married Ruark Gilbraith, she wouldn't be queen in her own right, and she wasn't ready to accept less. "I haven't completely given up hope of an external alliance."

One that would tip the balance in her favor, ideally.

He stared at her, all seething injury, and that set a pang of guilt through her. In her service, he'd lost so much: brother, best friend, most of his sword mates. She couldn't offer what he truly wanted, however, and any other comfort would be hollow.

"Do you honestly think outsiders will be of any real help?" he snapped.

This was the sharpest he'd ever been with her, and Thalia flattened her surprise into chilling reproach. "Perhaps I've been lax in allowing you to speak your mind too often."

Wounded, he fell quiet, and she could *see* him wrestling with the desire to confess. Gavriel was about to place his heart at her feet and if he did, she would lose him entirely. Nobody could stand to continue working closely with the person who stomped all over their private affections. She pretended she didn't see that warmth about to boil over.

Standing, she folded her arms, staring down at him. "Noxblade, is it your place to question my decisions?"

Gavriel gazed up at her incredulously for a few seconds

longer, then he broke eye contact first. "No, my queen."

"While I appreciate your service, *I* will decide what is best. If you have nothing further to report, you are dismissed."

A long tense moment passed before he sighed and stood up. Thalia had feared he might speak from the heart despite her discouragement. It was sad and tiring to pretend that she didn't know how he felt, but she would never be free to fall in love like a regular person. Her associations would always be weighed like she was purchasing supplies in bulk at the market.

"Unless you need me, I'll be scouting."

In his current frame of mind, that probably wasn't the best choice. Gavriel wanted to fight, and Thalia wasn't certain he cared if he won. Under those circumstances, she couldn't let him go.

"Permission denied. Right now, you need to rest and recover from your ordeal in Hallowell."

His jaw clenched on what she guessed was a protest. "I'm well enough."

"How long has it been since you slept?" she asked.

"Irrelevant."

"Since you can't or won't answer, my orders stand. Don't test me, Gavriel. I'm in no mood. Keep poking at me and I'll assign you to the archives."

Shocked, he eyed her with fresh wariness. "You wouldn't."

"I admit, it would be a waste of your talents, but at least I know you won't get yourself killed out of grief."

Gavriel stiffened, shoulders squaring. "I'm mortified that you would entertain that as even a passing thought. Whatever my emotional state, I will never willingly abandon you, my queen."

That's part of the problem.

"I'm glad to hear it," she said briskly, "but you still need to sleep and eat. Once Dr. Wyeth has cleared you for duty, you can return to the field."

She strode over to the door, throwing it open as a clear sign of dismissal. Gavriel left without protest, and Lil stepped in with an inquiring look. "Trouble?"

"Nothing I couldn't handle. He thinks we should give up on the idea of an external marital alliance." While she wasn't ready to surrender all hope, she had to admit that the prospects were grim.

"Do you have a secondary scheme?"

"Scheme is such an ugly word," Thalia said, smiling.

"I'll take that as confirmation. Gavriel would recommend that course even if your prospects were excellent, however. He hates outsiders as much as he lo—"

"Enough," she cut in.

She left the strategy room, irritated with both Lileth and Gavriel. Lil enjoyed needling her and after everything he'd suffered, Gavriel appeared to be ready to snap. She sympathized with him, and the orders she'd given regarding the leopard king in exile haunted her to this day. Sometimes the doubts grew teeth and chewed at her, whispering that since she'd already allowed her people to be killed at the retreat and permitted her father to unleash so much devastation, maybe she should—

No. Quitting wasn't an option. It never would be. She hadn't spent a decade locked away at Riverwind to turn tail now. Thalia passed through Daruvar, her footsteps echoing on the ancient stones. Occasionally she received a scrambled bow by a staffer startled to find her proceeding alone.

In her private quarters, she found messages waiting from two scouts in the field, footage to sort through from patrol drones, and an apology from the bear clan lieutenant. Still nothing from the cursed wolves. Sighing, she replied with orders, spent two hours scanning video, and then answered politely to the overture from the bears. While the marriage wasn't happening, it served no purpose to burn bridges.

Just then, her phone pinged with an urgent-coded message and Gavriel's face popped up. "We have movement on the border. Come to the battlements straightaway."

DARUVAR SAT PROUDLY atop the cliff known as Widow's Watch. This was a keep in every sense of the word with defenders on the ramparts, ready for action. Watchmen with silver lights also stood guard in each of the four towers, built at points north, south, east, and west. There would be a courtyard inside, Raff guessed, and a warren of corridors and secret chambers. The place must be drafty as hell, built from gray and crumbling stones no doubt quarried nearby and built by ancestors Thalia could recite by name.

Few modern amenities.

With a sheer, impassable rock face behind, crashing water below, Raff understood why the Eldritch princess had chosen to make her stand here. There was only one approach, and Eldritch scouts had been surveilling his group for several hours, keeping them under close watch. They had been traveling without urgency, breaking the journey into two days, because the roads were old and poorly maintained, jouncing his party until even Mags swore through clacking teeth.

"We're almost there," he said, stifling a smile.

"Don't smirk at me, wolf."

"Wouldn't dream of it."

At the top of the steep incline, the cracked asphalt simply stopped, yielding to loose gravel, which in turn ended in Daruvar's walls, perforated liberally with artillery slits. There was a single gate of black iron, scored from old battles and rusted where it had been damaged. The Rover juddered to a stop and Raff didn't wait for the all-clear. If Thalia opened fire, that meant the marriage was off.

He vaulted down and keyed her code into his phone. "The wolf is at your door, Lady Silver. Will you let him in?"

Thalia made a choked noise. The call dropped without the Eldritch woman speaking a word to him, and from somewhere behind him, Mags groaned, almost loud enough to challenge the grind of gears as the gates opened. The doors were wide enough to permit their vehicles to pass inside to the inner bailey, a crisscross of green and pavement. After they parked, the doors shut with a final-sounding clang. Though it was near dusk, no electric lights dispelled the darkness, just the flicker of portable solar lanterns.

"Not my best line?" he asked, grinning at Mags.

"Probably among your five worst."

"But the gates opened nonetheless. Should we wait for the welcome party?"

"Don't expect champagne," she muttered.

Raff hadn't liked leaving Korin on her own so soon after their losses at Hallowell, but he couldn't afford to have all wolf leadership away from Pine Ridge at this critical time, and he shouldn't need his second to complete a courtship mission that was more of a corporate merger. The time he spent here might be tedious, but it should strengthen Pine Ridge for the battles to come.

He milled around with the rest of his small entourage, no more than five minutes before Thalia appeared in black trousers and matching belted jacket. Her hair was twisted in a careless updo and atop that, she wore a winter cap. Currently, she looked more like a spy than a princess, and the idea kindled his imagination.

"Sorry to keep you standing in the cold," Thalia said. "But unfortunately, I had no notice of your arrival. Perhaps your response was lost in the ether?"

"I wanted to surprise you, but somehow you seem less than delighted. Don't you enjoy the unexpected, Lady Silver?"

"Not even a little." Her eyes pierced him, sparks of ire not shown in her buttery voice. "Come inside. I've requested that they lay the table for guests, but I fear you may find our hospitality wanting due to lack of preparation."

She's testy. This will be fun.

"I did note the lack of dried herbs and wreaths, there's no quartet caroling best wishes for our health and prosperity, and you haven't spoken a single ceremonial word in greeting."

Thalia paused. "Since this isn't an occasion of state, I didn't think you would wish to participate in the formal rite of hearth and home."

In fact, she looked a little surprised that he even knew about it. Raff figured that he probably should be offended, but it was so much fun to bait her that he decided not to pursue the issue. "It's fine. I know my part by heart, though. I'm not quite the barbarian that you seem to suppose."

Her fair cheeks pinked, though that might be the icy wind. "This way, then. It won't do to keep your people standing in the weather."

Winter's grasp had been broken, but the full bloom of spring was still weeks away. Since Daruvar stood poised between sea and sky in the foothills, it felt colder here than it did in the well-forested basin that Raff called home. Eventually, these fierce slopes would be covered in yellow and purple wildflowers, but he likely wouldn't be here that long. A few days, a week at most, and he should be able to melt the ice off Princess Thalia enough to get her to agree to his terms.

The wolves followed her small party across the courtyard and through an open arch that led into a dark corridor. There were niches with broken cables and dead bulbs, stacked crates full of supplies, and a constant parade of Eldritch warriors giving him the death stare. Raff ignored the chill atmosphere, keeping pace until they went up a couple of flights, stepped into another hallway—this one better lit—which opened into a salon decorated in what had surely been the latest style, two hundred years ago.

He took in handwoven rugs in red and gold abstract patterns, furniture that was solidly built as if to survive a shelling, covered with shiny, tasseled cushions. A long table dominated the space, ornate carvings of flowering vines on the legs, and the solar lamps were dim, lending the room a faintly sinister air. The food looked good, and they had been traveling long enough that he appreciated that she wasn't forcing a lot of officious nonsense on his tired, hungry team.

"Please, be seated," Thalia invited.

Raff wasted no time in accepting the offer. He couldn't recall if any of his predecessors had ever dined with the

Eldritch outside of the Pax Protocols. History wasn't his strong point; in fact, he'd hated books, not least because they made him feel stupid and inadequate. At every opportunity, he'd ditched his tutors, skipped out on classes, and spent as much time as he could in the wild, even before he learned to shift.

Once Raff was settled, his small entourage took their places beside him, leaving Thalia to sit opposite. Mags waited until everyone was seated, a move he read as a precaution in case someone tried something. If anyone came at him inside Daruvar, though, it wouldn't be with violence. The Eldritch were known to be cunning poisoners, so he might never see death coming.

Hopefully I'll smell it.

The food was simpler than it would've been, had he sent word of his intention: steamed vegetables and hastily grilled fish. For the Eldritch, there were also platters of fruit and cheese, raw greens tossed in oil. No fancy sauces or long-simmered nut and bean soups with complex layers of flavor. If memory served, many of the Eldritch were vegetarians or if not, they ate what could be pulled from the sea.

"Will you speak a blessing?" Thalia asked.

The woman to her left, venerable in age if Raff was any judge, curled her mouth slightly in dubious amusement. *Does she think we're heathens?* Lord Talfayen had certainly considered the Animari little more than beasts. If such prejudice persisted in his daughter or her people, this alliance was doomed.

"Dear Mother, watch and guard us from harm. Keep us from our enemies and help us walk your path. For the bounty we are about to receive, I bless and thank you."

"Well-spoken," the elder Eldritch woman said with a touch of surprise. "You have something of a silver tongue, a rare gift."

Raff smiled. "You haven't seen anything yet."

3.

AGAINST ALL ODDS, dinner progressed smoothly. The wolf lord was good at keeping the conversation moving without lingering too long on subjects painful and awkward. Judging from Lileth's surprised expression, she seemed to find him improbably charming. Thalia said only enough to be polite, instead observing interactions between her guests. There were six of them: Raff Pineda, Magda Versai, and four other wolves, whose first names she memorized dutifully—Janek, Tavros, Bibi, Skylett.

Janek was a tall, venerable wolf with weathered skin, silver hair, and a neatly trimmed goatee while Tavros radiated a youthful charm, tousled brown hair and wide gray eyes, slight of build and perpetually interested in everything. As for Bibi, she was a tall brunette with hazelnut eyes and golden skin. Sky stood no taller than Thalia, but her onyx curls made her memorable, especially when paired with tawny skin and cognac eyes. Really, the whole wolf party was quite attractive in various ways.

"Would you care for dessert or an after-dinner drink?" Thalia asked, belatedly aware that she had been studying her guests for a beat too long.

Raff shook his head. "My people are tired. They didn't rest well on the road, and we dodged a number of patrols on our way to you."

Thalia's brows shot up, but she waited until the rest of the guests filed out, Lileth shepherding them to the rooms they had been assigned. Once the two of them were alone, Thalia started to ask, "Are there Golgoth this far—"

"Eldritch. But we had no way of knowing what allegiance those scouts had, and it seemed best not to engage."

Unease prickled along her spine, dispelling the momentary comfort created by a decent meal and affable conversation. "What route did you take into the foothills?"

"Through Velder's Pass."

Thalia nodded. "How many groups?"

"Five, two close to Daruvar."

"Those were probably my people, but it was wise to avoid them. We didn't have word that you were incoming, and it might have escalated. We've gone wrong that way before." The rest of the troops, she had known were moving on Daruvar, but the arrival of the wolves changed things significantly.

"You mean when you attacked the cat king in exile?"

"It wasn't an attack!" This was a sore point, and she'd already apologized to Gavriel until her throat was raw. Only a not-so-secret love had paved the way to his continued service; she was less sure if he'd forgiven her. It also pissed her off that this bastard could refer to a personal failure so casually.

"That may not be how you meant things to go, but that's how it ended up," Raff said. "You don't win points for good intentions."

She set her teeth, so it was tough to get the words out.

"I don't require your advice."

"I can tell it's a touchy subject, so never mind. Can you show me to my room?"

She choked back the words 'if you'd gone with Lileth, I wouldn't have to' and offered a cordial nod. "This way, please."

An awkward silence fell as she left the dining hall and guided him through the stone hallways. Raff rubbed his hands over his arms. "Damn chilly. I should go wolf."

"Do as you please," she muttered. "Here we are." Thalia threw open the door and swept an arm, indicating the room, already lit with solar lamps. "If you're cold, I can have a fire lit in the hearth."

"How delightfully archaic, but I can build my own blaze, should I desire one." The wolf sent her a look that she gathered was meant to be seductive.

She ignored the innuendo. "I suppose you should know something about woodcraft. Good night, then."

Thalia left without looking back and by the time she got to her room, Lileth was there waiting for her. "It's a good thing the wolves didn't bring more honor guards," she said.

"Did everyone seem comfortable enough?" Half of Daruvar wasn't fit for habitation, but she wouldn't have it said that Eldritch hospitality was lacking, even under such haphazard circumstances.

Lil hesitated. "I had to send four of their folks to the barracks. Be prepared to hear complaints in the morning."

A strain of bias ran through her people, and some of them looked down on the Animari. She had to make it clear that she would give no space to such sentiments. While she wished she had a better solution than Raff Pineda, that was a personality preference. Under ideal circumstances, she would choose someone measured and rational, not a hot-tempered scoundrel. His attachment to Magda Versai hadn't escaped her notice, either.

Already she had questions; those two were close in Ash Valley and it was impossible not to wonder if Magda was the mistress she would contend with long-term, provided this marriage went through. Overall, it seemed more probable that the woman was the first of many, as the wolf lord didn't seem like the loyal sort. Their relationship would likely be for show, displayed primarily on formal occasions. A pang went through her, a fleeting wish that things could be different, but Thalia shook her head, putting the issue aside. She didn't need fidelity as part of their arrangement.

Still, she fought a tide of weariness as she said, "I always am. It all worked out, at least."

Lil always saw more than she let on. Her neutral response revealed none of her private conclusions. "You should get some rest. It will be a long day tomorrow."

Normally, she would ignore such suggestions and work until her eyes shut at her desk, but Lileth had a point. She needed to be both clearheaded and charming when she took Raff on a tour of the fortress first thing the next morning. Her aide had already put together a sample schedule of how she could best dedicate her time before they settled into the serious business of negotiating the marriage contract.

Thalia muttered an assent as Lileth left her quarters. The room still didn't feel familiar, as she hadn't been staying here long, and the gray stones held fast to the last of winter's chill, despite spring relative proximity. She threw the heavy maroon curtains wide to let in a faint trickle of moonlight and for a moment, she stared up at the starry sky. Thalia knew she shouldn't be weary so early in the game, but she had been fighting silently, slowly, for decades already.

Her heart ached too; there had been no opportunity to mourn her father's death. Her followers wouldn't understand that even if he had been venal and wrong, he'd still given her life, and before he passed the point of no return, he'd taught her to play Kingcross and always read epic poems aloud at her bedside when she couldn't sleep. Now, he was known as the maniac who had betrayed his people, the Pax Protocols, and allied with a murderous despot, killing his own in the process. Thalia might never be able to overcome that legacy because the Eldritch had long memories.

Sighing, she changed into her pajamas—utilitarian blue cotton that might surprise anyone who expected greater elegance—when a soft tap sounded. Thalia opened the door, expecting to find Gavriel with a list of issues that couldn't wait. Instead, it was Raff Pineda, leaning on the opposite wall with a bottle of wine tucked under one arm. He sauntered forward, offering a crooked smile like a flower bouquet.

"You look like you need a drink. And I owe you an apology. It's one thing to be feckless, another to be unkind."

It was impossible to be elegant or dignified in bare feet and blue pajamas, so she settled for returning an icy stare, ignoring his peace offering. "We haven't yet come to an agreement, and we are not in a relationship where such informality is permissible. Therefore, this is…" She couldn't find a word that encompassed both the audacity and impoliteness, so she settled for, "Rude."

"Lady Silver, I never would've guessed that you're such a stickler for the proprieties."

"Why do you insist on calling me that?"

"You are a lady and your hair is like molten silver," he said, sounding so reasonable that for a few seconds, Thalia felt like a dimwit for asking. Then he added with disarming perception, "Plus, I thought it might trouble you to be addressed by your surname."

Damn it, he was right. Until she redeemed House Talfayen, she certainly didn't want to hear the name on anyone's lips. "You may call me Princess Thalia."

A smirk curled his mouth as he ambled past her into the bedroom. "Who's crowned you? Isn't that why you want an alliance with Pine Ridge?"

Her weariness evaporated in a burst of iridescent anger. With a muffled snarl, she snatched the wine bottle and slammed the door behind him. "By all means, let's drink."

THE ELDRITCH PRINCESS'S room was impersonal, devoid of mementos. As Raff understood, she had led a failed rebellion against her father decades ago, and since then, Lord Talfayen had kept her in seclusion. Even that hadn't stopped her from exerting tendrils of influence. That took a level of determination that he would be a fool to disregard. This woman could be his chief ally or his greatest enemy.

Time to make an effort.

He pulled the corkscrew from his pocket and deftly twisted the cork from the wine bottle. It was a light, sweet wine he'd accepted as a gift in Ash Valley, before everything went to hell. It seemed like a melancholy moment, cracking this bottle open and drinking down the fermented fruit of more peaceful times.

"Do you have glasses?" he asked.

She was annoyed, he could tell, but he had no intention

of sticking to an itinerary. If Thalia couldn't be flexible, they had no future.

In answer, she brought two ceramic mugs, one slightly chipped. "Will these do?"

"Perfectly. May I sit?"

"As if you'd listen if I said no," she muttered.

"Of course I would," he said, startled and more than slightly offended. "If you want me to leave, I'll go. Never in my life have I lingered when someone wanted me gone."

Her gaze narrowed on him for a few seconds, then she seemed to accept his sincerity. "You said you were tired earlier."

"I said my people were," Raff corrected.

"That...is true."

"Now that they're settled, we should have a private chat." He hadn't wanted to spend more time with others judging their interactions, especially that angry, red-eyed Noxblade.

"I'm willing." Her tone was a little less grudging, at least.

The furniture was more comfortable than it looked since it was sturdy wood topped with cushions. Raff settled on the bench opposite and poured two mugs of Ash Valley Moscato. He liked the look of Thalia a bit more in the warm solar glow, her hair spilling like mercury over narrow shoulders. Even the blue pajamas suited her, tailored and crisp, a trifle too long so that the piped hem came down nearly to her toes. She sat like a child, curling her legs to the side. It was difficult to grapple with the fact that she was so much older and would live for many years after he was gone, unless she overused her gift.

"In such weather, we should mull this with cinnamon

and spice," he said.

"Wouldn't red wine be better?"

"It works with white as well. To your health, Lady Silver." Raff raised his cup and she surprised him by leaning forward to clack her's against his.

"Back at you, Lord Wolf."

"Until now, the only time we've spent alone was when we were on the ramparts, with you firing like a Valkyrie. You were impressive that night."

She smiled, coolly pleased. "I would be interested in sparring with you sometime. I'll even let you choose the weapon."

"I suspect you'll have the advantage, as I've never studied any weapon. There was simply no reason."

"Oh." She looked like she'd forgotten, momentarily, that he could shift. "I'm not sure how it would work out then, if I'm fencing and you're a wolf."

"I might get skewered," he said, taking a sip.

"Or I might get badly bitten."

"Such a possibility exists."

Thalia surprised him by laughing softly. "I thought you'd swear that you'll never hurt me, that you're quite a harmless wolf."

He liked the amused light in her eyes; someone without a sense of humor would make a dismal life partner. "I'll only promise that if we come to an agreement. I'm not in the business of making vows that I won't keep."

"That's good to hear," she said.

"Shall we play a game?"

"Kingcross?" She looked so hopeful that he couldn't bring himself to say that he'd intended to suggest something else. "There's an old board around here somewhere…"

Before he could respond, she got up and rambled around the room, opening drawers here and there, until she produced a gleaming wooden box. It unfolded to reveal the bone and blood hues of an expensive antique. Something like this would be an absolute heirloom in Pine Ridge, probably displayed behind protective glass. Her careless attitude spoke volumes about how different their peoples perceived the passage of time.

With eager fingers, she set out the pieces, artfully carved from alabaster and onyx. King and Queen, Knight and Squire, Priest and Nun. "Choose your color, sir."

Raff pulled the dark pieces to his side of the board. "What else can a black wolf be?"

"Is that what you change into?" Her curiosity seemed genuine as she arranged the pale figurines on her side.

"It is."

"Is there a lot of variety among your...pack? Is that the right word?" Her expression was solemn, lending the impression that she cared about the verbiage.

"Pack is right for wolves. With the cats, it's pride, and the bears prefer clan."

"What about the birds in the Aerie? Would that be a flock?"

It was an excellent question, but he'd never actually met anyone from the reclusive avian settlement. "I presume so, but it's always best to inquire about someone's preferences to prevent giving unintentional offense."

"Wise, sensible strategy," she commended, making her first move.

Raff hadn't played much Kingcross. It required a lot of predictive reasoning, focusing on his opponent's probable maneuverings; in short, it was exactly the sort of the thing that made him edgy and gave him a headache. This was why he had Korin as his second; she excelled in this sphere, freeing him for more enjoyable endeavors.

He chose at random, hoping he remembered the directions the pieces were allowed to travel and the jumps permitted. There were so many stratagems and gambits one could memorize, and he suspected Thalia was the sort who knew them all, forward and back. Therefore, he would play to make her happy, not to win.

Maybe he could still work toward his agenda of getting to know her better. "Shall we make this more interesting?"

"How?"

Mags would have immediately told him she wasn't playing strip Kingcross and possibly threatened his life. Because the Eldritch princess seemed less aggressive, at least on the surface, he said, "The winner gets a boon."

"Anything?" Thalia asked.

"Within reason. Nothing dangerous or…illicit."

"Agreed. But I'll have you know, you will likely be the one paying the penalty."

"I'm willing," Raff said.

Through losing, he might learn a great deal about her ambitions and her secret desires. They made small talk as the match progressed. As he'd expected, she quickly outclassed him, taking his pieces with all the ferocious glee of a gaming despot. In the end, he yielded.

Thalia eyed him while claiming his king and crowning her own. "Kingcross. I've won. Rather handily, in fact. I hoped you might offer more of a challenge."

"Not at this, alas, but I did enjoy your company. What's my forfeit?"

"Answer me a question," Thalia said.

"That's all you want of me?" An unlikely development, but the fact that she wanted to know more about him, enough to wager for it, that was...intriguing. Never in Pine Ridge's history had a leader brought home an outside mate, and the pack was divided, even now, as to whether this was an advisable course. They hadn't liked his overtures to the Golgoth Prince any better, for the same reasons.

"My curiosity is intense. I asked in Ash Valley, but no one would share the story. How *did* you get that scar on your cheek?"

4.

THALIA WONDERED IF Raff would answer honestly.

This wasn't a query so much as a test. In fact, she had heard a version of the story from one of the wolves in Ash Valley, but how Raff responded should prove enlightening. He sipped at his mug of wine, probably stalling for time, then he set it on the table nearby.

"It's not a particularly interesting tale, but I'll share it if you wish."

"By all means."

"A few years past, there was a woman from one of our settlements. She came to Pine Ridge to forget the bad memories. Her mate had been taken by the Golgoth and she was wild with grief."

"Wolves mate for life?" Thalia asked.

Raff glanced at her, but she couldn't gauge his expression. His golden-brown eyes were dark like shadowed amber. "When it's a true pairing."

"What does that mean?"

He sighed a little, as if her ignorance troubled him. "Do you know anything about Animari mate bonds?"

"Not really. It isn't something I've had cause to study

before."

"Animari mate bonds form in various ways. Sometimes there's an instant spark, a moment of recognition—aha, this is the person I'm meant to be with! In other cases, love and affection grows out of friendship and respect, or from repeated sexual pairings. However, the bond begins, that connection deepens over time, as trust and intimacy build. Some mates get to the point that they can sense what their other half is thinking or feeling."

"That result is a true pairing?" It sounded enviable, but also dangerous. Thalia could imagine treachery and heartbreak from someone knowing her that well…and then informing her enemies.

Nodding, Raff went on, "If one partner passes away, the one left behind suffers. I was trying to comfort her."

"That sounds harmless enough, but you must have crossed the line. Otherwise, there would be no scar and no story."

"People don't usually come back from the Golgoth dungeons," Raff said softly. "Her mate did. And misunderstood the reasons I had my hands on the woman. She used a specially treated black iron blade on me, stolen from the Golgoth armory."

"That's why it scarred?" From what she knew, normally the Animari healed so quickly that even deep, serious wounds didn't leave a mark when they sealed.

"It is. Are you satisfied with this answer?"

"I am. It's a sad story, though."

"I don't think so. It was such an unlikely happy ending."

"Not for you," Thalia said.

Raff raised a brow, then drained the mug he had set aside. To Thalia, it looked like a bracing gesture. "You make it sound like I'm perishing of want. It wasn't like that, I assure you. I'm glad that her mate came home."

Thalia sipped her Moscato, finding the flavor sweet and delicate. "I suppose it's true that you've been chasing that ferocious tiger lady with some dedication for a while now, so the...misunderstanding that scarred your cheek can't have damaged your heart too badly."

"My heart is pristine and inviolate," Raff said.

"Should you be divulging that information? It sounds as if you're boasting that you're an immovable object."

"Does that make you an irresistible force?"

She smiled faintly. "I hope so."

"It's late now, Lady Silver. I suspect I should retire before I test the bounds of your good nature."

"I won't carve up your other cheek, even if you do. Good night, Lord Wolf."

Raff left then, abandoning the wine he'd brought. Thalia considered drinking the rest herself, but unlike the Animari, she had a normal metabolism for alcohol, and she'd likely regret that decision in the morning. Pensive, she went to bed and crawled under five layers of covers meant to keep the Daruvar chill at bay.

It has been such a strange day.

Normally, she tossed and turned, but that was her last thought before she woke to pale sunlight streaming through the narrow windows, kindling a nimbus of color from the stained glass; it spread across the floor in swirls of green and gold. The stones were like ice; Thalia danced on tiptoes until she found her slippers discarded in the corner. Lil must have come and gone because there was tea and toast on the table in her sitting room. She finished both greedily, including the whole pot of lemon jelly. This sort of thing permitted her to keep her dignity in public, so her manner could remain polite and refined.

Quickly she bathed and dressed, hurrying Madu, the dresser who wanted to spend hours on her hair. Thalia settled for a neat twist, more in keeping with the military style she'd adopted since arriving at Daruvar. Eldritch staff and Noxblades alike snapped to attention as she strode through the keep, Lil close at her heels.

"Status," she said.

"The wolves are already in the small dining hall. You have eight new reports waiting on your desk. How shall we proceed?"

"I'll breakfast with them and give them a tour of Daruvar. Late morning, you'll need to take over to give me a chance to work. Can you cobble together some quick entertainment? This rebellion won't run itself."

A deep male voice asked, "Is it a rebellion, though? To an outsider, it looks more like a civil war."

Thanks to years of training, Thalia didn't startle as Raff glided out of the shadows of an alcove near the little salon. "Is skulking a wolf specialty or a talent particular to you?"

"Six of one, half dozen of the other?" But he was smiling, unoffended by the tartness of her reply.

If she let him, he'd draw her out and make her reveal...something. She had no intention of being diverted or charmed. "Regardless, since you've separated from the pack, please do tell Lileth what your people would find entertaining."

"A hunt," he said immediately.

"Would it be enough to flush out your prey and not kill it?" Lileth asked.

From the other woman's tone, Thalia could tell she

thought their guests were barbarians. Raff was nodding. "I'm sure you've no intention to starve us, so we won't ask our hosts to slaughter the wildlife."

"Perhaps one of the drones could be turned to this purpose?" Thalia cut in. "With a prize to the one who finds it first."

Raff nodded. "I like the sound of that."

"Go on ahead, I'll notify Gavriel, so he can start the arrangements." Lileth hurried off as Thalia fell into step with Raff, who offered his arm.

"Shall I escort you in?"

It felt...momentous, somehow, to curl her fingertips against his arm. "Certainly."

His muscles were harder than she'd expected. He didn't look bulky in his clothes, but his forearms *felt* different than an Eldritch male and his body heat penetrated even through his layers of shirt and jacket. Thankfully her composure held until they reached the table, where everyone else was already assembled.

"Good morning, Lady Versai."

The head of security glared at her. "Stuff your formality. It's Magda. Or Mags."

Her mouth tightened. Etiquette existed for a reason, and it was rude to insist that someone use your first name if that relationship had yet to be established. Thalia well knew that she'd only end up looking like a hateful witch if she protested, so she kept her mouth shut and smoothed her napkin across her lap.

"I trust everyone slept well?" She made polite eye contact with the four wolf guards, who seemed ill at ease.

A chorus of 'yes, thank you' came in response as the meal began. At least some of them knew how to play the game. She'd memorized their names last night, so she tested herself mentally. *The youngest is Tavros. The oldest is Janek.* Bracketed between the male guards were two female scouts, Bibi and Skylett. While she wasn't ready to use their first names, it was courteous to recall them.

"If everyone's eaten their fill," she said eventually, "then why don't I show you around? Daruvar is *not* a place where it's safe to get lost."

THE TOUR TOOK over an hour.

Daruvar was a sprawling place with hallways that doubled back or ended suddenly in a wall of rubble. Some of the stones were loose and the paths precarious. Raff tried to remember each twist and turn, but Thalia hadn't been joking when she said it was a perilous place to lose your way. He was awed by the sheer age of this structure, but at the same time, he couldn't wait to shift and run on the hunt they'd promised later in the day.

Probably he shouldn't reveal how impatient he was this soon, but he wished they could skip straight to the negotiations. That wasn't the Eldritch way, and if he couldn't last long enough for the marriage talks to begin, he might as well go home. Still, as Lileth started yet another story regarding the founding of Daruvar, he sighed.

"You look pissed," Mags whispered.

Raff shook his head. They shouldn't talk shit right in front of their hosts, who were trying their best despite this sudden imposition. "Have you learned anything?"

She dropped her voice lower still, so he had to lean close, even with sensitive hearing. "Too soon, I think. The Eldritch are secretive, even when it comes to shit we'd consider common knowledge. Took me damn near ten minutes this morning to get the staff to tell me where the fucking bathhouse is."

"Your room doesn't have private facilities?" he asked, surprised.

They dropped a little behind the main group, dawdling to converse. It seemed like they might be retracing their steps toward the courtyard, where their Rovers were iced lightly with dew that had frozen, now melting in the late-morning light. The steps leading down had crumbled at the edges, pebbles rolling underfoot. It would be easy to stumble here in the dark.

"It's got a toilet that looks like it's a hundred years old and a sink with broken tiles. How am I supposed to wash up like that?"

He grinned. "Go cat and groom yourself."

That earned him a punch in the shoulder that nearly knocked him down, and Mags was laughing as she did it. *Probably a good thing I never bedded her. She might've killed me.*

Thalia shot him a hooded look from the front of the group as she stepped into the greensward. "That ends our tour. Please feel free to rest, join our soldiers on the training grounds, or continue your explorations, carefully. It's not safe outside these walls for obvious reasons so venture out at your own risk."

Her aide added, "We will be hunting an hour past luncheon, so if you're feeling restless, look forward to that."

Janek executed a neat bow to the older Eldritch woman. "We're worn enough from recent events and our trip here that we will enjoy the chance to catch our breath. Thank you for seeing to our amusement."

"So that's why you brought him," Mags whispered.

Janek was the oldest hunter in the pack, not as nimble as he once was, but he was the closest thing Raff had to an expert in Eldritch customs. Before, it was never an issue. The Pax Protocols existed to keep everyone in check, and even if toes got stepped on, there were no grave consequences. Nowadays a diplomatic breach could turn a casual conversation in a charnel house.

"My pleasure," Lileth was saying.

"I must excuse myself as well. Unfortunately, work requires a little of my attention, but I'll certainly join the hunt this afternoon." Thalia smiled and waved, every inch the princess, despite her utilitarian garb.

With that, the Eldritch left them in the courtyard, the first time Raff had been unattended—apart from sleep—since their arrival. Mags took off at once; he presumed she had plans to do some snooping. What she hoped to find here, he had no idea, except that it must relate to the disappearance of the Ash Valley second.

His guards exchanged looks that told him they'd rather not stick to him like gum, so he said, "Feel free to do as you wish. I'm safe enough here."

He hoped.

As soon as he split from the group and rounded a corner, someone pounced on him from behind and slammed his face into the stone. Under normal circumstances, he'd use his exceptional strength to knock this asshole across the room and then possibly bite his face off. Raff stilled instead. He recognized this scent from Ash Valley, blood and cinnamon.

"Use your words, Gavriel."

With a sibilant curse, the Noxblade released him. "I warn you, wolf. The princess is not for you. Leave this place before something worse happens."

Before he could respond, Mags was on Gavriel from behind, twisting his arm behind his back until he let out a furious cry. "I'm something worse," she whispered, right in his ear. "And Raff is under my protection."

Funny as it would be to let this situation unspool, he couldn't afford to start marital talks from a position of damage control. "Let him go. We'll use our words too, Mags."

"You brought me as your bodyguard," she said, tightening her hold.

Any more force and she'd snap the bone. While Noxblades might be tremendous assassins, they probably took weeks, not days, to heal an injury like that. Raff pried her fingers away and Gavriel stumbled back a few steps, eyes blazing hate.

"How dare you bring your mistress here!" He spat the question more like a curse, and Mags balled up a fist.

"I belong to only myself." She took a step toward Gavriel.

Raff held her back, barely. It required all his strength. "Leave us. He won't hurt me. He respects the princess far too much to violate her oath of hospitality."

Gavriel spoke through clenched teeth. "That…is true. Come with me. Now."

He followed the Noxblade to the ramparts, where a chill wind sliced through his winter woolens like frosted steel. "Go ahead, speak your warning. If I hurt her, you will poison me, so I die in slowest agony, and then you'll carve out my heart and offer it to crows and so on."

The Noxblade simply stared at him. "None of that makes any sense. Slow poison makes it more likely that you'll be caught, an antidote administered. And if you died of poison, why would I feed your heart to innocent birds?"

"You take things far too literally," Raff said, laughing. "Didn't you bring me here to threaten me?"

"Much as I would like to, there are more important matters at hand."

"Then, by all means, continue convincing me not to wed Princess Thalia."

"You take nothing seriously and you seem to care only for your own pleasure. You are no fit match for her, and you will only add to her burden in time."

Raff lost patience then, itching to plant a fist in this bastard's face. "What the hell are you even saying, man?"

"Haven't you considered at all what a disastrous mésalliance this would be? When she's still bright and beautiful, she'll be chained to you, though you'll be a doddering, toothless old hound by then."

He *had* considered the disparity in their lifespans, but he wasn't about to share his conclusions. His tone was sharp as a naked blade when he replied, "Unless she asked you to speak for her, shut the hell up. It's embarrassing to see you froth jealousy that masquerades as concern for your lady."

Gavriel fell silent, his gaze drifting over the walls and toward the cloudy horizon. "I'll say one thing more, then. She may look cold and strong, but she has been alone for most of her life, fighting harder than anyone can imagine. Please, by all the gods you hold sacred, be gentle with her."

"I will." Raff was surprised to find that he meant it.

5.

*S*EVEN REPORTS, NO *good news*.

All three houses had forces in the field, trying to discern Thalia's true strength. After what her father had done at Ash Valley, none of the great families wanted to ally with her in case she turned out to be a traitor as well. Add in the grandiose ambitions of small minds that saw this conflict as a chance to rise to power and the situation became untenable.

With a snap, she closed the final dossier and rose, popping her neck and shoulders. She only had that freedom because she was alone; Lileth would have chided her for revealing the vulnerability. It seemed like a hundred years since she'd slept soundly, more than a few hours at a time, but it was probably only ten.

Only.

The strategy room smelled faintly of smoke, as the chimney hadn't been cleaned in who knew how long. On schedule, the knock sounded at the heavy door that guarded her privacy, and then her aide stepped into the room.

"Are you ready?" Lil asked.

Thalia inclined her head. "As I shall be. Did you bring

my armor and weapons?"

"You mean to participate fully?" Such a frosty, disapproving tone could only mean that Lileth thought she should supervise.

"Of course. I hope a few of the soldiers will as well, though I don't intend to order it."

Lileth let it go without commenting, escorting her from the strategy room to the half-ruined storage that had been converted to stables when they first arrived. "You should know there's dissent in the ranks. A few diehard purists would rather see everything burn than walk the path you've chosen."

Her mouth tightened. "They can burn without me. If we must be...harsh to set an example, so be it. I will have no talk of pure bloodlines or racial superiority."

"Understood." By the gravity of her expression, Lileth did grasp that Thalia was willing to execute her own if she must; she was that committed to this course.

"Have the vedda beasts been saddled?" Thalia asked.

"Your steed awaits."

Her steed was a majestic white creature with two polished horns jutting from a proud forehead. The creatures were stocky and mountain-bred, surefooted even on the most dangerous slopes, and a shaggy coat meant the animal stayed warm all winter long, shedding in the spring. They were also stubborn and cantankerous, not a mount for the faint of heart.

Today, she armed up only with throwing knives, eschewing the lightning bracers she preferred for actual combat. Though Thalia knew she was at risk every moment of the day, this outing should be a negligible risk since patrolling Noxblades kept the area around Daruvar clear.

We won't range far enough for it to be dangerous.

With Lileth's help, she fastened her armor and hurried to meet the rest of the party. It was no surprise to find Gavriel, Tirael, and Ferith waiting, the three Noxblades who had survived the hard-won Battle of Hallowell. Soon, he would need to accept the promotion she'd offered—Shadow Hand—which was equivalent to spymaster and head of the Noxblades. He also needed to recruit more young ones for training to fill out their depleted ranks, but she'd learned not to push him. Gavriel was more oak than willow and too much pressure would break him. In all these years, the fool had never learned to bend.

Tirael bowed quickly, not meeting her eyes. There was something odd about the woman, a flicker too much deference for Thalia's comfort. Ferith followed suit but she paired the respectful gesture with a genuine smile.

The wolves had already shifted, and she guessed the large black one must be Raff. Those golden eyes were uncanny, gazing out from a canine face, and he opened his mouth in what almost looked like a toothy grin. Thalia was momentarily dumbstruck by the sheer impressive size of these changed Animari. She didn't know much about wolves, but even she could detect differences in bone structure and fur patterns. Among the wolves stood an enormous tiger, pacing with barely concealed impatience.

I should learn more about them.

It wasn't like her to leave a task half-done, and though she hadn't initially planned to become the wolf lord's lady, if not his queen, she would throw herself fully into the role. Raff loped over to her, standing as tall as her thigh. Nobody would ever mistake a shifted Animari for a natural woodland creature. She extended a hand, then paused.

"May I?"

The black wolf dipped his head, so she touched two fingers to the plush fur between his ears. A little sigh slipped out of her. While she had no such desires where the man was concerned, she couldn't stop the thought that it would be lovely to hug him in wolf form and put her cheek against his warm head.

"I will be your hunt master!" Gavriel called. "We will be splitting into teams of two. If numbers allow, our Animari guests should choose an Eldritch partner, as we know the terrain best."

Since Raff was already standing at her side, Thalia said, "Partners?"

And received a little growl in response that she took for assent, especially since he didn't move while the others ran about. Once the couples were set, Magda was left without a partner, and Gavriel scowled. "Tiger woman, I will take you myself."

Probably in response to his tone, the great striped cat raked the air near his knees, forcing him to leap to avoid a nasty claw swipe. Thalia bit back a laugh. It wasn't often that someone got the best of Gavriel.

The stableman led Guthrie out, offering Thalia the reins. A less stalwart creature would be panicked to be standing among so many predators, but her mount only pawed the ground with diamond-sharp hooves as if warning the wolves and great cat not to venture too close. She swung astride without aid and waited for Gavriel to blow the hunting horn.

"Here is your prey," he called, as a drone whirred into view, white and silver, so it would be difficult to track visually in this terrain. "Bring it back intact or in pieces. The victor will receive a great prize from our treasury and, of course, full bragging rights."

The horn sounded.

As the gates opened, she raced out ahead of the pack, Raff running beside her. He seemed to match her mount's speed easily, and Thalia admitted they made an impressive sight: white vedda beast with Eldritch warrior queen flanked by her great black wolf. *This is a scene straight from one of the old stories, worthy of being captured in stained glass.*

She also knew that the others had given her a head start and Gavriel had probably told them to hold back—to let her win. As if she was such a poor sport.

There could be no reciprocal conversation in this form, though he understood everything she said. "You take point. I'm no tracker, but my beast can keep up."

Raff let out an affirmative yip and it gave her pleasure to see how joyfully he bounded forward, leaping over rocks and down snowy slopes as if he had been born in these hills.

"I'll follow you," she said, and wondered if he knew how strange it was, how long it had been since she made any such promise.

The drone had long since passed beyond her ability to detect, but he must be able to sense it, because Raff oriented himself straightaway, running west with complete assurance.

The wind felt lovely on her skin, and the sun was high in the hills, perfect weather for such an outing. For these brief moments, her worries blew away like dandelion down. Her vedda beast had grown fat and lazy while she studied maps and pondered strategies. On impulse, she let out an ancient Eldritch war cry, shrill and bloodcurdling.

Raff glanced back to check on her and stumbled, claws

slipping on a half-hidden cascade of rocks. Before she thought, she was on the ground checking on him—and that impulse saved her life.

A red bolt of light singed the tree Guthrie stood under, charring the bark to ash. Raff lunged at her, knocking her out of the path of the falling fir, and they hit the ground hard.

I wish I had my bracers.

She rolled to her feet, knives dropping into her palms. "Prepare to fight."

ALMOST BEFORE THALIA spoke, Raff had a lock on their enemies.

Fucking Eldritch. If they were trying to murder the princess, they couldn't be her people. Leaping ahead, he raced into the undergrowth to hunt down the rotten devils. They all smelled different, these elfkin. The ones he was currently tracking reeked of herbal smoke, underscored with a deep fungal rot, as if they'd crept out of some underground burrow.

Another burst of red light spattered the ground as he ran, a hiss of steam and stink of charred earth. They had powerful weapons, but it wouldn't help. Raff used the forest to cloak his motions and drew their fire. Thalia came on behind him, screeching and fearless. Knives flew over his head and he heard the muffled thump of a body hitting the snow, smelled the coppery tang of blood in the wind.

How many left?

If this was a war party, they might have bitten off more than they could chew, but he had the battle in his blood. Raff let out a howl to send word to the rest of the wolves

that there was a real quarry to face and then spun as
movement caught his eye. Eight Eldritch crept out of the
trees, ringing them slowly.

Thalia gave no orders as she vaulted atop her mount,
but he took his place behind her, dwarfed by her vedda
beast yet he had no worries that she would trample him.
The creature seemed calm and ready to fight, rearing in
warning when the nearest enemy crept closer. A blade sang
past him, slamming into a pale forehead. *One down.* Raff
leapt at the next, sinking his fangs in deep. The Eldritch
slashed at him with clumsy hands; clearly, he had no idea
how to fight an Animari. He bit down and snapped the ulna.
The weapon plopped from the warrior's bloody hands, and
then the screaming started.

Raff spat. Even the blood tasted wrong, sweet and sickly
at the same time. *There's something the matter with these
Eldritch.* It was eerie how none of them had spoken a word
and they attacked in mechanical motions. Raff glanced at
Thalia, but he couldn't tell if she'd noticed the abject
wrongness of their foes. The smell of damp decay intensified, until he could barely breathe. Ignoring the stench, Raff
circled and went for his prey's Achilles tendon this time.
More rancid blood in his mouth.

Four down, five left.

He checked on Thalia with a lightning-quick glance, and
hand to God, the princess stole his breath, so lovely in her
graceful violence that he nearly forgot to finish off his kill.
She had risen to her feet on her mount's back, flinging
knives like a goddess of the blade. He had no fucking idea
how she could stay on the beast as it stamped and spun, but
she was light on her feet, nimble as a flying squirrel. She
dropped two more as he watched.

No need to fret about her.

He dodged a barrage of red light and ran through the burn patches on the ground. With full strength, he launched himself and knocked the Eldritch back, the light gun somersaulting out of his hands. Raff went for his face and simply bit through the hands that came up in a protective reflex. Another look at Thalia.

No blades left, she dove across the vedda beast's horns and she twirled across them, as he'd seen acrobats do on rings or bars. Then her body became a weapon, lashing out with precise kicks. The vedda beast moved in unison with her, hooves striking out as she did. Blood sprayed in their wake as they stunned and tramped their hapless opponents. Reassured, Raff dove back into the fray, finishing those she dropped.

The last one produced a large weapon that looked like it was Golgoth made. Raff raced toward him as the bang sounded, and a metal slug slammed into Raff's shoulder, driving him into a tree. He spat red and charged, sprinting beneath the vedda beast. Without either of them speaking a word, she went high, and he went low. The final enemy screamed as Raff gouged his femoral artery and Thalia caved in the left side of his skull. Their bodies were still warm and twitching as she dropped to a crouch beside one.

Hurts. Sodding hell, my whole body is on fire.

Raff wished he could speak because she needed to know that this wasn't a normal gun, but something devil made, designed to hurt Animari. *But how the hell did they know she'd have Animari in her lands?* There were disturbing implications to this line of thought, but his brain felt scrambled, and he couldn't quite connect the dots on why he should be troubled. Trembling, Raff sat before he fell over.

Breathe. It'll probably pass.

"What do we have here?" With deft hands, Thalia searched their corpses. Raff couldn't ask but she must've thought he'd be curious.

And he would be, if his damned shoulder wasn't on fire.

"House Manwaring, a scouting party. It won't be long before they send numbers." She sighed softly. "I wanted to show some hospitality and keep my manners, but there's no time for niceties, I fear."

That seemed obvious to him as well. He bit back a whimper.

Thalia went on, "This cuts our hunt short, though this excursion has served its purpose. I'm certainly impressed with your prowess. But...there's something off about their warriors. Look at their blood."

It was too dark, he thought. For sure, the stuff tasted nasty; he could still feel it coating his tongue, more viscous than normal, too. Before she could say more, his four guards loped into the clearing, hackles raised. *Red wolf, timber wolf, gray wolf, steppe wolf, all present.* Normally, Raff would brief them, but the scene spoke for itself.

Gavriel and Magda arrived last; he'd never seen the Noxblade wearing such a grim expression. "Unfortunately, we will not be completing our course. Everyone, head back to Daruvar immediately."

In response, Thalia vaulted onto her vedda beast, leading the way back to the fortress. Raff stayed close and tried not to show much how his wound hurt. *What the hell did he shoot me with?* The injury should be sealing, even around the projectile, but he could feel blood gushing from torn flesh. The faster they got there, the better, since first aid had to wait until everyone was safe.

Gates clanked open, permitting their passage. The mood was a hell of a lot darker when they closed. He had the absurd thought that the drone might be lost forever.

It had been long enough that the sun was going down, and the chill came on fast with the night. Once they reached the bailey, Raff dropped out of wolf form and stumbled. Magda was beside him in two strides. All the Animari were naked but unlike the Golgoth, the Eldritch didn't seem bothered. Thalia was snapping instructions at Gavriel and Lileth, faster than he could process her words.

Not surprising, he was woozy from all the red he'd left behind, a river of it, seemed like, and it was still pouring out of his shoulder.

Mags slammed both palms over the wound. "I did a shit job of protecting you, I see. What the hell is wrong with this?"

"Not sure," he got out. "Think it's a special weapon. The Gols have something..." It hurt to speak and black nibbled at the edges of his vision.

To his surprise, Thalia turned and ran to him, setting her shoulder beneath his other arm, but Mags didn't let go. *Some bodyguard,* he tried to say, but his tongue was numb, and it came out as a strange choking sound.

"We need a doctor!" Lileth shouted. "No, get him inside, you idiots. Move. Now!"

Raff lost the light.

6.

"WHY WON'T THE bleeding stop?" Thalia demanded.

The scene was straight from a nightmare, crimson everywhere, and to make matters worse, the small medical staff wasn't trained in Animari physiology. Nobody had a spare breath to answer, working flat out to extract the bullet from Raff's shoulder. Judging by his expression, the doctor was completely baffled, which didn't bode well.

"Vitals dropping," the nurse called.

Thalia stared at the medical machines, uncomprehending. House Manwaring had a weapon designed to kill Animari in one shot. The horror swept over her in a chilling wave that prickled her skin. It could only mean that they had no intention of making peace or accepting Thalia as queen of the Eldritch. No, they meant to follow her father back to the old, murderous ways and would prefer to see the Animari and Golgoth both go extinct. House Manwaring didn't have that power, of course, which was why they'd allied with the tyrant Tycho.

"He needs a transfusion," Dr. Wyeth said.

Immediately, the four Pine Ridge guards stepped forward. The youngest, Tavros, said, "It should be me. I'm type O negative, universal donor."

Under normal circumstances, they'd take blood and run tests to make sure, but medical machines made it clear they didn't have time. Raff didn't have time. The emergency team glanced at Thalia, likely hoping she'd take responsibility for the decision.

Life and death, that's my job. I'll carry this too.

"Do it. Save him. If there are complications, I'll take responsibility."

Relieved of culpability, they got to work swiftly, pumping Tavros's blood into Raff.

Mags had been examining the bloody projectile and she suddenly dropped it with a shudder. "This is treated black iron with a beryllium core."

"What does that mean?"

"It's an Animari slayer. Treated black iron prevents wounds from healing. The chemical interaction hinders coagulation. And beryllium is toxic to us, as few substances are. We're resistant to most chemical weapons, most herbal poisons as well." Magda let out a long sigh, her gaze fixed on Raff. "Whoever designed this knows a great deal about Animari vulnerabilities."

It was impossible not to wonder about the Ash Valley second, who had disappeared during the attack. Dead people could not hide, so probability suggested that he had gone with the Golgoth. To Thalia's mind, the only question was whether he was a conspirator or if he had been taken captive.

Dr. Wyeth cut into her thoughts, stepping past her to ask Magda for guidance. "Do you have any suggestions for how to treat beryllium poisoning? I'm also unsure if our medicines will help with the coagulation issue."

"One way to find out," Magda said. "Test them on me, first."

Before anyone could react, she cut herself with a small blade and then rubbed the tainted bullet on the wound. Her skin reacted immediately, rays of red streaking her arm, and the blood kept flowing.

Dr. Wyeth didn't look pleased about testing on a live subject, but Thalia nodded when he silently asked permission. The nurse injected two different drugs, and the second one brought result.

"Hurry," Dr. Wyeth said.

The nurse fumbled the injector module in her haste but eventually got the medicine into Raff's body. By this point, Thalia felt like she was watching from above, distant from the blood spatter and the stained gauze, the tubing that piped Tavros's life into Raff. His vitals were stabilizing, slowly, but they had to figure out what to do about the toxins. The medical staff started arguing amongst themselves, and she could hardly blame them.

"We don't have time to develop a treatment plan, an antidote, or a cure," she finally snapped.

Likely thinking she meant to let him die, Magda went for her throat, but Thalia dodged and acted as if the big cat hadn't moved. "He's taken enough from Tavros. Connect him to the IC machine now, dialysis mode. It won't be quick, but it should clean up his blood. Animari natural resilience ought to do the rest."

Dr. Wyeth stared at her. "That…is brilliant. You heard the queen. Move!"

Confident now that they were on familiar ground, the medical team worked efficiently as Thalia let herself lean against the wall, more weakness than she'd normally show. She'd almost lost her prospective mate before the marriage talks began. This had to be some kind of record.

"Sorry. I misunderstood."

Glancing up, Thalia found Magda beside her, offering an unexpected apology. She shrugged. "It was a stressful situation."

"But you saved him...and I'm the one who agreed to protect him. I should have stayed close."

Thalia shook her head. "There's no gain in debating who is to blame. I could argue that it's all my fault for not guarding my lands better."

Janek joined the conversation then. "Perhaps it's because I'm old, but I've lost my patience for this sort of thing. The blame always rests with the one who did harm, not those who failed to prevent it."

"Wise words," Lileth said. "If only these young fools would heed them."

Thalia laughed quietly over being called young. She had nearly three hundred years behind her, twice the average lifespan of the Animari. Which meant the youngest wolf was hardly more than a baby, yet he'd freely given his blood to save his lord. She had a lot to learn about these people.

The wolves were all clad in robes, and they must be cold, yet they didn't budge a foot from Raff's bedside. Skylett and Bibi seemed quietly anguished, casting anxious glances at Magda, as if the tiger woman could heal him through sheer force of will.

Maybe she can.

The infirmary was cold and uninviting, like the rest of Daruvar. Now that Raff was out of danger and the IC machine was working to tip the balance, the environment had to improve. With bare stone walls and blood stains on the floor, this looked like a place where people routinely died in agony.

She made a swift decision. "Get a portable heater in here and call for domestic staff. I need a meal for our guests and some chairs they can use to wait."

Thalia understood that it would be pointless to try and shoo anyone out. It spoke volumes that Raff was loved so well by his pack. In passing, Thalia wondered who would mourn her so passionately. Gavriel, certainly, and Lileth.... But had she inspired such devotion in her people?

Perhaps not.

Therefore, since the wolves loved him too much to leave him alone, the infirmary must become a waiting room as well. In short order, her will was accomplished, and Bibi bowed deeply in gratitude over the food and hot, sweet tea. She joined them for the haphazard meal, eating only enough to keep the shakes from setting in.

A queen is calm and gracious, under all circumstances. Thalia had been reading and memorizing passages from that old etiquette book for as long as she could remember, and there was a truism for every event. She had been trying to meet the standards of that long-dead ancestor for most of her life.

Odd, it was only that adage that kept her from crying.

RAFF WOKE WITH a pleasant hum in his head.

A few seconds later, the sound resolved as distinct from him, emitted from machinery attached to his body. His eyelids weighed several kilos each, but he lifted them with heroic effort, the room swimming into focus.

Six meters away, his people dozed against the backs of

their chairs. Magda had curled up on the floor in tiger form, and nearest to him—*how unexpected*. Thalia had pulled a cot up beside his bed and lay curled on her side, facing him. It seemed to be the middle of the night.

Must've been out for a while.

His shoulder still hurt like hell, and the rest of his body didn't feel much better. As he studied her sleeping face, her eyes flickered open, instantly alert. She slept like a soldier, he thought, and not one who watched battles from the wall. No, more like a seasoned veteran who recognized that danger often crept in during the night.

"You're awake," she said, smiling.

Thalia sat up and leaned forward, touching her fingers to his forehead.

She was probably checking for fever, but it felt more like a gesture of possession, as if she was about to etch some arcane sigil on his brow and his thoughts might never be his own again. Raff half-smiled at that fancy, relishing the cool feel of her skin against his. The Eldritch didn't burn as hot as the Animari, and he wondered whether it was possible to warm her from head to toe.

Maybe he even wanted to try.

Those were probably the meds. Seemed like they had given him some good shit.

"What happened?"

It was an open-ended question, meant to let her say whatever she wished. He lacked the energy to ask more, but he didn't need to. She summarized everything he'd missed succinctly, starting with the attack and ending with the treatment for beryllium poisoning.

Sounds like I owe Tavros and Thalia my life.

"Do you have any idea what House Manwaring's true

objective was? To kill me, kill you, stop the wedding…?" His voice sounded hoarse.

Before answering, she set a straw to his lips. He sipped and cool water trickled into his parched throat. Raff wouldn't have guessed that the Eldritch princess would be such a capable attendant. At Ash Valley, she had seemed so much more imperious. Perhaps it meant something that he hadn't been delegated, but he couldn't fathom what.

"As yet, I'm not sure what they hoped to accomplish. Gavriel is in the field. If they've left other agents nearby, he will find them and extract more information."

Extract. Such a clean, clinical word for the terrible things the Noxblade would do in her name. Raff sighed.

"You said this before, and you were right. We don't have time to be proper about this, so let's start these marital talks, Lady Silver."

"Right now?" Thalia set the cup on his bedside table, eyes wide.

Objectively speaking, she was a fucking mess. Her platinum hair had long since escaped its precise confinement, and it frothed around her weary face in a fine, bright nimbus. Likewise, her clothes were wrinkled, and she had an imprint on one cheek, from resting it on the crook of her arm. A sensible man would back out of this arrangement, as the cost had already been prohibitive, but the benefits he'd noted before still applied, and he'd be damned if he allowed anyone to drive him from his chosen path.

Be they wolf or Eldritch, let the opposition burn and be damned.

"Right now," he affirmed.

"We should have witnesses…and scribes to take down our terms."

"Record what we say here and now, have it transcribed later. Is that good enough?"

Her gaze met his, for once uncertain. Somewhere in the long hours between midnight and dawn, she'd lost her queenly bearing. At this instant, Thalia was just a woman carrying more weight than it seemed her shoulders could hold. He remembered Gavriel's words about how long she'd been fighting alone.

"Yes, very well." She dug her phone out of a hidden pocket and activated the audio log feature. "You set your requirements first, Lord Wolf. If I have anything to add afterward, I'll say so."

I'm really doing this.

This was so far from customary courtship rites that a pang went through him. None who had come before had ever weighed what a mate could give the pack against what needed to be given. Such businesslike acumen made a mockery of what should be all joy and tenderness. Those feelings might have built in time, but that was in short supply, and he had to choose.

"I don't expect fidelity," he said softly. "Since we are not marrying for love. I will expect you to attend all formal occasions at my side and to spend at least three months out of the year at Pine Ridge. I will need a portion of your soldiers assigned to our borders as a sign of good faith. In exchange, I'll send you more drones to help you patrol your territories. We'll also help you consolidate your hold on Eldritch lands in exchange for aid against Tycho's forces later."

"That's fair." Her voice was faint, eyes flat and steady. "I agree. I will require reciprocation on all points, including three months at Daruvar or wherever I am posted.

Depending on how the war turns, we may live the rest of the year at our discretion, separately if the situation requires."

Raff already felt like shit, and for some reason, all of that just made it worse. "Understood. But don't hesitate to send word if I'm needed. Whether we're together or not, you will be my wife."

"I'm offering you the title of consort," Thalia went on, as if he hadn't spoken.

That pissed him off, too.

"I don't even fucking want to be king of the Eldritch," he muttered.

"That is another reason you're a desirable choice. If I wed an Eldritch, I'd have to worry about their ambition my whole life long. At least with you, there should be some peace of mind."

"I can't say anyone's ever claimed that about me before."

"Color me unsurprised. One last question, then—do you expect an heir of me?"

He hadn't thought that far ahead. How damn ridiculous. "I don't really know how that works among the Eldritch. Animari women choose when they get pregnant, so—"

"That must be nice." Her tone was wistful. "We rely on science for such matters. In all honesty, it's not easy for Eldritch women to conceive due to our long lifespans. It's best done while we're young, as aging decreases the chances even more."

There were probably technical explanations about declining sperm counts and decaying ovum, but Raff had no interest in any of that. If he wanted an heir, he could find someone in the pack to carry his genes forward, preferably a woman who didn't care about his complicated marital status.

Fuck all of this and fuck Talfayen who ruined the conclave, and fuck Tycho Vega especially. *I just wanted to drink and hunt and—*

Thalia was staring at him like he'd stabbed her with his silence. He scrambled for the right words, a task made tougher by his addled mind and persistent pain.

"I don't expect that, but if it happens, I'll welcome our child and be the best father I can."

"Then let's move on to my final request. I'd like to frame this marriage like a contract with the terms put in writing and with an expiration date. Ten years should be more than long enough to accomplish what we need together. Oh, and if we finish sooner, there should be an option for early mutual dissolution. Either way, you'll still be young enough to follow your heart, afterward."

"What about you?" Raff asked.

Thalia only smiled, a bittersweet expression that didn't lighten her eyes. "I've never been free to do that. Nor will I ever be."

7.

TWO DAYS AFTER the attack, Raff had rallied more than Thalia would've thought possible.

She'd seen some of that Animari resilience in the aftermath of the attack on Ash Valley, but it was still a relief. For the last forty-eight hours, she had coordinated the war effort from his bedside. Now that he was ambulatory, she could relax a bit.

"Message for you, Your Highness." A young page cut into her reverie, offering a handheld with a deep bow.

The communication was already queued up, so she plugged in her headset and hit play. Ruark Gilbraith's pale, narrow face appeared on screen. Thalia had never liked or trusted him; he tended to take credit for things he hadn't achieved and eliminate rivals who might dispute those claims. Not quite a Tycho Vega, but the seeds were there, along with excess arrogance and avarice.

"Good day, Lady Talfayen." That was a slight straightaway, tacit refusal to acknowledge her royal claim. "It has reached my ears that you are experiencing some difficulty uniting the other houses. By now, House Manwaring will have declared against you. I will give you one opportunity to make good the promise your father made to mine."

She set her jaw, glaring at the message unit. *I'll marry you when all the seas freeze, and I can walk across them.*

"If you choose to break our old bonds of allyship, I will take it...poorly. Manwaring will come to me, and I've already sent enticements to House Vesavis. I doubt your little resistance can stand against the collective might of all three houses. I will give you one day to decide, so choose wisely, lest you drive your own people to extinction through delusions of grandeur. You are no queen, but you *could* be my consort. Think well."

A cold shudder crawled down her spine, and she controlled the urge to fling the comm pad against the far wall. For long moments, she controlled her breathing along with the fury racing like wildfire in her veins. Sometimes she wanted to scream until her throat ached, until she couldn't breathe for the uncontained fervor.

"Bad news?" Raff asked quietly.

She hadn't realized he was awake. This morning, he looked much better, good color in his cheeks, eyes bright as chips of golden agate framed by truly disarming dark lashes. His skin was burnished brown against the pale gauze wrapping his shoulder. His restless hands tapped endlessly against the white sheets, as if he were searching for something. With a whimsy quite unlike her, Thalia wondered what that might be.

"More of a nuisance." She hesitated. Ordinarily, she would delete the message and share the worry with no one, but for the duration of their marital contract, her enemies would become his, so he should be fully informed. "See for yourself."

At the end of the playback, Raff tossed the unit onto the

foot of his bed. "What an ass. Should I kill him?"

That casual tone almost made her laugh, but the wolf lord's expression suggested that he might not be joking. "Are you serious?"

"He's threatening you. I have a zero-tolerance policy for aggression against my own."

"Am I, though?"

"What?"

"Your own."

"We've come to terms. Unless you change your mind, yes. That means if you say the word, he's done."

Thalia tried not to show the ripple of pleasure she felt at that simple statement. "You make yourself sound like a sword in my hand. I aim, you strike."

"That's not a bad description, Lady Silver. Your grasp of the big picture is likely better than mine. My old man called me a hotheaded fool more than once, and..." Here, his words trailed off, his eyes going distant.

"And?" she prompted, curious what might make him look so.

"I only lead Pine Ridge because my older brother died young."

"I thought rulership wasn't dynastic among your people."

Raff shrugged. "We say it's not, but it takes some damn serious incompetence to get passed over, once a family takes power."

"We always strive to keep what we hold. This is true among my people, too."

"Then maybe you know how much it sucks having a legacy to live up to."

Thalia considered. "Not as such. I'd already destroyed

all my father's hopes for me, long before he turned traitor."

"Can't have been easy." Such a gentle tone, as if he cared.

She couldn't let herself get pulled into his charm. From what she'd seen at Ash Valley, Raff offered that same warmth indiscriminately. To him, women were like a field of wildflowers waiting for the sun. It would be a severe tactical error to mistake his charisma for personal interest.

Time to change the subject.

"While you were sleeping, the clerk brought the transcription of our conditions. Would you like to look them over?"

"I trust you," he said at once.

That...was odd. He didn't even want to glance at the documents? Mentally, Thalia shrugged.

"Then we just need to sign and get ready for the ceremony. Under the circumstances, it seems best to hold a simple wedding and then get down to business."

Raff smiled. "The business of crushing your enemies?"

"I wouldn't have put it quite that way, but...yes." Even to her own ears, she sounded prim. "If the doctor allows it, I think you can leave the infirmary this afternoon. You must have preparations to make."

"I do feel like I'm growing moss," he admitted with a roguish grin. "But...not sure what you mean by preparations?"

"There's no one you want to invite from Pine Ridge?"

"I wish Korin could be here, but she shouldn't leave the hold while I'm away, unless it's an absolute emergency."

"Korin is your second. Is she...special to you?" Thalia couldn't believe she'd asked the question. It just sort of popped out.

How humiliating.

Raff cocked his head, all wolfish curiosity. "What does that mean?"

"Never mind."

"Korin's my second. I'm not sure how else to explain who she is to me, so I'll say this. When I was a pup, my father dragged her in and said, 'this girl will save your ass someday, boy. She's as clever as you are stupid, so keep her close.'"

That information was both blunt and startling. She hadn't much liked her own father, but even so, he had never denigrated her. Well. Not until she stood against him. After that, they stopped talking entirely and he had her confined to Riverwind under heavy guard 'until she saw reason'. She had heard of the things he said *about* her, however.

"You're not stupid," she said.

"That's sweet, Lady Silver, but you don't know me. In time, you'll wish you could eat those words."

She narrowed her eyes, controlling the impulse to smack him, and wrapped herself in poise as if it was a cloak. "I find that statement offensive. My acumen is excellent. My father told others that I was a worthless, brainless brat, more than once. Does that make it true?" Outrage swelled in her head, so much that her skull almost couldn't hold it.

"Easy. I won't insult your judgment again. If you've agreed to take me, I must be top drawer, right?"

A week ago, she might've said that their alliance was pure expedience, but that was before they fought together, and she witnessed firsthand his extraordinary valor. Maybe the elder Pineda had wanted a tactician for a son, one who studied old tomes and memorized battle tactics. Instead, he'd gotten a bit of a clown with a smile warm enough to melt the heart of winter.

"Precisely."

Briskly, she rose to find Dr. Wyeth, who pronounced the patient well enough to go about his business. The medical procedures eased the strange atmosphere, so things felt normal by the time Raff got dressed. She walked with him back to his quarters.

"Is tomorrow too soon to hold the wedding?" she asked.

"I'm up to it. Seems like you should ask your people, though, not me. They're the ones who will have to scramble all night to get it done."

"The service and decorations will be simple. Don't expect too much." On some level, that bothered her. This shouldn't be rushed, promises made haphazardly, under duress.

"I never do," he said softly.

For some reason, hearing that hurt her heart.

THE FIRST THING Raff did was call his people to his quarters. Tavros turned up first, then Skylett and Bibi, and finally Janek. Magda didn't answer to him, so he didn't expect her obedience.

"We thought you were going to die," Tavros said.

"I have a lot to do yet," Raff said.

"That didn't save Beren," Janek pointed out.

While that might be true, such pessimism didn't help. "Come in, all of you. I need to brief you." Once everyone was settled, he filled them in on his decision. "I'll send word to Pine Ridge shortly regarding allocation of soldiers and technology. I intend to stay here for the next three months to fulfill my part of the bargain."

"I have mixed feelings," Bibi said.

Since she looked so young, most would pay no heed to her words, but she was also the youngest Seer in pack history, so he had to ask. "What troubles you?"

"The portents are dark down this path. I see betrayal and shadows in your near future and I could not find a glimpse of you emerging from that darkness."

Skylett shivered, wrapping her hands around her arms. "You know she wouldn't make such a revelation lightly. Perhaps—"

"I should go back on my word because two crows flew past your window at daybreak? It's not that I don't believe in your gifts, Bibi, but my options are limited. In times like these, fortune favors the bold."

"Then you're determined to move forward?" Janek asked.

"I'd all but made up my mind before we arrived, and nothing I've seen here makes me want to withdraw. The time for considering input has passed."

"Understood," Tavros said. "When is the grand event?"

"Tomorrow, provided her people are up to the task. The place will be bustling. Janek, will you stand beside me in place of family?" In truth, they were only distant cousins on his father's side, but it was better than nothing. Sky was closer to him in terms of friendship, as she was like a younger sibling, but she wasn't an actual blood relation and that probably mattered for Eldritch ceremonies.

"I'm honored."

He ignored that; it was the sort of thing the elder wolf said, even if he didn't mean it. Old school manners had no modern equivalent.

"I'm not sure what the ceremony will be like, but please

be tolerant, even if it seems strange."

"Princess Thalia appears to be thorough," Tavros said. "She will strive for something that honors both Animari and Eldritch ways."

"That's true enough," he said, pleased that one of his people didn't hate this prospect.

Thalia's time in Pine Ridge would be a lonely nightmare if people didn't warm up to her. He could well imagine the whispers, sideways glances, and the subtle exclusion from pack socialization. Just because three months was a flicker of light to her, that was no reason for her to suffer.

"Do you have other news?" Bibi asked.

"For now, I need you to focus on the issue of defending her lands and defeating her enemies."

"As you wish." Her flat tone said she wasn't thrilled with the assignment or having her warning disregarded.

I already knew this wouldn't be easy. Doesn't take a Seer to know that.

He turned to Tavros. "Get with the guards and see if you can find anything out about House Gilbraith. I need to know what kind of numbers they can field, how much sway they have over the other two, Manwaring and Vesavis. Learn what you can about them, too."

"I can help in terms of historical house power, if not current military standing," Janek said.

Right, that's why I brought him. Of all the pack, he knows the most about Eldritch doings.

"Stick around and have a drink with me, old wolf. The rest of you are dismissed."

The three young ones bowed and hurried off, leaving Raff to pour a drink for Janek. Handing over the tumbler, he said, "My attention span isn't long, so try to make this a teacup history lesson."

"As best I can. Vesavis is the least of the houses, politically insignificant and eternally hungry. They're known for treachery and would not hesitate to make a deal and then break if they saw advantage elsewhere. On several occasions, they've nearly been wiped from existence when some intrigue imploded. I would not depend on them for support."

"Noted. And Manwaring?"

"Informally, they're known among the Eldritch as the Gray."

"What does that mean?"

"They put up a pretext of neutrality while secretly working toward their own ends. The fact that they've come out against the princess so early in the game is quite disturbing."

Times like this, Raff would've traded a year of his life for a quick brain like Korin's. "Spell it out for me."

"It means they don't see her as a true threat. If they feared her reprisal, they wouldn't have acted so fast. In my opinion, this heralds a power shift. You should prepare yourself for the other three houses to align with Gilbraith."

"Tell me about them."

"They have been vying with House Talfayen for centuries, and they have a sprinkling of royal blood in their lineage. Not a direct declination like Princess Thalia, but enough through a distaff family connection that it has been impossible for anyone in either family to take the throne."

"Do you think her decision to ally with me will ultimately hurt her cause?"

Janek hesitated.

"Don't swallow it. Tell me the truth!"

"Likely, yes. The Eldritch will see it as weakness and desperation instead of a wise strategic maneuver."

Raff showed his teeth; it did not qualify as a smile. "Then we'll prove them wrong, old wolf. Give me something I can use."

"Since Vesavis is known to be untrustworthy, we could work to weaken the cohesion of those allied against us."

"You mean, make Gilbraith and Manwaring think that Vesavis is hedging its bets, ready to flip if things look good for Thalia?"

"It's probably not even that far from the truth," Janek said. "We'd only be hastening that conclusion."

"Divide and conquer, works for me. Put together a concrete plan and tell me what resources you need to get it done. Thalia will want to know, as soon as you're ready."

"As you say." Taking that as dismissal, Janek drained his drink and rose. "She will help us, won't she? When the time comes."

Raff couldn't even blame the old wolf for his doubts. It was hard not to fear the worst since historically, wolves had no close ties to the Eldritch. If she was like the assholes in House Vesavis, she might take their help and then later, let Pine Ridge burn when Tycho's forces hit the border.

It's not like she loves me, or my people. But...

"If I'm good at anything, it's reading people's hearts. And I'm betting my life that she keeps her promises," he said.

"That's good enough for me."

Raff walked Janek to the door and was startled to find Thalia frozen, her hand suspended as if she'd been about to knock. The old wolf greeted her like a courtier in passing by. Heat flooded Raff's cheeks, blazing worse than any fever.

Dammit all, she caught me being sincere.

"Did you mean it?" she asked.

No pretense that she hadn't overheard.

This, this was why he thought that. While she might be good at scheming and intrigue, with him, she was as straightforward as an arrow to the heart.

He answered in a gruff tone, wishing she'd go away. "I'm not in the habit of saying shit I don't mean."

"Neither am I, Lord Wolf. But then, you seem to know that quite well already." To his astonishment, she kissed his cheek before rushing away.

8.

THALIA DIDN'T SLEEP that night.

Not because she'd yielded to impulse, but because there was so much to prepare for the wedding service. First, she stopped in the kitchens to see how the food for the feast was coming along. The staff was too busy chopping to spare more than a moment.

"Do you need anything?" she asked.

"Please don't trouble yourself," the head cook said.

Which translated roughly to, 'please get out of my kitchen'. Thalia was familiar with such code and didn't dally among the boiling pots. She met Lileth in the back corridor, and it seemed as if the older woman was looking for her. Lil wore a grave expression, one that heralded nothing good.

"Problem?" she asked.

"Gavriel wants a word."

Thalia swallowed a sigh. "Can it wait?"

"I don't think it can."

If he deemed it important enough to interrupt her work, she'd better make time. "Is he in the strategy room?"

"He was when I left."

"On my way. Why didn't he call me?"

Lil's expression darkened. "The connection may not be secure."

As she headed to hear Gavriel's grim tidings—which could be the name of a particularly gloomy children's tale— it occurred to her that this was a hell of a way to spend the night before her wedding. While Thalia had never fantasized about what it would be like, she had never imagined that she'd be forced to such a strategy by threats from all sides. There would be no tender words or floral bouquets, no time spent putting scented lotion on her skin in hopes that her chosen mate found her beautiful.

Thalia didn't have close friendships, either, nobody to gather in her room and giggle over how wonderful or terrible her first night might be. For her, such relationships constituted vulnerability. She had supporters, not confidants, and while she didn't regret the choices that had kept her safe, sometimes security was lonely.

Gavriel stood before the window, staring out the narrow opening into the dark. He turned as she entered, a shadow with red-hot coals for eyes. Sometimes his intensity gave her the shivers, for devotion like his could turn dark under the right circumstances. He executed a brief bow, waiting for her to reach the grouping of chairs arranged on a worn antique rug.

"Sit down," she invited.

"I'll be brief. I know that you're busy."

"Go ahead."

"I would like to be discharged from your direct service," he said quietly.

Of all the words she could've pictured Gavriel speaking, those never came to mind. She covered her surprise with a question. "Will you tell me why?"

"Magda Versai is pursuing an investigation related to the disappearance of the Ash Valley second. I believe the trail could lead us to an insurgent stronghold, where your father's followers are hiding."

"So it's likely that the jaguar cut a deal with my father and is now working for the traitors and the Golgoth?"

Gavriel lifted a shoulder, never one to make judgments before all facts were available. "She picked up a hint of him from one of our patrols, but everything was in such disarray that we can't be certain if he was a captive or actively cooperating."

"What I'm gathering is that you would like the freedom to pursue this on your own?"

She didn't say what else she knew to be true—that this was likely an excuse to get out of Daruvar before the wedding. Sometimes it was so hard pretending to be oblivious, but she'd thought it best to salve his pride this way. Otherwise, she would've had a candid conversation with Gavriel long ago. Thalia suspected he loved the idea of her more anyway, a sort of knightly devotion.

"Exactly so. Will you release me from your service?"

A pang of regret went through her. Through the years, there had been nobody more dedicated or loyal than Gavriel. If she released him, she didn't doubt that he would keep working for her benefit, but he would no longer take orders directly from her. Replacing him would take some doing, as she'd been counting on him to lead the Noxblades and train replacements in the future.

She let out a soft sigh and then nodded. "Follow your own path from here. Send word if you learn anything important."

"Thank you, Your Highness."

"When are you leaving?"

"As soon as the tiger woman is ready." The descriptors sounded vaguely pejorative spoken in that tone.

"Then be safe." She didn't say she would miss him, though that was true, it might also foster false hope.

"You as well." He hesitated, but in the end, he chose to swallow whatever words hovered at the tip of his tongue.

Just as well.

"Could you do me one last favor?"

"What is it?" He looked wary, wisely enough.

"Recommend your successor of the two who returned with you from Hallowell."

"Ferith, definitely. She has the most experience. Tirael is too young and is impulsive in the bargain. Was that all?"

"Yes, thank you. Take care, Gavriel."

With a bow, he excused himself and Thalia didn't watch him go. *End of an era.* Once, she'd taken for granted that he would be the silent sword behind her throne. Their roads had diverged unexpectedly and might not join again.

Wearily she went to the hall to check on the decorations. They seldom used this room, as it was large and cold, but apart from the courtyard, there was no space large enough for everyone at Daruvar to bear witness. The staff had dug out some truly archaic decorations and were bedecking the halls with them, no time to order anything or wait for supplies. If this wedding seemed rustic and rushed, so be it.

"How are things going?" she asked.

A young page dipped at the waist in a nervous obeisance, twisting her hands before her. "Well, Your Highness, there aren't enough chairs, not anywhere in the fortress, and we don't have a red carpet anywhere. I'm sorry—"

"Don't worry about it." Thalia cut into the apology with a careless gesture and a reassuring smile. "You can only do what's possible with the resources available and the time allowed."

"Understood, Your Highness."

Her eyes burned, dry and sore, but she had one more stop before she could snatch a few hours of rest. At this hour, the chapel was deserted, moonlight streaming in the etched silver stained glass. The mosaics were so old here that she could scarcely make out the pictures, and the candles had been dark for decades. It seemed a minor miracle that the sparker allowed her to light the tapers, one by one. They were melted, ancient, and misshapen, but lucky for Thalia, they still kindled to flame.

In the best of all possible worlds, she wouldn't be doing this alone. Her family should be beside her, gathered to pray for her happiness and prosperity, but their numbers had never been great, and now she was alone, the last of her line. At this point, Ruark Gilbraith was her closest living relative, and he wanted to *marry* her to unite their bloodlines, so he wouldn't be lighting any candles. Still, while she had abandoned some of the old ways, she wouldn't omit this quiet vigil.

"Mother, guide me as I take my first steps to my new life. Help me remember that truth is not always wisdom and that compassion is always required. I will do my best to be worthy of the task you have entrusted to me. Watch over me and keep me from harm." She whispered a few more words in Old Eldritch, her pronunciation rough and slow.

Traditionally, she ought to pray to her father as well, but she couldn't bring herself to ask for his aid, not when their ideology had diverged so completely. *He'd probably hex me if he has any power in the afterlife.* Thalia knelt on the cold stones for a long time, until her knees went from sore to stiff to numb and she had to use her hands to pull herself upright.

That should be enough reverence.

Carefully, she blew each candle out and sat in the darkness, unable to move. In the morning, everything would change.

SLEEP WAS IMPOSSIBLE.

Magda had just left, after offering a cryptic, 'I have a trail to follow'. If Raff had any illusions that they had formed a bond, her casual departure would've dispelled them. His body hurt with a low-grade ache, but the wound was healed, at least. It looked like it would scar, making him unique among Animari.

In the middle of the night, they had only a skeleton crew on watch, which permitted him to wander the hallways unimpeded. A few guards bowed or asked if he needed directions. Raff only shook his head. He didn't even know what he was looking for, but he was too restless to sleep. The days he'd spent laid up took a toll since he was used to grueling physical activity. As he rounded a corner, he smelled the distinctive odor of burning tallow and the sharp scent of a flame recently extinguished.

That was how he found her, kneeling in a stripe of moonlight. He'd seen relatively few expressions from Princess Thalia, so her naked loneliness hit him hard. She had her face upturned to the window, eyes closed, and he could imagine what might be running through her head. He hesitated, as interrupting her might make her feel worse.

There must be some attachment between her and Gavriel and Raff had just watched the Noxblade leave the fortress with Mags.

Well, he'd never been known for prudence or caution. Raff strolled into the chapel and sat beside her. A mark of her absolute introspection, she didn't notice his arrival for a couple of minutes. Then she started, her breath coming in a sharp inhalation. In such a restrained person, that qualified as a shocked scream.

"I'd apologize for intruding, but I'm *not* sorry, so let's bypass the part where I feign remorse, as I'm not very good at it. I rarely regret yielding to my various impulses."

"Good evening to you as well," Thalia said.

"Does it bother you that I've omitted a traditional greeting? Then how about, 'Hello, fair princess, why do you tarry in this desolate place?'"

"I might tell you if you truly wished to know and were not just mocking my preference for good manners."

"That's unfair. I was *teasing*, Lady Silver. Mockery has unkindness at its heart while teasing springs from affection."

"A spurious claim. You scarcely know me. Therefore, it can only be the former."

"Is that so? Well, my curiosity was sincere at any rate. What are you doing here?"

"I *was* praying," Thalia said. "And now, I'm sitting."

"Alone, in the dark?"

"Not anymore, though it *is* still dark. We have a couple of hours yet before sunrise."

"How should we spend them?"

Thalia tilted her head. Even in this light, he could see her clearly. "You should get some sleep before the festivities start." Impossible to miss the faint tinge of bitterness, the emphasis on the word 'festivities'.

"If you have doubts, it's not too late to stop this. You could marry up with the Gilbraith wad who issued such a lavish ultimatum."

"I'd rather die," she said softly.

"No need to be dramatic, 'no' is good. Works for so many unpleasant occasions."

"I'll remember that. Even if you can't sleep, we should go. Except I'm not sure if I can. My legs seem to be asleep."

That was easily enough solved. Raff rose first and pulled her upright; she hadn't exaggerated, though, and Thalia stumbled against him. He supported her, noting the way her heart sped up. That might be simple nerves, however. There was no reason to read it immediately as attraction.

"Better?" he asked, after a long moment. "Can you walk now?"

"I think so." To prove her assertion, she took a step, then another, steadying herself on the cool stone wall.

"Then I'll see you to your room."

"You offer as if I'm in danger," she said lightly.

"I'd rather not test it. It's not like I expected to get shot with anti-Animari rounds while we were out hunting."

Her shoulders rounded slightly, as if he'd added to her burden with that reminder. "Fair point. I'll welcome your escort."

Great, they weren't even past the wedding night, and he was already making shit worse. Raff had seldom felt more useless. While the Eldritch princess might need his troops and his technology, the odds didn't seem promising that she'd welcome anything he had to offer personally. That shouldn't even bother him.

Being purposeful wasn't his strength anyway. Life of the

party? Yes. Leading the way out in the wild? Certainly. He could also drink most people under the table and beat nine out of ten challengers in a bar dust-up. None of those skills would keep his people safe like the Pax Protocols.

"My pleasure," he mumbled.

She sighed audibly. "Do you mind if we detour? I'd like to get some air and see the stars before I turn in."

That would be the perfect atmosphere to make a move, flirt a bit and see if he could thaw her out. Only it seemed...wrong to look on her that way, but he didn't know how else to be. People fell into two categories: those he could charm and those who saw him as a nuisance. Thalia didn't seem willing to join either camp, currently.

"It's cold. Do you have a coat?"

"I'm already numb from crouching on the chapel floor and I'm used to discomfort. Indulge me for five minutes, won't you?"

"Easily done."

In silence, she led the way to the stairs that wound upward through the west tower, closest to the chapel. There was nobody stationed on the wall, but she likely had motion detection drones deployed that would sound the alarm in the security room. Too dark to see the sloping hills, and above, it was all blackness and stars. Even in Pine Ridge, they didn't shine so sharp and clear, too much light pollution.

"It's breathtaking," she whispered. "But at the same time, it makes me feel so small...and I need that, so I don't get lost in my own nonsense."

"What do you mean?"

"Perspective. I can't believe my own propaganda, or I'll become a queen people fear, not the leader they need."

Maybe it was the late hour, but that just seemed so wise and profound that he couldn't figure out what to say. So he offered, "I didn't mean to upset you, before. With what I said about needing protection here."

"You didn't say anything that was untrue. I let you come to harm after I promised safe shelter." Her lips compressed on more words before she shaped them into a smile.

"Sod that noise. I'm alive and I've got another pretty scar to show off. You know how rare that is?"

"Is it? I didn't realize. If I'm honest, I haven't spent much time among your people."

"Or your own for that matter, if stories can be believed."

"Pardon me?"

"I understood that you weren't allowed to leave Riverwind for quite some time, after you openly opposed your father."

"That story is circulating everywhere, I suppose. Damn Gavriel. He thinks I'm a martyr to the cause." She whirled away from the wall and headed down.

Just as well, she must be chilled to the bone.

"Princesses locked in towers always suffer," Raff said. "It's enough torment to have your freedom stripped away. I'd rather have a whipping."

"I'd rather not talk about my time at Riverwind, if you don't mind. Those are not good memories, hardly anything I should have in my mind the night before our wedding." Thalia marched down the hall, her shoulders set.

"Hearing you say that, it almost sounds...real." One day, he'd lose the dratted habit of blurting things out. Maybe.

"Instead of an affair of state?"

Her tone made him wish he could eat his words. This must be hard for her as well, and he was making it worse. Raff tried to find something to say that would make it better, but they were already at her door.

She opened it without hesitation. "Thanks for seeing me in. Until tomorrow, Lord Wolf."

9.

THALIA CRAWLED OUT bed five minutes before Madu trotted into the room, carrying the case she used for work.

The dresser clapped her hands in excitement. "You bathed last night, yes? Tell me the answer is yes. Otherwise, I'll never get you ready in time."

Thalia nodded. "I'm a blank canvas, ready to receive your best work."

"Then wash your face and we'll get started."

Water couldn't rinse the weariness away, but Thalia took her place at the dresser. "I'm ready."

Three hours later, she was more than tired of sitting, but Madu finished at last and spun the chair to the mirror. Thalia's hair gleamed silver, fastened in coiled plaits with jeweled pins. She tilted her head, taking in the lustrous shine of eyes that almost looked purple in this light. Her lips were outlined in pale pink, a deep red in the center, making her mouth look like a flower. Madu had gone traditional with the rest of the cosmetics, so instead of a more modern blush, her face was pale, highlighted in silver.

"How is it?" Madu asked.

"You did well, thank you."

"I had no choice but to resort to the old ways with this face and these dark circles." Madu pinched her chin and angled it with a critical eye. "You look as if you haven't slept in years." This scolding was more than most of the staff dared.

"Noted. Where's my gown?"

It was a lace and taffeta confection that had been in her family for generations. Both her mother and grandmother had worn this to be married. Madu did up the pearlescent buttons in the back and Thalia smoothed the fabric over her hips. The dresser gave an approving nod.

"You look splendid. Do you want me to send a bit of something for breakfast?"

Thalia shook her head. "I doubt it would settle. Besides, we'll be eating after the ceremony anyway."

"Well now, that's a cheerful assessment of your wedding," Madu said pertly.

"It's fast. And...reckless. But I can't see any other path. Let's go."

Setting her shoulders, she strode out of her private quarters and set off for the main hall. There was nobody to enter with her as she heard the music, so she pushed the heavy doors wide alone. At first, the room was a burst of sunshine and crystal that resolved into a sea of faces. For most, she could recite their names, and they all looked serious as the music swelled, a chorus of pipes that rose with each step she took into the room.

There was no red carpet, so they had gone with winter wonders instead: wreaths of fresh evergreen and a carpet of pine needles that crunched beneath her feet. It was a nice touch, incorporating the pack's predilection for the wild with more Eldritch touches like the mixed dry herbs burning in censers that sweetly perfumed the hall. The aroma was soothing; she relaxed at once, as the organizers likely intended.

Clad in black, the wolf lord stood at the far end of the hall, waiting for her. Raff was stocky, but he wore the formal wear well, his beard neatly trimmed and dressed, dark curls untamed as they tumbled about his face. The half-hidden scar on his cheek lent him a piratical air. Thalia proceeded toward him in measured steps and trembled only a little when he took her icy hand in his. *He's always like a furnace.* As one, they turned to face Lileth who would speak the first part of the service. The pipes quieted.

"Gentle guests, we gather to unite two houses as one and bear witness to their promises today." Lileth proffered a white candle to each of them before continuing her speech. "As you light your separate candles, you salute your separate selves. All that makes you who you are, you honor with this flame. Princess Thalia of House Talfayen, please kindle yours."

She held the wick to the censer and waited until she was sure the candle had caught before pulling back. At least her hands were steady while she waited. Lileth studied her for a moment, then her gaze flickered to the wolf lord. "Lord Raff Pineda of Pine Ridge, please bring your flame to life."

He was faster and less cautious, plunging the candle halfway in, and then he flashed her a roguish grin when he pulled it free with a flourish.

Lileth continued, "As you blend your flames to light the third candle, you celebrate the power to ignite a common flame of commitment. From each Numina, there rises a light that reaches to infinity and one day will join with our mothers and fathers, both earthly and divine. From this moment forward, you swear to walk the same path, your two shadows become one. May the road you tread together be full of truth and light, happiness and honesty, purpose and peace."

That was the signal for them to step forward together and unite their flames. For some reason, it seemed momentous when the larger tallow lit up. "Lord Pineda, give your breath as a sign that you take responsibility for her light."

His exhalation not only extinguished the flame, it also smelled of peppermint. Thalia smiled in response, waiting for Lileth to invite her to do the same. "Princess Talfayen, give your breath as a sign you take responsibility for his light."

This is the end of the Eldritch portion of the service.

Efficiently, she blew out his candle and Lileth took them back, placing one on each side of the unity candle. She had tailored the service to omit all the awkward language about love and desire, which Thalia appreciated. It wouldn't help the situation to force them to speak false vows.

Her part done, Lil made way for Janek on the dais. The elder wolf was soberly garbed and dignified in demeanor. "Friends, we are here to mark the joining of these two. Promises are ties that bind. Today, you have chosen one another. Raff, please turn, face your bride and offer her your hand."

His quick compliance saved her pride. While everyone had to know that this wouldn't be the first choice for either of them, nobody could gossip about the proprieties.

Janek stepped down and wrapped a thick cord around the wolf lord's wrist and then he pulled the other end around Thalia's. She hadn't known that the wolves had this sort of tradition, but she didn't object as Janek deftly fastened a loose knot. If she exerted the slightest pressure, it would fall off, probably a bad omen.

"The first, fragile link has been created. One may be conquered, but two can defend, back to back, joined in common cause. Likewise, a rope woven of many threads does not fray easily. Will you two pull it tight as a symbol of your union?"

"I will," she said, in unison with the wolf lord.

They each drew on the rope until there was only a little slack and the knot was tight enough to hold. Normally, there were probably a lot more words about love and devotion, but the wolves had cut to the chase as well. This must be almost over, right? Janek misted them both lightly with water.

"The bond is made and blessed. House Talfayen is joined with the Pine Ridge pack. From this moment forward, we acknowledge your kith as our kin. Let these witnesses recognize the promises made today and let no man separate what we have joined. Friends, I give you our newlywed couple. Please support their union with your applause."

At first, the response was lukewarm at best, but a few enthusiastic witnesses in back motivated the crowd to sufficient fervor. Once the clapping died down, Janek bowed and then raised their arms high. People started taking pictures, as if the occasion truly needed personal commemoration.

I got a rope instead of a ring. How...odd.

"WHEN CAN WE take this off?" Thalia demanded, about an hour later.

They had proceeded through the customary Eldritch fertility dance and the pack receiving line, which was short as hell, since most of Raff's people were still at Pine Ridge. Now they were about to eat, so he could understand her aggravation.

This should be fun.

While it might be wrong to tease her, he still intended to wring every drop of satisfaction from imparting this info. "You didn't know?"

"What?"

"We wear the handfast cord for twenty-four hours. It ensures we stay close, build intimacy, and enjoy a playful first night."

"You can't be serious." Her eyes shot purple daggers, and her free hand balled up, the most temper she'd shown in his presence. It made a nice change from icy composure.

But…she wouldn't really hit me?

Fortunately, Janek overheard the sharp tone and stepped up to offer moral support. "He's not jesting, your highness. It's a pack peculiarity. I suppose you're free to disregard our traditions once you're out of the public eye, but I would ask you to bear with us at least until you retire. Otherwise, Bibi will not waste time informing everyone upon her return."

The seer was going to be a pain in Raff's ass; he just knew it. While Thalia's jaw clenched, her fingers relaxed, so the crisis must be past. She lowered her arm and stayed close to his side as he moved off. It seemed like there was an endless stream of Eldritch wanting a word, some impassive, others actively hostile.

"I don't think I have many fans in your holding," he said lightly.

"Do you want a candid reply or a tactful one?"

"That's an answer already, Lady Silver. Or did you not realize I could read between the lines?"

"From the way you play Kingcross, I wouldn't guess you could read at all."

It was a joke—he knew it was—but the sting bit deep anyway, because that was so much like what he'd heard from his father, years ago. Only back then, it was more, and longer, and worse. Grim memories beckoned like a murky sea. If his contract bride started down that road, he might not even be able to stay for the promised three months.

"Ha," he said.

Raff didn't think he'd shown any outward sign that the quip bothered him, but her brow furrowed. If she was as adroit as Gavriel seemed to think, however, she might have a gift for reading nuances. "I'm sorry. I meant it as a gentle poke at your gamesmanship, but it didn't come across, did it?"

"Forgotten already. Do I seem like the sensitive sort?" It was an offhand question, but she seemed to be considering seriously.

"Yes."

When her gaze locked with his, the noise in the hall faded. He had the unnerving sensation that she could see through him, right down to his bones. It took Sky's hand on his arm to pull his eyes away, and even then, he could still feel the princess next to him. *What the hell?*

"What is it, pup?"

"Don't call me that," she snapped. "Janek and Lileth say it's time for you to lead the procession to the dining hall."

"I hope there will be speeches and toasts to our health. You know how much I love that sort of flummery."

Skylett shot him a dark look, but she stepped back so they could take their place at the head of the queue. Since he was still tied to Thalia, he let her set the pace. She solved his minor dilemma by setting her bound hand on his arm. Raff measured his pace to match hers. Since she knew the way, it was best to let her lead. Silence prevailed as they proceeded to the dining hall.

Though he knew little about such matters, it was clear even to him that the princess's staff must have worked long hours to transform the cold stone. Old tapestries covered the walls, and the sweet herbs burned here as well. Winter woodcraft wreaths graced every table, and Eldritch workers were still scurrying, even as they stepped in.

"I don't know if the food will be up to par," she said softly. "But we weren't expecting to push the schedule forward so much, so please understand that my people have done their best."

"Are you asking me to be gracious?" Amusement flickered through him.

Raff headed for the table with the largest centerpiece and a placard that marked it as 'RESERVED'. If that was wrong, she'd surely correctly him. Since the princess maintained her courteous hold on his arm, he trusted this was where he ought to be. He pulled out her chair and seated himself once she was settled. There was room at the table for his four guards, two more seats as well. At that moment he realized he had no idea who might sit with them as Thalia's family.

Soon, Lileth took her place on the other side, but the final chair remained empty. Until a lean, foxy-faced Eldritch woman slipped into the spot five minutes later. She had darker hair than most of her people, a burnished gold instead of white or silver, and her eyes were a piercing green, hard as agate, and intensely watchful. She smelled...strange, a tang of something chemical and unfamiliar. He had seen her before—and not just while wandering Daruvar. A bit later, it came to him.

I encountered her first at Ash Valley.

Which meant she had been among Gavriel's people who survived after Lord Talfayen turned. Raff's attention sharpened, and sure enough, she was wearing twin daggers that marked her as a Noxblade. *Is she protection or close kin?* The only way to find out was to ask.

Raff tried a charming smile. "I don't believe I've had the pleasure."

Unlike Gavriel, this Noxblade didn't scowl like it was part of her training, but he noticed that while her mouth curved, her eyes were still as cold as a mossy pond. "We haven't been introduced, though I did see you at Ash Valley. I'm Tirael."

"She's my...cousin," the princess said.

"You're being generous." With an expression as blank as that white linen, Tirael smoothed a napkin across her lap. "It would be wrong of me to rely on our distant connection, so it's a privilege to be included at the head table."

Lileth chose that moment to rise with her glass in hand. "It's time for the wedding toasts and then we can finally eat. Thank you all for your patience."

Surprisingly, Janek stood as well, possibly in response to a prior arrangement. Raff hadn't been informed how the wedding would go; just as well, he wasn't interested. His stomach rumbled, reminding him how long it had been since breakfast. Plus, they didn't serve protein-dense fare like he was used to. *Unless we do some hunting, living here will kill me.* Even the princess's white vedda beast was starting to look delicious.

But there should be red hart somewhere in these hills. If we take one down, the venison will last a while.

Come to it, he needed to decide who to keep with him for his three-month tenure. *Probably not Bibi, Pine Ridge needs her. Janek would be an asset here...*

The old wolf cut into his thoughts by tapping a small spoon against his glass to quiet the room. "May you be poor in misfortune and rich in blessings. This day we saw two shadows become one, a single thread binding you to the other's fate."

Still, why does that sound so...ominous?

Lileth continued the toast. Despite his general antipathy for formal nonsense, Raff had to admire how smoothly they'd orchestrated the occasion. "From this day forward, neither of you is alone. May you always have walls for the wind, a roof for the rain, a hearth with a merrily crackling fire, and everything that your heart desires. Raise your glass and drink to our fair princess and the wolf lord."

The elder Eldritch woman lifted her goblet high, so it caught the morning light, refracting sunbeams, then she drained it, likely showing her commitment to the marital alliance her princess had chosen. Reflexively, Raff brought his glass up and it smelled strange, bitter and—

"Stop!" he shouted. "The wine's been poisoned!"

10.

THAT WAS IMPOSSIBLE, it couldn't be true. *We had security. The fortress is secure*—

Can't breathe. Thalia's throat tightened as fear became a vise on her neck, rising, rising, floodwater that would choke and drown her. "No!" The word burst free before she could lock down her panic.

A queen is always—*oh, fuck that. Fuck being calm.*

Nothing could happen to Lileth, who had been like a mother to her for so long. She leapt from her chair as the older woman collapsed. Janek's reflexes were fast enough, even at his age, that the old wolf didn't let her hit the floor. Instead, he swung Lileth up in his arms and moved toward the exit.

"Don't eat or drink anything," she called to the guests, rushing after him to bark more orders. "Take samples from each plate and bottle, then discard the rest. I need to know how broad the attack was."

Tirael nodded. "I'll get Ferith. She can supervise the investigation."

Since Raff had been treated after the disastrous hunt, Janek must know the way to the infirmary. He proved this was true with his sure but hurried footfalls. Thalia called Dr. Wyeth as she ran, the rest of the wolves close behind. "We have an emergency. I need you right away."

"What's happened?" He'd been one of the few exempted from the festivities, given permission to keep watch on a couple of patients instead.

"I'll tell you when I see you. Prep the IC machine."

Dr. Wyeth met them outside the makeshift hospital, his gaze flying to Lileth's prone body. "Not Lil!"

"She's been poisoned," Raff said. "I'm not sure how much was in the wine, but she drank the whole thing. I smelled bitter almonds and a sharp medicinal tang in addition to the fermented grapes and the essence of the wood cask—"

The doctor shot him an incredulous look. "You got all that in one whiff?"

Thalia might've been amazed if she hadn't watched the cats sniffing for mines ahead of her convoy. "Animari senses are incredibly sharp. Help her, please."

Responding to her urgency, Dr. Wyeth took command of the scene. "Get me bloodwork and pump her stomach."

The nurse leapt to do his bidding, taking samples even as the rest of the medical team hurried around the infirmary. Thalia barely noticed when the wolf lord took her arm, but she did resist when he tried to pull her from the room.

"I have to be here."

"We're in the way. Let's not hinder the rescue efforts."

"Then you go," she said sharply. "This woman practically raised me, and I will *not* leave her."

His hand dropped away. "I didn't know." It was an indication of his character that he didn't force the issue. "Then let's move to the doorway. You can still see everything from there, but we won't interfere with treatment."

"Fine." Thalia let him lead her that far. Her heart thundered in her ears, an infinite onslaught of dread.

Raff turned to his people. "Please go check on things in the dining hall and work with the head Noxblade to figure out who did this…and why."

"I'm the target," Thalia whispered.

"Why would you assume that?"

"Because poison just makes your people sick. It's not an efficient means to eliminate a wolf, but our people have been ending each other this way for centuries. We're *good* at it. And it doesn't make sense that they'd strike at Lileth…she's a low-value target. Therefore, they must not have realized that you'd detect the toxin before we all ingested it."

The whole time she spoke, she didn't take her eyes off Lil's pale face. It was terrible to see the tube go down her throat, worse to imagine the worst coming to pass. *This is because of me. My choices.* This nightmarish tableau also summoned diabolical images, those she'd spent a hundred years trying to forget.

He didn't respond to her assessment, which probably meant he agreed.

"It seems like she's very special to you." It was an invitation to talk, open-ended.

Normally she wouldn't be drawn so easily but it felt like her tongue was unhinged. "I barely remember my mother, only how she died. Lileth was always there."

"How your mother died…?" He trailed off, gentle but curious, and she supposed discretion didn't matter.

He'll learn what sort of unholy bargain he's made, soon

enough.

"She was poisoned by my father's mistress," Thalia said. "Right in her afternoon tea. By nightfall, she was foaming at the mouth. By sunrise, she was gone."

"Shit," Raff said.

It was the first time she'd thought of him by his first name instead of his title or what he represented to her people, but there was no point in mental formality when she was making such revelations about her family.

"How old were you?" he asked.

"Ten. Scarcely more than an infant."

"We'll agree to differ there, but...I'm sorry. This must be bringing back some dire memories."

"That's true enough."

Thalia watched as Dr. Wyeth worked frantically to save Lileth, trying every hope they had. The dialysis setting on the IC machine didn't seem to be helping fast enough, as Lileth lacked the supernal Animari recuperative process. The older woman was paler than death, so still that she scarcely seemed to be breathing.

Raff tugged lightly on the bond that connected them at the wrist to draw her attention. "What happened to her? The mistress."

"My father had her publicly executed, head on a pike."

His eyes widened. "You mean that literally?"

She sighed, wondering why she'd thought it was wise to open this Pandora's box, especially now. "Yes. The birds ate her eyes, pecked away at her decaying flesh, until she was only a skin-pocked skull with tufts of hair. An example of what happens when you're caught going against the hierarchy."

"Caught?"

Each of his questions underscored how different they were, how little he could understand her. "Tradition is valued here. The same four families have held power for generations. Nobody escapes their birth rank, outside of truly diabolical scheming."

"I'm not sure I understand what you're getting at."

"If she'd succeeded, she would've married my father and become my stepmother. People judged her more harshly, not for committing the crime, but for leaving evidence. A whisper of unprovable suspicion probably would have enhanced her reputation."

Raff let out a slow whistle. "That...is deeply fucked."

"I know." She would change that, if she could—so it didn't require a perfect crime to change your social status.

Lileth still hadn't moved. The wine was out of her system, now swirling in the IC machine. Dr. Wyeth didn't appear hopeful; Thalia watched his mouth tighten, the pleat between his brows deepening. She dragged the wolf lord over to join the doctor, unable to stem the questions.

"What have you learned? What are her chances?"

"It's bad." The bald words nearly made her knees buckle, but the wolf lord grabbed her elbow and held her up with such casual strength that gratitude suffused her.

I'm glad he's here.

"Tell me," she ordered.

"We've identified three separate toxins: chokevine, widow's veil, and some kind of venom. The database can't tell if it comes from spider, snake, or reptile. I've given her the first two antidotes, but if my hypothesis is right..." He hesitated.

"Just fucking speak," Thalia snapped.

"I believe these substances were specially chosen because they blend into a fast-acting super poison, and if we can't identify the last one, it's impossible for us to counteract. And that's not even the worst news in this situation."

"Breathe," Raff said.

His arm went around her because she suddenly had no strength in her legs. *How can I lead? I can't even save Lil.*

"Which means..." she whispered.

"I've never seen a toxin get into the blood system so fast. At base, this is a designer, next-level Eldritch killer. She has internal bleeding and her organs are failing. We can make her comfortable, but it's unlikely she'll awaken. I'm sorry. You should begin the death watch and prepare for the worst."

"STEADY," RAFF MURMURED, as Thalia sagged into his arms.

She would've hit the floor if he hadn't been holding onto her, and that would've strained the marriage knot beyond what it could bear. It might look like superstition to an outsider, but this was already the shittiest wedding day ever. They didn't need a bad omen on top of an assassination attempt.

"There's truly no hope?" she asked, all desperate eyes and tissue-thin voice.

The doctor shifted, hesitating, but he finally shook his head. "Even if we could identify the final agent, we couldn't synthesize an antidote fast enough to save her."

Thalia straightened, likely trying to compose herself, though her grief was palpable. "Bring in two chairs and make sure she feels no pain. We'll stay until the end."

"It's fine if I'm here too?" Raff expected an argument over stupid wolf customs, a queenly demand for solitude.

"You're my husband," she said simply.

Hearing that, it pulled a cord within him, as if she'd twined her fingers in silver strands and tugged them taut. "Would you like to talk?"

"About what?"

"Anything."

Sighing softly, she shook her head. "I'd rather you did, if you have something that will fill the silence."

Before he could respond, the medical aide, a burly sort, considering most Eldritch were lanky and lean, brought in the seats she'd requested. "Will these do, Your Highness?"

"Fine, thank you." Blank words, blank eyes.

She was like a piece of paper devoid of ink. Raff sat first and pulled her with him, or she might've hovered beside the chair for hours. They still hadn't eaten, and he was hungry as fuck, but it would be an asshole move to demand a meal delivered to a death watch. Mentally, he snarled a warning at his cavernous stomach.

"Would you like a personal anecdote or something that will teach you more about Pine Ridge?" Mentally he sifted through his stories. Nothing too dirty or outrageous; it wouldn't fit the mood. *Maybe I could just talk about—*

"I don't care. I'm not trying to be difficult. It's just…" She trailed off, her voice wispy and broken.

Watching Lileth die was practically killing her too; he could see her pain and despair, smell it on her skin. "Got it. I wish I wasn't witnessing such a sorrowful occasion, but you're not alone, Lady Silver."

"Thalia."

"That's your name," he agreed.

"Call me by it. I'm giving you permission, which is significant among my people. We're bound at the wrist for the next day, so it seems silly to insist on a title."

"Ah. It's pretty. What does it mean?"

"To bloom."

"Well, sure enough, you're a flower tightly furled." In other circumstances, he would've added some flirtatious nonsense about petals and dew, but this wasn't the time. Even he could see that she needed solace, not seduction.

She reached out and took the older woman's hand, pressing her two over those pale, limp fingers. By virtue of their wedding knot, his hand went with hers, offering comfort to two women, both of whom he barely knew.

"Weren't you going to tell a story? Lileth even said you have a silver tongue."

The hell of it was, he couldn't think of anything to say. "I...think I'm having performance anxiety."

Thalia tilted her head; she was so out of place in the bare infirmary in her wedding gown with a formal cascade of hair, blue gems glittering amid silver tresses. "There's a joke to be made, but I don't have the heart. Not when she's dying for me."

"You said she's like a mother to you. If you feel that way, she does too. Which is why she'll go to the afterworld happy she could protect you until the very end." He was trying to console her, so panic rippled over him when her eyes welled up.

"Faith and fire, why did you have to put it like that?"

"Because that's how it is."

She didn't make a sound, but tears spilled over and trickled down her cheeks. In his life, Raff had made a few women cry, but never like this. They were usually throwing things at him and cursing as they did. Slowly, hesitantly, he took her hand and laced their fingers together. It seemed like a juvenile attempt, not a move that would help in this situation, but she stared at that point of contact with puzzled, blurry eyes.

"Nobody's ever just...held my hand," she said faintly.

She's been fighting alone for longer than you can imagine. Gavriel clearly knew what he was talking about in regard to Princess Thalia. Raff wished like hell that the Noxblade hadn't already left. From what he'd seen at Ash Valley, the bastard was good at getting answers. Plus, he'd taken Mags with him; she would've been such an asset.

"I guess that's my job now. No escape from the big, bad wolf."

The IC machine shrieked then, an alarm so shrill that it made Raff flinch. *Vitals dropping,* it intoned, and the whole medical team came running. He pulled Thalia out of the way, but he knew—and she must too—that even if they won this fight, they couldn't win the war. She started crying in earnest, something he couldn't even have imagined. Her face was wet and splotched red, her painstakingly perfect cosmetics smeared down her face as if she were the sad clown everyone avoided at carnivals.

The life line dropped lower as Thalia wept. Raff pulled her to him as their bound wrists allowed, and silently cursed whoever had murdered Lileth. If he hadn't understood the stakes before, he did now. Sure, they had talked a lot about loss of land and forces arrayed against them, but that was all abstract, theoretical harm. Real damage was the blood slowly trickling out of Lileth's eyes, her mouth, her ears, and her nostrils.

"She's a martyr," Thalia was whispering.

"What?" Not a smart question, but he was so fucking tired and hungry that his brain wasn't working its best, and even in peak conditions, it wouldn't be his strong point.

Rage boiled up to the point that it was getting hard to be gentle. Raff wanted to go wolf and bite somebody's face off over this. Their wedding might not have been romantic or born of mutual love, but he'd meant those promises, and some asshole had the *nerve,* the fucking nerve—

"In our faith, it's said that if someone dies with a pure heart, pure sacrifice, she will take her place at the Mother's side for all time. Blood tears are one sign of martyrdom."

"She'll become a goddess or something?" He wasn't clear at all on Eldritch theology.

"A saint, perhaps, if other portents appear. She'd laugh at the notion."

The line flattened out completely on the medical machine and the tone of the alarm changed, dropping from a klaxon's blare to a mournful drone. No mistaking what it meant. Thalia collapsed against him, sobbing so hard he feared she might be sick. She gave him all her weight, and it was no burden to hold her. Her body was so slim and light that her bones might be hollow, like the bird-kin Animari up in the Aerie.

Raff barely heard the doctor call time of death. He looked away as the nurse drew the sheet over Lileth's face. The blood on her cheeks soaked through, lending her death linens the grim look of abstract painting done in blood.

"Go," he said sharply. "Give us some privacy."

The medical staff left, making him think he had some authority here. *Unexpected. Looks like I'm not entirely a paper tiger.*

With his right arm, he supported Thalia and with his left, he held onto her hand, otherwise, she would be tearing at her own skin. He'd never seen grief like this, never

imagined the icily contained Eldritch princess had that much
fire below the skin, like a molten river running beneath
snowy tundra. He didn't tell her to calm down or hold it in.
It felt like it *meant* something that she was breaking down in
front of him. Even when she screamed and scratched him,
he let her rake those welts and shrugged off the blood she
scraped from his skin. The wounds healed so swiftly that it
hardly mattered.

A courier knocked on the infirmary door, and Raff took
the tablet he proffered with an impatient gesture, guarding
Thalia with his body. Her people shouldn't see her like this.
He played the message because she couldn't.

Only a few words from that bastard Gilbraith: "I told
you you'd be sorry."

Eventually, Thalia cried herself out and pulled out her
phone with trembling hands. He didn't know who she was
calling, but her steady words sent chills down his spine.
"Lileth d'Aquitane of House Talfayen, last of her name, has
passed from this world. Begin the funeral rites. Her death
anniversary is also my wedding day, and as the All-Mother is
my witness, I will not rest until Ruark Gilbraith's head is
mounted on a pike."

11.

THALIA COULDN'T REMEMBER the last time someone else had washed her face. Painted it, certainly. She routinely sat so that Madu could render her suitable for some formal occasion. Afterward, she was always alone in wiping her skin clean, alone to see the vulnerability reappear as if by magic. Cosmetics were like armor in a sense, or perhaps more of a mask that permitted her to reveal only what she chose.

Not today.

Today, Raff lathered her face with one clumsy hand, splashing her clothes and scrubbing with an enthusiasm that could double as an exfoliant. Afterward, he patted her face dry, and she wondered why she hadn't protested. Numbness only went so far as an explanation; she needed to step up, demand answers. Somebody had to pay. If she didn't take swift action, it would undercut her ability to lead. The people would remember this crisis and the way she'd folded like a paper flower.

"I should—"

"Ferith is on top of things," Raff cut in. "You haven't slept well since I've been here, and you *just* lost someone dear to you. Part of being an effective leader is knowing when to delegate, so you have the strength to carry on long-term. If there's any new information, they'll notify us."

"I wish we had the kind of surveillance tech here that they used in Ash Valley." After she said it, she realized the futility. Didn't Gavriel have the ability to circumvent such equipment? If his gift had manifested so, someone else's might have, too.

"That would help, but your Noxblades know how to get answers. Trust in them and rest. Tomorrow, the funeral will be taxing enough."

Thalia sighed and gave in. She lacked the fortitude to drag him along to question the kitchen staff, who would be more likely to offer honest answers to Ferith. Thalia's presence tended to end in stuttered answers and hasty, repeated obeisance. Few of her people knew her as more than a symbol of resistance to her father's adherence to the old ways, where bigotry and isolationism prospered.

"We haven't talked about where we'll sleep while you're here," she said.

"Tavros is packing my things. I'll vacate the rooms you set aside for me, so Janek and Tavros can share it. Magda's quarters are empty now, so Skylett and Bibi are moving there. That should provide some relief from the tension between your guards and my people."

"Nicely resolved. Was there a lot of friction?" she asked.

"Some, but that's to be expected. It's late, let's get ready for bed." Raff punctuated that comment by turning down the covers and leading her over to the light switch. The room was plunged into darkness.

She had no idea what time it was, but they'd sat for hours on Lileth's death watch, so it was probably getting on toward midnight. "I hope you're not offended but I'd rather..." There was no polite way to say she was in no mood for bedsport. Even under better conditions, the necessary consummation would be awkward.

"I'm a wolf, not a demon. I'm not trying to get between your legs tonight." He tugged gently on the cord that bound their wrists. "What do you usually sleep in?

"Nothing," Thalia said. "If you close your eyes and move your arm as I do, maybe I can get undressed."

If I can't, I'm taking this damned knot off and a pox on your pack customs. There's no way I'm sleeping in this dress.

His obedience almost made her smile, despite the steady thrum of grief that beat through her as regular as her heartbeat. It took a little maneuvering, but she managed to get out of her dress without destroying it, thanks to the many buttons in back and sleeveless design. There was no way for Raff to disrobe without ruining his suit, but he didn't seem to care. He looked away until she climbed under the covers and then he flopped on top, fully dressed. His groan echoed her own sentiments perfectly.

Folding his free arm behind his head, he kicked off his shoes. "I could sleep for a week."

"We can't, unfortunately."

"Do you ever think about running away from it all?"

"Never," she said.

"Me either. Hardly ever. Only like six or eight times a day."

Thalia laughed. Unbelievable in this situation, and she felt immediately disloyal. "You make it sound as if you're a figurehead in Pine Ridge, and I know that's not true."

"How?" he asked.

"Would you think it's uncouth if I admit to acquiring

certain intel on you?"

"I suppose that depends on the nature of what you've learned. Do you have any naked photos? If so, I hope they're flattering. Or perhaps you've got a sex vid? I *had* been thinking of making one, so you can save me the trouble."

She opened her eyes wide, conscious that he was being absurd to leaven her spirits. It seemed he didn't mind mocking himself for her amusement. "I don't have anything like that," she said softly. "As for what I do have, I suppose you must wait and see."

"Ah, secrets and intrigues. You exhaust me with such innuendo."

"You pretend that you aren't clever, Raff Pineda, but I find that you know what people need exceptionally well."

He propped up on an elbow to stare at her in the dark. "You think I'm clever and striving to hide it?"

"Not very well," Thalia muttered. "Yours is a rare gift, for the hearts of men cannot be calculated or reckoned with pure intellect."

She sometimes feared she was too much her father's daughter to be a good leader. Not an *effective* one, nobody could argue that she got results. But goodness? That was a separate issue entirely. Thalia had learned too much about subterfuge and deception at her father's knee, not enough about personal warmth.

"You say the strangest things," Raff mumbled.

"I applaud the tactic. It's best if people underestimate your prowess. Such poor assessment leads to overconfidence, and that generally ends in abject defeat."

"Go to sleep, Thalia. It will be another long day tomorrow."

Since he was right, she tried her best, but her mind

wouldn't shut down until he set a hand on her stomach, blazing warm even through the covers. "Stop rolling. It's like sharing the bed with four restless pups."

A grumpy admonition, but it settled her down nonetheless. And then she slept.

In the morning, she woke much later than she'd planned. Late enough that Raff had untied the knot binding them. *It's been twenty-four hours already.* She found a meal waiting for her, toasted bread with melted cheese and a dish of sliced fruit. Thalia ate quickly and washed up, then she donned simple black mourning clothes. Lileth wouldn't care if she wore formal attire, after all.

The door opened as she was pulling on her boots, militant, not fashionable. "Good morning," she said.

"Everything is set for the funeral. Are you ready?"

Not for this. Not ever.

"Of course."

Raff's four wolves waited outside, along with Ferith, Tirael, and some young Noxblades who had probably been promoted from their apprenticeships. Ferith needed to choose some likely children to begin training, or the numbers of capable agents in the field would diminish, a disastrous outcome with House Talfayen hovering on the brink of war.

She led the procession, all stately poise, but she might have stumbled if not for Raff's arm beneath her hand. Everyone was already assembled in the hall, swiftly repurposed to honor Lil's passing. They had no furnace here at Daruvar, so her body must burn the old way, in a fire built by hand. It was a sin that she should be laying Lileth to rest under such circumstances. Ruark Gilbraith had taken credit, but the one who had done his evil bidding was still roaming free. To make matters worse, Gavriel wasn't even here to sing, so Tirael was filling in, but her voice was light and thready, lacking Gavriel's resonance.

Offering Lileth such a second-rate Song of Death broke Thalia's heart.

RAFF HAD NEVER attended an Eldritch funeral before. Among the pack, the ones who loved the deceased best would be singing and telling stories. This affair was quiet, after the eerie chorus. Thalia blew out a candle and moved about with a censer of heated oil and made a sigil on everyone else's forehead. Then, a company of Noxblades took the linen-wrapped body out to a bonfire they'd built in the courtyard.

The wolves had been asked to move their vehicles to one side, making space, but he didn't know why until now. With great ceremony, they consigned Lileth to the flames. It all seemed short and simple, but he didn't ask about the reasons behind their rites. It didn't make sense to ask about battle strategies in the middle of a fight, and the same principle applied here.

The mourners all threw something into the fire. Some had herbs, others had books or household articles, and Thalia dropped a whole dress on the fire. He would've liked to ask Janek about it, but the old wolf was out of earshot. That would've also meant letting go of Thalia, and she had such a desperate grip on him that her fingers might leave marks.

Another first.

"You're probably wondering about the death gifts," she said softly.

He glanced at her in surprise, hesitant but interested. "I am, but don't let my curiosity distract you from proper reverence for the occasion."

"Lil wouldn't mind. We're offering her favorite things in life. We believe that by burning them, she can have them with her in the afterworld."

"Then she'll be wearing that dress you sent and reading that book that Ferith gave her at the All-Mother's side."

"You learn fast," Thalia said.

That wasn't something that Raff had heard a lot, before. Here in Eldritch lands, it seemed like Thalia said it every other day. If she kept it up, he might start believing it. Come that, he *had* always learned better from interaction than books or classroom teachings.

Frowning, he muttered, "I don't have anything to give her."

"Here." She pressed a square of cloth into his hands—white linen embroidered with blue flowers. "She made this for me when I was small and crying for my mother. I'd like for her to have it back."

After the myriad struggles of this life, Raff hoped like hell that there would be no tears in the afterworld, but he took the handkerchief in the spirit in which it was intended. He joined the queue of those waiting to drop their offering in the fire and found the orderly array interesting as well. The blaze was big enough that twenty people could've chucked things in, but that would also probably be disrespectful, if you imagined Lileth on the other side, collecting her tribute. In life, you wouldn't want folks chucking stuff when it was supposed to be a special occasion.

He moved up in the line and heard Ferith whispering,

"May you be well with our dear Mother. You pass from our sight, but you do not travel alone. Our love goes with you and will carry you to our beloved dead. Pass from love into love."

Simple and heart-wrenching.

Raff repeated, "Pass from love into love," as he dropped the handkerchief into the crackling flames.

After he returned to stand with Thalia, he kept watch on the fire. His eyes watered from the excruciating smell of burning flesh, and the rest of his wolves did no better. The Eldritch tolerated it, but they lacked the enhanced senses that came with being Animari.

Thalia touched his arm lightly. "If you want to go in, you don't have to stay until…" Her voice broke, and she tried again. "Until it's finished. That's my role."

He heard what she didn't say. *Until Lileth's gone.* As he hesitated, Bibi made a noise in her throat. It wouldn't do Thalia any good if his people got sick in the middle of the service. Making a quick decision, he beckoned to the wolf guards.

"We've paid our respects. Let's withdraw."

The smell was more bearable inside the fortress, thanks to sturdy stone walls. Raff herded the group to the room the wolf women were sharing, formerly allotted to Magda. *Can't believe she hasn't called, not even once. Faithless cat.* While his romantic pursuit had been singularly unsuccessful, he'd thought that they'd become friends, at least.

Bibi made a hot, strong tea to wash away the smell of death that they all had in their nose and throats. They settled with cups in the sitting area, and Raff let them drink a bit in silence. Nobody seemed to know exactly what to say; he'd already heard and overruled their objection to this marriage, and now an Eldritch elder was dead. Given half a chance, Bibi would talk more about the dark portents she'd seen in her dreams.

"They'll be at it all day," Janek said. "Maybe into the night as well. It's fearsome slow, burning a body down to ash in such a way."

"I could help them fell some trees. They'll need plenty of wood," Tavros offered.

The young wolf always had far too much energy, but it seemed harmless enough, so Raff said, "Speak to Ferith once we're done here. I wouldn't know if they need aid."

"Grunt work is all he's good for," Skylett teased.

"At least he's good for something," Bibi said. "Exactly what you have you contributed since we've been here?"

The seer valued her privacy and sharing a room must be making her cranky. Raff cut off the conflict before it could escalate. "Let's not debate who's most useful. Instead, I'd rather find out what you've learned."

"About what?" Tavros asked.

He stifled a sigh. It had seemed like a good idea to bring someone guileless, but the young wolf might be too green to realize if he heard something important. Fortunately, he also had Janek, Bibi, and Skylett to serve as his eyes and ears.

"The murder, you dolt." Janek rapped his knuckles lightly on Tavros's head.

Raff went on as if people hadn't interrupted. "That or anything related to House Gilbraith. I haven't mentioned it to Thalia, but she must have a traitor inside these walls."

Bibi nodded. "Someone with kitchen access. My dreams aren't clear, but you're right, Raff. It's someone close to her, closer than she knows."

Closer than she knows? What does that even mean?

"Is there anything you can do to make your visions more specific?" That earned him a poisonous look from the seer.

"I don't have a magic mirror," she snapped. "Nor can I pull answers from the ether."

"Well, it narrows the list of suspects," Skylett said thoughtfully.

The old wolf rose and clapped Raff on the shoulder, then headed to fetch the teapot for a refill. "Hell of a thing, packmaster—and on your wedding day, no less."

She'll always remember Lileth's death on our anniversary. Since they weren't a normal couple, maybe that didn't matter, but it gnawed at him along with Bibi's fearsome whispers and the hints of a dark fate that they couldn't avoid. Yet it pissed him off to think that in such a modern age, people were still against inter-marrying on principle.

"We stop this Gilbraith asshole. That's our mandate. Find out what you can. You have my permission to poke around and ask awkward questions."

"At last," Janek said. "My purpose in life is revealed."

As Raff opened the door, he was startled to spot the lead Noxblade pacing the halls outside. At his appearance, Ferith seemed to make a decision.

She strode into the room and bowed. She had a sturdy build and she favored blue-black hair and was meticulous with the dyeing, so you'd never see a glimpse of silver or white at the roots. The contrast of white skin, onyx hair, and pale blue eyes made her look like a character from a children's story, but her attitude was all-business.

"I've come to make my report, Your Highness."

12.

THALIA STAYED WITH the fire until everything was finished and then she filled an urn with the ashes, more symbolic than complete. Full dark had fallen, so it was risky to venture out. Rather than put her people in danger, she climbed to the highest point in Daruvar—the roof of the west tower—and let Lileth go. She didn't weep or say good-bye.

Despite the cold, she lingered, staring up at the starry sky. None of it seemed quite real. How could the world have changed so much in a short time? She was married to the wolf lord, and she'd lost Lil. It was hard not to see this as a trade, considering that Ruark had tried to murder everyone at the head table as the price of her alliance.

Enough. She'd want me to step on Gilbraith instead of wallowing in grief.

Squaring her shoulders, she climbed down and went to her room, where she found Raff waiting with simple food and a thermos of herbal tea. He offered a tentative smile. "I wasn't sure when you'd get back. Ferith came by to talk about what she's learned."

"Let me wash up and then we'll talk as I eat."

"Go ahead, don't mind me."

This give-and-take was so awkward, but at the same time, it would've been worse to come back to a silent room and sit with the knowledge that she'd never see Lil again. Quickly, she took a shower, mostly so her meal didn't go stone cold. *It doesn't matter. It's fuel.* She dried off haphazardly and shrugged into her robe.

Sometimes it seemed as if she'd spent her whole life embattled. Before she left the confines of Riverwind, it was a cold war, waged against her own father in secrets and schemes. Now, it would become an outright battle, fought against her own people—because they preferred a return to the old ways, or because they didn't trust her to lead them in a new direction. Two sides of the same coin.

"What did Ferith say?" she asked, stepping out of the bathroom with towel in hand.

"She's compiled a list of everyone who had kitchen access. There are like thirty names to eliminate, though. It won't be easy."

"Anything else?"

Raff shook his head. "She didn't mention any particular suspicions, if that's what you mean. I'm volunteering my services as your food sniffer, going forward. We won't be caught like this again."

"Thank you."

If they'd thought to do that before, Lileth wouldn't have died. Thalia should've known better, should've realized that if the other houses were acting in opposition, she couldn't be safe anywhere. As if he sensed those thoughts, Raff stood and fetched her by the hand, tugging her toward the tray.

"I've already checked this out and tasted everything. If there was anything wrong with it, I'd be sick by now."

She stared at him, wide-eyed. "I never intended for you to become my taster. That...it's not part of our agreement."

"Then take it as a bonus service. As you noted before, poison isn't a good way to do in a wolf."

"I don't know what to say."

"Don't talk, just eat. I've got a shipment of drones on the way. They'll help guard the perimeter and the surveillance feature should allow us to detect incursions faster."

Since he'd said he didn't want her thanks, she ate her food silently. It was lukewarm but filling, and she pictured him tasting each dish to make sure no harm came to her, a level of protection she hadn't expected from their marital agreement. Once the tray was clear, he set it outside like this was a fancy hotel. Still, someone would probably pick it up eventually.

Thalia cleared her throat. "Things were...chaotic. At our wedding. Which means we left an important task undone."

How am I supposed to bring this up?

"...Task?" Raff repeated the word with obvious bafflement. "Is there another part to the ceremony?"

"Consummation," she said firmly.

In her whole life, Thalia had never propositioned anyone. She'd taken a few lovers at Riverwind, but only after mutual feelings developed and desire built on its own, over time. Her husband's face reflected sheer astonishment, so she guessed he hadn't thought of this.

"It's not the time. Don't worry about that. We have other problems—"

"This *is* one of our problems. If we fail to consummate, the marriage can be annulled, and I can be forced to wed Ruark Gilbraith. He will then use me to claim the throne and lock me away as my father did."

"Like hell," Raff snarled.

Thalia savored the bittersweet feeling for a moment before she responded. "We must join, whether you want me or not. Divorce is complicated among my people, and your claim will offer security from Ruark's ill intentions."

"I don't want to *own* you," Raff protested. "I didn't realize your society was so..."

"Patriarchal? Yes, it always has been. That is one of the many things I'd like to change, if I survive long enough."

"What I'm hearing is that we need to have sex."

She sighed. "I'm sorry if you don't want to, but we *must*."

"Look, you just lost someone who was like a mother to you, and I'm not into coercion. I only take people to bed who are eager for it."

On a deep breath, she untied her robe and let it drop. "Then get me there. I've heard that you can seduce damn near anyone."

This was pure bravado. Her body must seem thin and frail compared to his Animari lovers, and she couldn't read his expression at all. If he refused, it would damage her pride and she'd still have to worry about a potential annulment because of Ruark Gilbraith.

"You're sure this is what you want?" Raff finally asked.

She didn't know him well enough to want his body, but she did want to get this over with. Thalia nodded. "Yes, please."

"Then let's see how we do together. Under these circumstances, I'll take willing instead of eager. But get this, Thalia. If I can't make you hungry, we won't finish tonight. Even if it takes a month of trying, I won't make you mine until you're shivering for it."

That seemed unlikely and quite a waste of time, but she didn't protest his intentions. It spoke well of him that he cared about her satisfaction, and maybe she could fake the necessary enthusiasm. She'd done that when she didn't want to hurt someone's feelings, and they weren't getting the job done. Most of her best orgasms, she'd given to herself, possibly because it was so hard to let her guard down.

"Very well," she said.

"Get in bed. I'll shower and join you soon."

While she hadn't expected him to be overwhelmed with lust at the sight of her bare skin, *some* reaction would've been nice. She kept her dignity as she padded across the room and slid under the covers. *Think sexy thoughts.* Thalia ran her hands down her body, and it had been long enough that a whisper of pleasure flickered to life. With so many worries whirling in her mind, she couldn't fan the spark to life.

Sighing, she dropped her hands to the cool sheets. Pretense would have to suffice.

A few minutes later, he came out of the bath in a swirl of steam. With his dark hair tousled and beads of water dotting his beard, he looked...wilder than she'd seen before. His body was very different, brown, broad and hard, dusted with hair. Raff moved to the bed and got in beside her, chucking the towel after he did so.

"Was that to protect my modesty?" she asked, amused.

"Maybe it was to safeguard mine. Come here."

RAFF HAD NEVER been in a situation like this.

Well, hell. You pride yourself on being good at three things:

drinking, fucking, and hunting, not necessarily in that order. Time to prove yourself.

That didn't give him any insight as to what she liked, though. She was naked beside him yet still cool and remote. He knew she wished he would just get on her and do the job like a contractor, but few things sounded less appealing than making love to someone who didn't really want it.

Tentatively, he pulled her into his arms. *We'll start with body heat.* Raff kissed her temples and touched the fine, silky hair that streamed down her back. The strands were still damp from her bath, and she shivered a little. *Does she like that?* He sifted his fingers through her hair, but she didn't move, still and quiet against him.

"Tell me about the hottest thing that's ever happened to you."

"What?" She jerked, lifting her head.

Thalia probably couldn't see him well, but her features were clear, along with the rapid blink of her eyes. Such adorable surprise.

"If you don't trust me enough to talk about dirty things, how are we supposed to do them together?"

"It's not hard," she muttered. Then her small hand darted out and she grabbed his cock. "Shit. It's really…not hard."

"I like sex. You could even say I love it, but I don't bone up on command. You know what turns me on more than anything?"

"What?"

"Being wanted."

She let out a sigh of a breath that he felt against his shoulder. "Does that mean it won't work otherwise?"

"What, sex in general? Or my cock?"

"Both, I guess."

"You were planning to fake it." It didn't take a genius to figure that out, but she seemed so surprised. "I'd rather not take you that way, Thalia. Honesty is all we have."

"I understand," she whispered.

"It's all right not to want this. All things considered, it would be a little strange if you did, right now."

"But I want that peace of mind."

"You have my word that I won't let Ruark Gilbraith take you away from me or force an annulment. Is that enough for tonight?"

"Then...should I get dressed?"

"Only if you want to. I like sleeping this way, and your skin feels incredible. You're like silk all over."

She made a little sound, pleasure or embarrassment, or both combined. Hesitantly, she put out a hand and touched his cheek, rubbing the curls of his beard between two fingertips. "It's softer than I expected."

"Will you answer my question now?"

"About the...hot thing?"

"Yes, princess. Tell me a filthy bedtime story."

Beside him, Thalia squirmed in his loose hold and her small breasts scraped against his chest. He wasn't impervious to her beauty, but right now, she didn't need a quick dicking. Her requirements ran a lot deeper, and Raff didn't even know if he could meet them. This represented his best effort in good faith, though.

"That was an endearment, wasn't it? Not my title."

"It was indeed. And you're dodging. Again."

"I'm organizing my thoughts, and I guess...one incident stands out."

"Incident? You make it sound like a sexual accident."

"It was, a little. I was in the bath at Riverwind…"

Oddly, her shyness was getting to him. Raff never would've guessed that she was so prim. He imagined cutting her loose from all that propriety, and his cock jumped a little. *Not now.* In encouragement, he stroked her back in long sweeps.

"Big tubs like in Ash Valley or a small, private one?"

"It's large enough for two, but it's private. At first, I was just washing up, but at some point, I started…feeling good."

She hardly seemed to have the words to describe the event, which struck him as endearing. "You got turned on, touching yourself?"

"I suppose. Yes. Well, that, and the warm water. It…I liked it."

"Mm, that's lovely, Thalia. So you're all slippery and wet and naked. Where did your hands feel best?"

"I know this is strange, but…my lower belly. And my thighs."

"Everyone has different sweet spots. See, this is helping already, I'll know where to start when the time comes."

"You—you're going to touch me there?" She seemed startled for some reason.

"Eventually. Probably not tonight. I'm a patient man. Continue your story?"

"Oh. Well. As I started…doing more, someone from the staff came in. I could hear them moving in the other room, and the bathroom door was ajar."

"Did you stop?" he whispered, already knowing the answer.

Making her say it was half the fun.

"No. I was scared of getting caught, but…that only made it better. I had to bite down on my hand and be quiet."

"This story has taught me a lot about you. I'll keep it in mind for next time."

"Are we really...not going to?"

"Not tonight."

She huffed out an angry breath. "I only struggled through that humiliation because I thought it might offer sufficient enticement."

"Don't consider it a humiliation. It was only a confidence, one that I will cherish. My wife's preferences are nobody's business but mine."

"You say that with such conviction. If I'm not careful, I'll start believing in you."

"Lots of people do, I haven't been able to work out why yet."

"It's because you're careful with their hearts," Thalia said. "You're a fraud, aren't you? I don't think you're a wolf at all."

"But you've seen me change," he protested.

"Sure, you can *turn* into a wolf, but at heart, you're a lamb."

Ah, she's joking. For a terrifying moment, he'd feared that she saw straight through him—that she knew he wasn't fit to fill his brother's shoes. If not for the entrenchment of his family name, Korin would be leading the pack. As it was, she stood in his shadow and helped him make the right decisions.

"I'm taking that as a compliment. In the morning, I'll help with deployment of the drones and then I'm taking my wolves to hunt, unless you object."

"Hunt what?"

"Meat," he answered, wondering if she found it repugnant. "Though if we run across any intruders, we'll take care of them, too."

"I'm sorry we're not better provisioned."

"It's not your fault. I chose to surprise you." Raff closed his eyes then, listening to the steady thump of her pulse. He could *hear* her relaxing bit by bit, now that she was sure there would be no naked pouncing.

"And you keep doing it," she whispered.

"They do say that variety is the best spice for a relationship."

"Is it? And do we have one?"

"Have what?"

"A relationship." Her tone made him turn onto his side, so he could see her better, but long hair tumbled across her face, hiding her expression from view.

"That's a ridiculous question. We chose to get married. We've fought together more than once, you saved my life, and we sent your foster mother to the afterworld together. We're in bed naked. I've never had more of a relationship with anyone."

"Damn," she said. "When you put it that way, it *has* been eventful, has it not?"

"All the more reason why we shouldn't rush the rest. We have three months here and three months in Pine Ridge. At some point, you'll want me. I mean, just look at me. I'm irresistible." He offered what he hoped was a charming grin. "And if we spot Gilbraith's shadow, I'll put his head on a pike, as you wanted."

"Oh, I do like you. That pillow talk is remarkable."

"This criticism, from a woman who thinks a story about wanking in the bath qualifies as foreplay."

Thalia made a sound low in her throat and swatted at

him, but it was a playful move, and she didn't roll away from him.

It was a start.

13.

THE NEXT MORNING, Ferith called Thalia to alert her that she had guests in need of her attention, currently milling about her strategy room. She hurried through her morning routine and dressed like a commander, not a fairy queen. Which meant black trousers, heavy matching sweater, and her ass-kicking boots.

Four wolf guards were waiting for her, two sitting and two pacing. This was her favorite place in Daruvar, her books and maps, and all the things that represented her plans to lead their people to a better future. It also helped that the staff kept the fire burning in here, so the chamber was warmer than most.

She offered a polite smile. "Good morning. Has everyone eaten?"

"Sort of," Skylett mumbled. "But we're all bloody tired of fish."

"Sky," Janek cautioned.

"It's true. When the hell are we hunting? Raff promised—"

The old wolf took the younger woman's arm, a clearly cautioning gesture. "Let's see to the niceties first, shall we?"

"Oh right, they're going. Sorry, Your Highness." Skylett didn't *look* remorseful.

Nor did she seem to mind acting like she stood in her own living room. In fact, she radiated defiance, like she had something against Thalia personally. The Animari didn't favor politesse or protocol; that was for sure. Thalia kept her social smile in place, though she'd like to lose her temper at this fractious little wolf.

She turned to Tavros and Bibi. "Are you departing, then?"

"I'm sorry that we're leaving in the middle of...well, everything." Tavros bowed deeply, and Thalia waved away his regret.

"It seems sudden." Unless she'd misunderstood before, Raff had given them assignments at Daruvar, and those tasks remained incomplete. They had also been talking about laying in supplies, hinting at a longer stay.

"There are...issues at Pine Ridge. Korin can solve them with my help, but I can't tarry here any longer, and I need Tavros to watch my back as I travel." The wolf seer folded both arms, as if daring Thalia to poke into their business further.

Issues? Like a Golgoth attack? That would be worrying.

Nonetheless Thalia took the hint. "I understand. Please take care of the demesne while your packmaster is away." She included both Tavros and Bibi in the request, but the seer scowled, her thick brows pulled together.

I have a long way to go before I'll win this woman over.

"Of course," Tavros said quickly.

"Did you say farewell to Raff already?" Asking the question revealed that she didn't know as much as she wished.

They might know I'm fishing.

In all honesty, Thalia wasn't even sure where Raff had gone. This was the second day that she'd woken without him and it was starting to set her teeth on edge, not least because she was normally a light sleeper. Yet somehow, that rogue wolf could vanish without rousing her. If he had any consideration, he'd leave a note informing her of his plans for the day. Instead, she was sleuthing among his own people, hoping not to make a fool of herself.

"Yes, we saw him on his way out," Bibi said.

That told her nothing. Janek and Skylett stood nearby; they'd decided to remain with Raff for the remainder of his time at Daruvar. With any luck, she'd have a better grip on Eldritch leadership and they'd have put Ruark Gilbraith down like a rabid pig by the time she was supposed to go spend time at pack headquarters.

"Take care on the way home." Thalia rose and bowed to each wolf emissary in turn.

Tavros scrambled to return the gesture while the seer remained impassive. Finally, Bibi dipped her head in acknowledgment. "We'll see you soon."

Once those two wolves left, she relaxed a little. Something about the seer made her feel like she'd turned up for a formal meeting in her underwear. Thalia rubbed her hands up her arms, conscious of a chill that permeated down to her bones, cold that couldn't be countered with scarves or blankets.

"She doesn't like you," Skylett noted.

"I hadn't noticed," she lied.

You don't, either.

Janek was a true diplomat; he changed the subject. "Raff should be back from setting the mines and programming the drones soon."

When the elder wolf threw her a wink, that made his intentions clear. *Totally clueing me in.* Thalia pretended not to notice. Now she remembered Raff saying he intended to get on that first thing, and relief swelled through her on a warm tide, like stories she'd heard of tropical seas in human lands.

"Are the mines safe for wildlife?" she asked.

Skylett nodded. "They have different settings. Raff will use the shock feature, so if an animal gets too close, it'll be stunned, not killed. When a mine goes off, a drone is dispatched. Measures will differ depending on what's been caught in our traps."

"No action for a hart or a hill cat," Thalia guessed. "But if you find an Eldritch spy—"

"The drone will deploy a tranq dart, so we can take the intruder alive," Janek said.

That worked. Better for intel if they could interrogate those creeping around Daruvar's borders. Now she needed to identify the traitor who had murdered Lileth and then she'd go after Ruark Gilbraith.

Ferith had been waiting quietly during the discussion and she cleared her throat, drawing Thalia's attention. "If I could have a moment, once you're finished?"

"Of course." She turned to Janek and Skylett. "Would you excuse me?"

"Certainly. Let's go look for Raff, little pup."

"Don't call me that," the young wolf snarled.

After the wolves left, Ferith shut the door firmly. "It's not that I don't trust our new allies, but it seems best to share this information with you first. If you decide to disseminate further, that's up to you."

Shit. This must be bad news.

"Don't be dramatic. Tell me already."

"I really don't know how to say this because it's such a tremendous Noxblade failure. It would be easy for me to blame Gavriel, as he was in charge when we arrived, but I've had security for a while now, and I *just* noticed the problem."

"Which is?" Thalia snapped.

"There's a secret tunnel in and out of Daruvar. We didn't notice it at first because it leads to the portion of the fortress that we condemned as uninhabitable."

The implications hit her at once. "Then it's possible that someone slipped in and poisoned the food and drink for our table?"

"Possible," Ferith allowed, "but not probable. I still think inside help would be required to execute the op with such precision. None of the other samples came back tainted. Which likely means the toxins were added after the food was plated."

Thalia considered, then nodded. "That's a small window of opportunity. They needed to be fast and accurate."

"That's why I think the escape route is being used for another purpose."

"I'm listening."

"You won't like this," Ferith warned.

Thalia twisted her mouth in a bitter smile. "When have I liked anything since my father set off a bunch of bombs in Ash Valley?"

"Point taken. Well, if someone inside our walls was transmitting intel to Ruark, we'd have spotted it by now. Between our tech and what the wolves have added, we're essentially a locked data fortress. I'm jamming all non-official comms and scanning everything that comes in or goes out. Let me say, the wolves weren't thrilled."

She waved that away, following the thought to its logical conclusion. "Then you suspect low-tech espionage. Someone's slipping out the back and rendezvousing with Gilbraith's forces."

"Whoever it is, they're also responsible for Lileth's death," Ferith said.

Nodding, she tapped her fingers against the wooden arm of her chair, pensive. There were two ways to handle this. Part of her wanted to plug the hole quickly, so no more information could leak out, but she could also see the merit in setting surveillance on the tunnel. Anyone who used it instead of the front gate—well, that was tantamount to an admission of guilt. While risky, setting a trap might be the best and quickest way to catch the traitor in the ranks.

"What do you think?" she finally asked.

"It's hard to get to with all the ruined walls and fallen stairs, so simply reaching the access point requires a certain fitness level."

"Understood." There was one solution, and she didn't hesitate at the hard choice. "I'll check it out. Alone. You stay hidden, keep me in sight at all times."

"You're playing bait? Your Highness, that's—"

"Objection noted. Unless you have a better idea, let's do this."

RAFF DIDN'T LIKE to delegate, so he made good on all his tech promises personally. Unlike the day they were attacked, it was all quiet, nothing to disturb the countryside, which made for good hunting. Silently, he shifted and stalked a hart, reveling in the thrill of the chase and the blood-bright satisfaction of making the kill. He field dressed it himself with the knife he always carried.

He returned to Daruvar triumphant, with the carcass slung across his shoulders. After the fact, he realized he probably looked like a fucking barbarian, smeared red and glorying in carnage. *Too late to dial it down.* Pretending he couldn't read the looks from the Eldritch, he carried his bounty to the kitchen. Raff half expected they wouldn't know how to process the meat.

Though the head cook's eyes widened, she didn't react otherwise. "The smokehouse is this way. We're using it to cure fish, but there's space for the venison, too."

"Thank you."

The 'smokehouse' was a bare room at the back of the fortress, chilly even for him, and full of racks of fish. He hung the field-dressed hart from hooks dangling from the weathered timbers. From the bloodstains on the floor and the scars on the wall where equipment had been removed, it seemed likely that this had been a torture chamber.

"Daruvar has a dark history," the head cook observed. She seemed to be guessing his thoughts, her gaze on those stained stones.

"We've all got our skeletons," he said.

She offered a brisk nod. "Indeed, that's true. I'll take it from here. You must be tired of our cuisine by now, but if you can bear with it for another week or so, I'll make you something lovely from this venison."

"Thank you."

Maybe now, Skylett would stop complaining. Sixty pounds of meat would feed three of them for quite a while.

Raff inclined his head at the cook and headed off in search of his wife, who should be relieved to hear they had mines in place and drones on patrol. He was tired and cold; normally, he didn't work this hard, and he wanted a pat for his uncharacteristic industry. Failing that, some of her burden might be relieved, at least. He knew all too well how it felt to worry about the people under your protection.

He did wash up and get dressed first, though.

One perk of having a wolf's nose, even in human form, was that he should be able to find Thalia anywhere in the fortress. He picked up her trail near the strategy room and followed it toward the unused portion of the keep. *This can't be right.* But the scent markers only got stronger, leading him over piles of rubble and down damaged staircases.

Where the hell is she going?

Deeper in, he caught another scent, fainter but unmistakable. He'd encountered this person before, but not enough to be able to name them in one whiff. It seemed like this person was stalking Thalia, though, and that sent a cold chill down his spine. Raff quickened his steps, relying on enhanced senses, but while he felt like he was getting closer to both of them, he still didn't *see* anyone.

Must be a Noxblade.

He raced on, over tumbled stones and ice-slick rubble, nerves prickling with the desire to change. With effort, he controlled the urge because he'd already left one set of clothing in the hills, and he hadn't packed *that* much stuff. The hair stood up on the back of his neck as he came to a dead end, just a shadowed corner, only he could feel the whispers of chill wind crawling over his feet.

Raff felt around, half with his hands and half with his senses, until he found the trigger mechanism, just a minute depression in the wall. Which swung open to reveal a dirt passage descending into darkness. Both the scent trails he'd marked went this way. If Thalia didn't know about her stalker, something terrible might happen.

The door started to close, and he dove through. *Seems like it's on a timer.* The chilly wind got stronger inside the tunnel that smelled of ancient graves and fetid damp. No telling what might be down here...or why the Eldritch buried it. Better question would be why Thalia was going after it.

Up ahead, he glimpsed movement. The gloom helped him narrow in on his prey, and with a snarl, he pounced on...Ferith, slamming her against the wall. "What're you playing at?" he demanded.

The Noxblade struggled against his hold, futile at best. "Let me go! Every second you delay me, the princess is in danger!"

He let go in reflex. "What are you talking about?"

"We laid a trap and caught only a foolish wolf. You might have ruined everything."

"Explain. Quickly."

"There's no time for that!" She broke his grip as the ceiling rumbled above them.

Raff flung her away as a ton of rock and soil dropped; with superior reflexes, he twisted away from the worst of it, though his lower body was pinned. Crushed would be a better word. *That was almost enough to kill a wolf.* Snarling in pain, he dug himself out by increments, a feat possible only due to his Animari strength.

No telling how long it took, but Raff finally crawled backwards, fresh blood trickling from wounds that healed and cracked open all over again from the rough treatment. He lay against the packed dirt wall, conscious of the dead roots jabbing into his spine. He was filthy and injured, but at least he was alive. Raff had a feeling he wasn't supposed to be and calling out might alert their enemies. Hopefully, Ferith could backtrack to the door and get out on that side.

He pulled out his phone, but the screen was cracked, and it wouldn't power on. Unsurprising, the rubble that shattered his femur also broke the phone in his pocket. The bone needed to be set, or it would fuse crooked, then doctors would have to break it again when he got out. Inconvenient and painful for an Animari but not permanently debilitating yet he didn't want to go through all that shit if it could be avoided.

Currently, it was all he could do to breathe. Even Animari healing took time, so Raff rested, his senses sharpened by the darkness. He heard the scrape of shoes and smelled Thalia above the dankness of the tunnel, long before she spoke. She must've heard the cave-in and come to investigate.

"Who's there?" she whispered.

"Just me."

"Are you all right?" A narrow beam of light appeared, necessary for her, not him.

The yellow glow skimmed over him and then she knelt with a muffled exclamation. "Raff, your leg!"

"I'm well-aware of my predicament. Do you think you could help me set it? Time is of the essence."

Raff expected her to protest, but she surprised him by setting her light down and taking hold of his foot. "I'm not a professional, but I have basic medical training. Count to three and clench your teeth."

He managed not to scream when she pulled on his foot and guided the bone back into position. The ends ground together, which meant it should be good enough to set on its own. He just needed to rest a bit. Still, the pain-sweat trickled down his forehead and other injuries hurt more as if in some awful sympathy.

"Thanks," he got out.

She sat beside him and presented her shoulder. Raff wouldn't have thought she was strong enough to hold him, but she didn't budge when he dropped his head on the perch she offered. *She smells like flowers...and the ocean.*

"What happened? And what are you doing down here?"

"Isn't it obvious?" he asked in a wry tone. "I'm saving you."

14.

"I SHOULD'VE REALIZED." Thalia kept her voice gentle, but she smelled the blood, cloying in the gloom. "Thank you."

Too conscious of his warm weight leaning on her, she used a hand torch to check his pupils for potential concussion. Thalia leaned in, peering at his eyes. Raff's face was smeared with red and she spotted myriad cuts and bruises, but the broken bone seemed to be his most serious injury, and she'd already set that as best she could.

"I know I'm handsome, but the light hurts my eyes. Do you mind?"

Quickly, she clicked it off, drenching them in darkness. "Sorry. I can't see much of anything without it. Did you happen to encounter Ferith on the way in?"

She was supposed to have my back.

"I pushed her clear of the collapse. She should be working to free us on the other side. Sorry, I didn't know this was a sting."

Thalia winced. "No, I should have told you. There are no excuses, really. I'm just...not used to being part of a unit."

"You're a lone wolf who wolfs alone?" Despite his obvious pain, he was still trying to make her laugh.

She did let slip a reluctant smile. "Isn't that ironic? When you're the actual wolf."

"We don't, though."

"What?"

"Wolf alone. We're pack animals who thrive on social interaction. I suspect that's true of you as well. You've just never had much opportunity."

"You make it sound like I was raised by a witch in an iron tower."

"Not what I meant. It just seems like the Eldritch have a stronger sense of hierarchy than we do among the Animari. I'm packmaster, but nobody hesitates to tell me when I'm full of shit. I've noticed that your people treat you with a particular reverence."

"What about it?" Thalia wondered why she felt defensive.

"That makes it tough for intimacy to develop. They serve you, but other than Lileth, it didn't seem like you socialized with anyone."

Regret and sorrow warred within her. She missed Lil, but she still didn't grasp what he was driving at. "What is your point?"

"Don't ice me out, Lady Silver. If I'm wrong, I am, but I'm just saying—I don't see you playing cards or drinking with anyone. No friendly sparring matches or trips to the city. That's what friendship is all about, and people *need* that. You may not be alone in this fortress, but you must be lonely."

"Not anymore," she said. "I have you."

The words came out before she reflected on them, but

that lack of consideration made them no less true. He drew in a soft breath, one she felt against the side of her throat when he let it go in a long puff of warmth. "Even if I mess up your careful plans?"

"Ferith might've been killed without your intervention. This is certainly an attempt to isolate me and the consequences could be dire, especially if the enemy is waiting on the other end of the tunnel."

"I suspect that's a generous view of my interference, but...thank you."

Thalia reached for his hand and found it with an accuracy that seemed faintly surprising. "I'm grateful that you came running because I might be in danger. But...I'm starting to suspect that marriage to me might be hazardous to your health."

His fingers were warm when he wrapped them around hers. "I am notoriously hard to kill. Many have tried. None have succeeded."

"That makes you uniquely qualified for your current role," she said with mock gravitas.

Raff sounded serious when he went on, "I think about it sometimes, exactly how much catastrophic damage is required to take me out."

At first, that seemed like an odd thing to say but sorting through, she found a mutual memory that might be troubling him. The bear clan leader had died at Ash Valley, killed instantly in the first explosion. "Is that because of Beren? It seemed as if the two of you were close."

Long pause, in which she wondered whether she had overstepped. Finally, he said, "We argued a lot. Drank twice that much. But yeah, I'd say we were close. He gave better advice than my father."

Why didn't you look to the bear clan for an alliance then? Thalia almost asked. She didn't, largely because the question sounded too much like, *why did you marry me?* And his reasons didn't matter—or they shouldn't, if the wolves kept up their end of the contract.

Instead she said, "I'm sorry for your loss. You must miss him."

"I do. I also miss living with the protection of the Pax Protocols. His death represents a much larger problem...the fact that the world as we know it has changed."

Once, such an acute observation would have surprised her. Not anymore. Raff only *pretended* to be a hapless rogue.

"And not everyone wants peace," she said softly. "Some would rather profiteer and sell secrets."

"It's one thing to defend your home, quite another to feel as if you deserve to take what someone else has."

"I agree. This probably won't come as any great shock, but Ruark Gilbraith is every bit as dangerous as Tycho Vega."

"Gathered that when he killed Lileth and tried to take out the entire head table at our wedding. No worries, Lady Silver. We'll get him. Once I've rested a bit, I'll be ready to wreak some havoc."

How could he be so confident *all* the time? It didn't seem like bravado, either. Thalia found this wolf disturbingly hard to read. Maybe his physical prowess gave him the conviction that all enemies could be bested eventually?

"That is so perplexing."

"What is?"

"In a few days, your leg will have healed? I don't understand how it's possible."

"An Animari physician could explain it better. I just

know our enhanced senses and healing kick in after the first shift."

"What's *that* like?"

"Shifting?" At her nod, he seemed to consider the question carefully. "That's hard to put into words too. Nobody's ever asked me before."

"Other Animari wouldn't need to."

"That's not entirely true. Latent Animari probably do wonder but they don't ask."

She thought she understood why. "It would be like a wingless bird asking how it feels to fly."

"Yes. I'm going to sleep for a bit. Keep watch?"

It was mind-boggling the way he just switched off. His weight sagged against her and Thalia had to wrap both arms around him to keep him from toppling across her legs like felled timber. She cocked her head, listening, but the tunnel was eerily silent. It would've been nice to hear scraping from the other side of the blockade.

Maybe Ferith is still trapped?

Best not to imagine worst-case scenarios. If the traitor had laid a trap, they might investigate why she hadn't stumbled into it yet. It seemed likely that the cave-in was meant to separate her from Ferith and drive her toward the exit in a panic. Since theirs was a political marriage, the enemy couldn't have planned for a meddling wolf. Who was apparently willing to put himself in harm's way for her.

Repeatedly. Thalia had mixed feelings about that.

In any event, she wasn't the sort to panic, even when her plans went south. This time, she'd come ready to fight, fully geared with shock bracers and both knives. She also had five different poisons and twice as many antidotes in her pack, but any conflict had to wait until Raff could walk properly. Down here in the silent chill, she might've been cold if not for his body draped over hers.

Though she'd had lovers before, brief moments stolen for physical pleasure, nobody had ever given themselves over like this. The implicit trust was daunting. *What if I don't hear them coming?* Thalia half-wanted to turn on her light, but that would give away their position, and they were trapped with the blockage behind.

Stay calm. This isn't how it all ends.

She sat in the dark and held him and breathed.

NO TELLING HOW long Raff had been resting, but he snapped awake instantly, his muscles tense. *Movement in the tunnel. How many?*

He tested his leg. It still hurt, but it was fused enough to hold his weight. Gently, he touched Thalia's shoulder. She probably didn't mean to sleep but staring into the dark was monotonous. Raff had counted on his ability to hear an intruder from a long way off, and these trespassers weren't even trying to be quiet. Eldritch from the smell of them, but he couldn't distinguish between the houses yet. In time, he'd be able to tell where they came from, based on the olfactory clues.

Not soon enough to help us.

It took a second shake to get her attention. She snapped upright, and he silenced her instinctive question with a press of his fingertip against her lips. Raff set his mouth against her ear, barely making a sound.

"We have company, let's greet them. I'll take point."

Ignoring the twinge from his bad leg, he stripped swift-ly. In this terrain—in the dark—he'd do much better fighting as a wolf. It would help his balance too since a wolf could move better on three legs than a man could dragging one. Thalia didn't question his decision; she was on alert as she scooped up his clothing and stowed it in her pack.

Helpful, that.

Over the years, he'd lost lots of garments, the price you paid to be Animari when the shit hit the fan. Since Thalia wasn't a shifter, she could keep up with all the clothes he discarded, and he'd have something to put on later, after the fight. It was such a little thing, but it felt good to realize that this mixed marriage wasn't all doom and dire portents.

He slid into wolf form—like diving into cold, deep water—and stretched, testing the strength of his injured leg. *Better now.* Raising it still let him prowl ahead smoothly, breathing in the nervous tang of the enemy's sweat. Closer, he heard the whisper-light scrape of leather soles against the dirt and loose stones of the tunnel floor. Thalia was quiet as a Noxblade behind him, more skilled than the Eldritch creeping toward them.

Eighty meters and closing.

Raff wished he could warn her, but she wouldn't understand even if he tried. He rushed, leaping at the nearest enemy and tearing into the Achilles tendon. Wolves in the wild normally didn't hamstring their prey because they hunted as a pack, but he didn't have any other wolves at his back today. The Eldritch went down, his leg buckling, and Raff tore out his throat in a sticky-sweet rush of blood.

Different than the Manwaring strike team. Why is that?

He circled, dodging the slashing knife strikes that told him the Eldritch didn't see as well in the dark. A blue lightning arc crackled in the dark and the second target juddered in place, then dropped his weapon. The stench of charred flesh and burning hair filled the tunnel, so he hacked a breath and backed off. He saw it clearly when Thalia finished her opponent with a knife, a quick thrust and twist to the kidney.

"I think that's all of them," she whispered. "At least the ones who came in the tunnel. There are probably more outside."

A reasonable assessment. For obvious reasons, he stayed quiet.

She switched on the torch and said, "I won't leave this on, but I need to ask some questions. Reply with a nod or a shake of the head. Shall we continue?"

Raff nodded.

"Do you want to lead?"

Another nod.

"All right then. I don't like leaving the bodies here, but we can't take them with us. They'll slow us down and we'll probably need to fight again."

That seemed likely to him, too. He trotted off, setting a pace she could keep up with.

Her whisper reached him a few seconds later. "They're not used to fighting Animari. It almost seems unfair, how fast we killed them."

It's kill or be killed, princess. And I won't let them hurt you.

Raff couldn't say that, of course, and maybe that was just as well. Her regret was natural. If harming her own people didn't trouble her, she shouldn't rule them. Something he'd read in old history books came to him, along the lines of 'those who seek power are not worthy of it'.

The tunnel sloped downward and stretched on for quite a while. There was no further opposition, and eventually, the darkness diffused with a trickle of daylight. A cold wind blew through his fur, and Raff rushed toward the promise of freedom. Caution reined him in at the last minute as he recalled there were probably more Eldritch hunting for them. Their recourse now depended on why they'd collapsed the tunnel. Was it meant as an attack on Thalia or an attempt to cover someone's tracks? Without knowing that, it was tough to be sure how to proceed.

He waited for Thalia to catch up. She stepped out of the cave mouth to shade her eyes against the winter-pale sun. To Raff, it looked like they had tapped into a natural cavern system with that secret passage into Daruvar.

"Let me get my bearings," she said.

As she fiddled with her phone, he oriented himself by scent. Mountains to the west, forest to the south. There was rain or snow in the air, a heavy storm threatening. He tipped his head back to study the clouds. *It will hit soon. We don't have much time.*

"We're farther from Daruvar than I realized…"

With a bad storm threatening and an Eldritch hunting party on the move, they couldn't linger. He growled and pawed her leg.

Thalia glanced at him, one fine brow arching. "What is it?"

Like I can answer. Shifting to reply would burn energy he couldn't spare, so he stared at her, ran a few paces south, and growled again.

"You know the way back?" she asked.

He nodded. *Not exactly, but we can't stand in the open like this.* It was a miracle that they didn't have to fight as soon as they left the cave.

To his vast relief, she fell in behind him and even increased her pace to a graceful lope when he ran faster. There was old smoke this way, the remnants of a fire, and that probably meant shelter. The precipitation he'd scented earlier dropped on them in a wet wave, half-rain, half-sleet, and it iced the ground. He had less trouble than Thalia, who slid and cursed behind him.

"I don't think this is right," she called as a tree branch slashed her cheek.

Raff snarled.

Nearly there.

From the forest proper, he ran into a clearing that held a small hunting cabin. There was no visible smoke, but he could smell the remnants of the fire, doused a few hours ago or so. He dropped out of wolf form, and the shift left him shivering, between the sudden cold on naked skin and the expenditure of energy. Raff didn't expect to find a lock and he was right; the door opened easily.

"I thought we were going back," Thalia snapped.

Before answering, he got his clothes on. "My concern was getting us out of the weather. Don't you see that ice?"

"I do, but—"

"It will kill us, Lady Silver. Freeze us to death before we reach Daruvar. We don't have winter gear with us or the necessary provisions. We have to wait it out and hope that Eldritch strike team doesn't find us before I recover fully."

"But Ferith will think we're dead!"

He sighed at her outrage. "Better than being actually dead. Help me get a fire started and see what the last tenant left us to eat."

15.

THALIA WAS PISSED off.

Mostly because Raff had a point. The hail had turned into sleet, slush when it hit the ground, and the ice was sticking, enough that the ground was half-covered in white, as far as she could see. The cabin was rustic, at best. Primitive would be a better word. There were no indoor hygiene facilities; a shack out back had a hole excavated for such a purpose.

Inside, everything was built of unfinished wood, a few shelves with random tins, a rag braid rug on the floor—even the furniture looked handmade, from the bed stand to the rough-edged mattress and table and chairs. The lack of trophies made her think this was no normal hunter's retreat. As she thought that, Raff built a fire efficiently from the wood that was stacked against the wall near the hearth. Even the stones that had been placed were asymmetrical, found rather than quarried.

"This is an Animari hideaway," he said then.

She asked, "How do you know?" before she thought better of it and then wished she could swallow the question.

"Scent markers. The last person who used this cabin

was a cat, no one I recognize from Ash Valley, but there are traces of bear and wolf, too, along with something strange, like nothing I've ever encountered before."

That was interesting. "Could it be someone from the Aerie?"

The bird shifters were notoriously reclusive and lived in a stronghold in the northwest that was said to be unreachable except by air. They'd stayed out of all Numina affairs for the last several hundred years, so if they'd emerged from hiding, it could portend an important power shift. Regardless, Thalia didn't like the implications of an Animari hideout so deep in Eldritch territory.

Raff shrugged. "It's possible. These other olfactory trails are old, though, barely discernable even for me. Only the cat is recent, but we already knew that from the smoking fireplace."

"Do you think they'll be back?"

"In this weather? Not likely. I think they knew the storm was coming and got out ahead of it."

"Wish we'd done the same," she muttered.

He glanced up from the small blaze he'd coaxed to life, narrowing his dark eyes. "Hey, it's impossible to monitor the weather in a tunnel."

"I'm not blaming you. It's just that I'm worried about the situation at Daruvar."

"Worry is a waste of energy. Focus on what you can change." Saying that, Raff straightened from the hearth with effort.

Belatedly Thalia remembered his bad leg. Since he'd come here in wolf form, it hadn't been as evident. As a human, he was limping.

"Does it hurt a lot?"

"Some," he grunted.

"What can I do to help?"

"If you're asking sincerely, fill that bucket with ice from outside and hang it on the hook on the fireplace. We can't take a bath, but we can wash up a bit."

"On it." Normally, there would be five servants fighting to take over such mundane chores. It was novel to do it herself. "What else?"

Raff settled onto the nearest chair with a strangled groan. "Fuck me, that's enough moving for a bit. Ah, see what's in the tins, I suppose."

"Two are potted meat. Two are mixed vegetables. One is fruit compote."

"You have the veggies, then. I'll take the meat. We can share the fruit."

"Sounds good."

There were no cooking facilities, so she opened the tins and heated them by setting them at the edge of the hearth. Carefully, Thalia pulled them free with the fire tongs and she was hungry enough that nothing else mattered; she raked the contents out with her fingertips and barely chewed the corn, beans, peas, and carrots. Raff was equally efficient with the meat, and she let him have most of the fruit.

"You sure?" he asked, offering the tin.

"You burned more energy shifting and you need the calories to mend that leg."

"True enough." He tipped his head back, his hair a dark tangle down his back as he swallowed.

For some reason, Thalia was riveted. She couldn't look away from the movement of his throat, from the curls of his beard, and the way it framed his mouth, now slightly smeared with peach juice. It was impossible not to notice that he had gorgeous cheekbones and that the scar that peeked out from his beard looked as if it needed a soft touch, a vertical stroke, and then her fingers would be on his beard, on his lips—

She tore her gaze away with effort, conscious that her heart was pattering in her chest. *I thought it was sheer arrogance when he said I'd want him eventually, but...now? Like this?* There was nothing elegant or gentle about this man or their surroundings. She was used to candlelight and carefully orchestrated seduction, measured pleasures, and orgasms that left her lightly satiated.

This...would be something else entirely.

If she let it happen.

Briskly, Thalia rose to check on the ice bucket and found that it had not only melted, it was also warm enough to wash. "I'd give you some privacy, but there's nowhere for me to go, except out into the cold."

"I wouldn't do that to my good wife," Raff said.

His dark eyes twinkled as if he knew how little she considered herself to fill that role. *In name only* had never seemed so sad yet apropos. As he shucked his shirt and pants to sponge off the blood, that seemed wrong suddenly. No matter what, he'd shattered his leg coming to her aid, and it felt rather despicable to let him struggle when she was perfectly capable of helping.

"Let me."

He glanced up in surprise when she plucked the rag from his hands. Thalia didn't speak, conscious of rising heat in her cheeks. She washed away the red, rinsed the cloth, working on automatic, until he was clean. Though she tried to feign a certain clinical detachment, her hands trembled when she moved upward to clean the blood from his chest. The scrapes had already healed, but he still bore the signs of old injury on his skin. Without her volition, her hands lingered on the scar at his shoulder.

Suddenly, warm fingers wrapped around hers. "Are you bathing or seducing me? I'm not opposed, mind, but I need to know your intentions."

"I wish I could answer that." Flustered, she tried to pull back, but the wolf lord didn't let go.

Instead, he raised her hand to his mouth and kissed each knuckle, one by one. The whisper-light rasp on his beard against her skin sent a shiver through her, a promise of illicit pleasures. Thalia imagined it chafing her thighs, his mouth moving lower, lower, and suddenly, she was all liquid heat, quivering and breathless. Longing never hit her like this, ferocious and relentless, but now she was squirming, legs pressed together.

"Lady Silver, you're on your knees, caressing a naked man's chest. How can you *not* know your own intentions?"

When he put it that way, everything clarified in her head. She raised her chin. "Then...I suppose I'm seducing you. Any objections?"

FOR A MOMENT, Raff didn't think he'd heard correctly. Teasing this woman almost never turned out the way he expected. *Take now for instance.*

Instead of scuttling away like a nervous crab, she was magnificent on her knees before him, eyes like a night sky full of stars. Hesitantly, he reached for her hair and realized she was serious when she let him take it down. The strands spilled like quicksilver into his hands, light and silken. He brushed it back from her face and breathed her in.

She's serious.

Her scent was subtly different, spiced with pheromones, and he reacted instantly. There was no faking this, no chemical substitute for real desire, and he had spoken honestly when he told her nothing got him hotter than being wanted. His cock perked at the promise of enthusiastic sex, and she *watched* it happen. That only turned him on more.

"Your interest is powerful," he said softly. "Shall we go to bed, my good wife?"

He offered her a hand up, which she accepted gracefully. She surprised him again when she pulled off her shirt and skimmed out of her trousers in careful, precise motions, then she folded her clothes and set them on the chair he'd vacated. The air in the cabin was still chilly, not enough to make him shiver, but her skin was delicate.

Raff pulled her to him, warming her with his body as they moved toward the bed together. She also tried to lend him her strength, though his leg was just a residual ache now. A night's rest would put him to rights, but if she wanted to coddle him—well, he wouldn't say no.

Does that make me the wolf that cried wolf?

"Are you all right?"

"Well enough to make you feel wonderful, I'll wager. I wish this wasn't happening in a stranger's bed, but here we are."

Climbing in beside him, Thalia seemed relatively unconcerned about that. "You're excited this time," she observed.

"Is that surprising?"

"Well, we've been together before, and you didn't—

you weren't—"

"The difference is you, Lady Silver. You didn't want me then. Now your body is soft and sweet and silky-hot. It seems you like a little misguided heroism."

"Don't tease me."

He felt her flush, felt the heat shimmer up from her shoulders past her neck into her cheeks. With gentle fingertips he traced her fey features: sharp cheekbones, elegant little nose, pointed chin. Before he got to her soft mouth, she bit him.

"Is it all right if I kiss you?" he asked.

"You have my permission for...everything."

That was heady, carte blanche to touch her, but it left him oddly tentative. He already knew her stomach was sensitive and that the idea of being caught turned her on...*ah, I can work with this*. Raff swept aside her hair and set his mouth on her throat, just below her left ear.

"Hope the cat who used this cabin last doesn't circle back because of the storm. Might be shocked by the deliciously dirty things I'll be doing to you."

A small sound escaped her, and he'd barely touched her yet. *She's so responsive. This will be fun.* He didn't tease her further, taking her mouth in a kiss that was softer and sweeter than he planned, first just a series of pecks that deepened when her lips parted and clung, when she let out a breath that he drank in.

When she raised a hand to touch his beard, he pulled back a little. "Does it bother you?"

Eldritch males were hairless bastards from what he'd seen, so it startled him when she shook her head swiftly. "I like how it feels."

The cabin was dark apart from the orange crackle of the

fire, but it seemed to give her courage. Thalia trailed her
fingers lower, brushing his shoulders and settling on his
chest, flexing her nails like a cat. He drew in a breath and let
it out as a groan as she tested his pectoral muscles. His
nipples responded to each tease and scrape. Before, he
wouldn't have said he was especially sensitive, there, but her
light, experimental touches made his abs tighten and his toes
curl.

Passive acceptance wasn't his style, so when she paused
to nuzzle her cheek against his chest, he tangled his hands in
her hair and kissed her. From the little gasp he swallowed,
she liked the tug that brought her mouth to his. This time,
he went slow and deep, tasting her while he ran his hands
over her back, long, luxurious strokes that made her squirm.
Her scent bloomed all around him, a deepening arousal that
went to his head like strong liquor.

"You really want it," he whispered, right against her
mouth. "You're so hot and hungry. If your loyal soldiers
could see you now..."

That little nudge at her secret predilections sent a shiver
through her. Thalia's eyes closed, and Raff thought she'd
never been more beautiful than with her breath coming fast,
lashes fluttering against smooth cheeks. He kissed a path
downward, skimming over her breasts toward her stomach,
such a sweet, strange erogenous zone.

"Oh, you wish they *could*. See you. You want them to
watch you take my cock? I bet you do. It would be the
sexiest thing they've ever seen."

"Stop," she whimpered.

"Stop what?"

"Saying such—"

"Don't pretend. You're trembling, that's how much you

like it." Raff bit down on her shoulder, gently. "I don't mind if you fantasize about people watching us. I'm not shy, I'll make that dream come true someday, if you want."

"Oh *fuck*."

"That's the idea, princess. But I'll make you come a few times first."

She startled at what he guessed sounded like a bold claim and then her entire body arched when he pressed his mouth to the silky skin at her hip. Raff kissed a path across her belly, gauging her response by the way she twisted and shivered and finally sank her hands into his hair, not trying to tug him away, but silently pleading for more. He used his mouth and his teeth, slowly working lower, until she was writhing under him, hands urgent on his back.

"You're too slow!"

"Calm down, we have all night."

"Unless that cat interrupts us...or the Eldritch who are hunting us see the smoke. We need to...*do* it, so I can think straight again."

"I'm flattered," Raff said. "I think. And your complaint is noted."

He buried his face between her legs then, and she shrieked, a breathy, shocked sound that turned him on so fiercely that his dick throbbed. A little trickle of precome slicked the head and he shifted it carefully. *No squeezing, no friction, not yet.* Her thighs parted around him as he kissed each labia with tender precision.

Thumbing her sex open in a soft motion, he went in lightly with his tongue, learning her tastes by the way she squirmed and sighed and moved his head. Soon, she was rolling her hips upward, whimpering sexy little incoherent sounds. Thalia wrapped her legs around his head, gasping, moaning, and it was like nobody had ever eaten her before, like each lick, each caress felt brand new.

Her soft sounds got louder, taken on a frustrated edge. "You're driving me crazy, but...I can't go like this," she finally panted out.

He lifted his head and planted a kiss on her quivering belly. "What do you need?"

16.

"FOR YOU TO ask that question. Let's switch things up." Thalia had seldom hovered at such a fever pitch for so long, and it made her voice ragged.

"Then just tell me...or show me," Raff said.

"You wanted me to come, right? Before we do it."

"If possible."

Part of her couldn't believe she was about to do this, but she just went for it, straddling his face with her thighs. "It'll be better like this, from this angle."

Raff couldn't answer readily, but from the eager way he put his mouth on her sex, he must be enjoying himself. Leaning forward, she moved tentatively against his chin, his lips and tongue. Thalia moaned over the scrape of his beard on her thighs, the feel of his hair on her belly. Need tightened her muscles; it had been so long—

He sipped at her clit, and her back arched. The orgasm spilled over her in quick, convulsive waves; she rode his chin, hunching against his face until the pleasure receded. His hands were gentle on her hips, steadying her, but never trying to control her. Thalia milked the last shivers from the experience and then slid off his face to tumble beside him.

"Good?" Raff trailed a fingertip between her breasts, so light and teasing that she lifted her hips, though she'd just finished.

"Very."

She half-expected he'd go straight between her legs again, but instead, his teasing touch meandered to her belly, where he scraped little patterns on her skin with his nails.

It shouldn't feel this good.

Her nipples had softened, but they perked up again in direct response to the game he was playing on her lower abdomen. Normally partners took that as a cue that she wanted her breasts touched, her nipples sucked, but Raff didn't make a move. Thalia turned on her side, curious.

"Are you ready for more?" His voice was midnight dark, so deep that she felt it like a sexy growl in her bones.

"Yes. I want to fuck you now." She'd never said it so explicitly before, in such raw language, but from the flash in his dark eyes, it was the right move.

Raff took her hand and guided it to his cock. Beneath the covers, she couldn't see what she was touching, so she learned him with delicate fingertips. Hard, so very hard, and long, too. Too thick for her to encircle completely with her thumb and forefinger. Thalia explored further, found the fleshy head slick with precome. He jerked in her hand and rubbed against her fingers, his breath coming faster.

"See the difference, Lady Silver? That's because you want me."

"I do."

Pure curiosity, she put her fingers in her mouth to taste him, and his lips parted as she sucked the salt from her own skin. Raff swallowed a groan, eyes locked on her lips. Then he moved, slow enough that she could've rebuffed him at any point. He was such a tender, gentle wolf.

Never would've guessed.

He also surprised her by lifting her leg and nudging closer. It was absolute seduction when he nudged her labia open and snugged the tip of his cock against her, luxuriating in the friction between their bodies. She sucked in a sharp breath over how good it felt and how impossibly patient he was, watching her face for each nuanced reaction.

"If you want my cock, take it."

At this angle, it wasn't easy to do alone, but she arched and wrapped her thigh over his hips, and then he pushed. His cock stretched her to perfection; once he slid inside fully, he paused to assess her response. Evidently encouraged by what he saw, Raff lifted the leg she'd draped over him, making room for long, slow thrusts. He held her close with his other arm, so that her breasts nestled against his chest.

Each time he pushed, measured and rhythmic, he kissed her throat, her clavicle, her shoulder. As his pace got faster, he bit down on her neck, and she trembled, wildly unable to process how purely *good* it all felt. His cock, working inside her. His mouth, hot and open on her skin. His teeth sinking in.

"*Oh.*"

Thalia had no experience in this position, no frame of reference for how intimate it was. Before, she'd taken her pleasure from him, but now there could be no mistaking that he was *giving* it, with each push and pull, each luxuriant slide. Even when he angled her hips to provide the perfect pressure inside, it was in response to her moans.

"Getting there, princess?"

"Yes." It was all she could do to speak.

"Let's go together." He took her mouth, tongue sliding over hers as his cock stroked inside her.

She bit him when she came, savaged his lower lip, but he didn't withdraw from the kiss. He held still while her body tightened on him, gasping in her ear so it sent shivers all down her spine. Once she quieted, he pulled free and fisted his cock once, twice, quick and vicious, and then liquid heat spurted against her bare belly.

"Why...?" Thalia tried to whisper the question, but her voice was too unsteady.

But he knew what she wanted to know, offering a lop-sided smile as he eased down beside her. "The way I understand it, you can't just decide to have my baby. That sort of thing's left up to fate among your people, isn't that right?"

"Well, yes." She'd heard that Animari could decide when to reproduce, and until then, there was no risk in sexual pleasure.

"Then I shouldn't take that choice away from you."

She raised a brow. "It's unlikely that one encounter would do the job, even assuming we're a fertile pair."

"Even if the chance is slight, we should decide to try together, or avoid the risk. It shouldn't be a whim of mine since it's your body at stake."

Understanding broke over her at last. This was a measure of his concern. "You're trying to protect me."

"As best I can."

Softly she kissed away the trace of blood from his lower lip. "I appreciate it. If you like, we can ask Dr. Wyeth about the probability of conception, and in the meantime, there's medicine I can take for prevention."

"If that'll put your mind at ease."

Sighing, she said, "You're too casual about this. Aren't you supposed to want to—"

I can't say it.

"I already marked you, Lady Silver. Maybe your people won't be able to tell but the wolves at Daruvar will have no doubt at all what happened here today." The wolfish grin curved his mouth, tugging at the scar half-hidden in his beard.

Irritated with his smug teasing, she got up and scrubbed her stomach, trying not to blush. "That's not funny."

"It wasn't meant to be. They won't bother you about it, and I'm sure Janek will be relieved that we're getting along so well. He likes you."

That revelation caught her by surprise. She laid down the damp cloth and came back to the bed, mostly because it was so damn cold. The fire in the hearth could only do so much against the ice storm outside. "He does?"

"Indeed. Just the other day, he called you a tactical genius, in fact."

"And what's your opinion?"

"You need to get under the covers before you freeze your pretty tits off."

It wasn't obedience, Thalia told herself. Just common sense. Yet it still gave her more joy than it should have to comply with his suggestion and snuggle up against his hard, hot chest. His arms felt so nice around her that she could've purred.

Maybe a marriage of convenience to a wicked wolf wasn't so bad after all.

RAFF COULD HARDLY believe his eyes.

The soon-to-be Eldritch queen lolled in his arms, her mouth slightly open and so completely unconscious that it was impossible not to take it as a compliment, either to his sexual skills or his trustworthy nature. Either way, he found her faith endearing if a little puzzling. After all, reliable wasn't the word that usually sprang to mind when people described him.

Idly he ran his fingers through her hair, marveling at how the silver strands caught the firelight and shone like platinum. Her body felt so fragile to contain so much determination, and damn, from what he'd seen, the odds were *not* good. The Eldritch didn't like coming straight for conflict; instead, they lingered in the shadows and winnowed away at the foundations, until suddenly, your house toppled over.

He spared a moment to wish his phone hadn't been smashed in the cave-in. It would be good to touch base with Janek and Skylett, maybe even call to see how things were going in Pine Ridge. Through technology, it would also be possible to check on his traps and drones to verify the status of the holdings around Daruvar, though the storm might jack up the signal. Raff sighed.

Ah, well. No point fretting over what couldn't be changed.

Pulling up the rough, thick covers, which had been stitched together out of random fabric and then stuffed with bird feathers, Raff closed his eyes. Their body heat made the strange bed feel cozy, and with his belly full, it was a decent place to ride out the storm. In time, he slept, and then—

I'm on the floor, bleeding. I can't remember when the beating stopped or when the next one will begin. Nobody says anything. It's all right, because I can heal the hurt and shake it off. It's not like I'm a Latent or a pup in need of protection.

Nearly grown, that's what everyone says.

The room is cold and dark, Father paces in the hall. I can hear his curses, the half-coherent rantings. He's calling me the devil that killed his mate? That means he's had far too much liquor, enough to kill a Golgoth, and he'll be coming for me soon. Evert will try to stop him. He'll try.

I should take the punishment, even if I don't exactly understand why.

"Stupid accursed whelp, where are you?"

I know I shouldn't, but I can still feel the belt and my mouth is still bleeding. If I'm fast, I can escape to the woods and live for a few days, until my father's in his right mind again. When the door opens, I bolt, shoving through to the corridor. Hard hands reach for me, but Evert is there, struggling. Behind me, they're struggling—

He jolted awake, heart hammering hard in his chest. It had been a long time since he had the nightmare, but he could still see his brother at the base of the steep steps, sprawled at unnatural angle, blood spilling from his cracked skull. Such accidental deaths were rare among the pack, yet another reason for his father to hate him. Sometimes he wished the old man would simply *die,* but he wasn't gone, even now. Instead, the pack had called for a vote of no-confidence and quietly confined him, and the outside world heard from Rand Pineda no more.

Wonder how she'll take that news.

"Raff?" Her hand was suddenly on his cheek and he pulled it away before he could stop himself.

Even between normal lovers, there were boundaries, and the dream left him feeling like he was one raw wound, bleeding freely beside her. "What's the matter?" he asked, trying for his usual tone.

"You're trembling. Are you cold?"

"How could I be, with such a hot little bundle beside me?" He thought he sounded fine, should be enough to get her to go back to sleep.

It wasn't.

"Bad dream?" she guessed, with an acuity that was as impressive as it was intrusive.

His first instinct was to snap, as wolves did when unfamiliar hands went after their sore spots, but then he remembered how she'd told him about her mother, poisoned by her father's mistress. That couldn't have been an easy thing to share, but she'd trusted him with it, long before she curled into his arms. Such candor was a rare sort of courage, an example he should follow.

"You want to hear about my long, dark night of the soul?" he asked quietly. "It's not in our contract."

"That's a baseline agreement, as in, this is the minimum we will do for one another. There's no reason we can't give more, if desired."

"What a long, roundabout way to say, 'Yes, Raff, I want to hear your story'."

She curled into him, sliding one thigh over his and rested her head on his chest. "I want to listen, Raff."

"Better. I like things straightforward." He closed his eyes, aware that he was about to tell a story that most of the pack knew, but he'd never really spoken about before. "If things were different, you might have married my older brother, you know."

A jolt of surprise went through her; he felt it. "You have a brother?"

"Not anymore. Which is too bad because he was brilliant, years of training and so many incredible ideas. Pine Ridge lost a lot when he died."

"You feel responsible." It wasn't a question.

Thalia opened her palm on Raff's chest, clearly an attempt to comfort him. Some of the horrors of the dream faded, leaving him more grounded. He covered her fingers with his and tried to keep it together. It was one thing to confide in her, another to break down.

"No denying that. He was trying to save me from a beating and paid the ultimate price for that interference."

"Your father didn't have him…" She trailed off like she couldn't even ask the question.

"Executed? No. Officially his death was an accident, but if I hadn't tried to run, it wouldn't have happened." Now that he was talking, it was easier than he'd expected, as if this was a dam that badly needed breaking.

Under the cover of darkness, Raff told her everything— how his mother had died in childbirth and his father hated him irrationally, so that nothing he ever did was good enough. About Evert, who was always his shield, until that terrible night when he wrestled with their father like gods of old, and how in the end, the whole pack paid the price.

"My father was never…right, afterward. He kept it together long enough to install Korin as my second, but that was the last sane decision he ever made."

"Grief drove him to madness," she said softly. "Where is he now?"

"Safely confined in Pine Ridge. Are you shocked?"

"I'd be lying if I said no, but mostly, I feel sad. Because like me, you never knew your mother, and like me, you never had your father's love."

Astonishment flared in him, bright as a match kindled in

absolute darkness. "Are you saying we're two of a kind?"

"Maybe I am. Of the two of us, I think you've had the better outcome."

"Why do you say that, my good wife?"

"Because you had a brother who loved you so much that he was trying to protect you to his last breath...and even though he's currently lost, there's still a chance your father could come back to you."

His chest hurt with the unexpected sweetness of her words and their undeniable truth chipped away at the awful residue the nightmare had left behind. "Mm, well, I do concede that I'm a lucky devil, not just for those reasons."

"Why, then?"

With gentle reverence, he kissed her temple. "Because I married you."

17.

IN THE MORNING, Thalia woke hungry.

Nothing had been solved, so she shouldn't feel so serene, but she couldn't muster sufficient ambition to haul herself out of bed. The room held a fearful chill, as the fire had died at some point during the night, so she was wrapped around Raff like he was the flame that could keep her alive.

Getting out of bed would be torture.

Still, even knowing that didn't stifle her whimper at the cold shock against her bare skin. She scrambled into her torn and filthy clothes, for once missing the luxuries she'd enjoyed during her confinement at Riverwind. There in her gilded cage, she'd had heated floors and an endless supply of hot water.

"You're so eager to leave," Raff mumbled.

Layering up only helped so much. Thalia's hands were so cold that the joints hurt. It had been such a long winter; this should be that last hurrah of ice and snow, yielding to spring and warmer weather. She tried to imagine the dead ground coming back to life as she went to the window, but found it impossible to superimpose verdant growth atop the white field and the icicles dripping from the trees.

It was just warm enough that they were melting, slow-ly. That would make it dangerous to pass through the woods. People always told gruesome stories of those who died with ice spikes in their eyes.

"I should call Ferith," she said.

They had to be worried at Daruvar, search parties combing the woods. Last night there had been no signal, but before she could touch the screen, Raff snatched her phone. He didn't seem to feel the cold as much because he was completely naked, paying no mind to the frigid air or his bare skin. In the full daylight, she could appreciate his raw strength, musculature quite unlike the more delicate Eldritch build.

Don't get distracted.

"What are you doing?" she snapped.

"Let's take a minute to think about this," he said. "We've been given a chance here. If they think you're dead, it may flush out the traitor."

Thalia paused. That was…coldblooded and strategically brilliant. She hadn't set out to fake her own death, but with everything that had happened, she'd be a fool not to exploit this opportunity. But that didn't mean playing the leader of the Noxblades.

"You suspect Ferith can't be trusted?" she asked at last.

"I'm not saying that. Look, I don't know any of your people well enough to say. But if you make contact, the channel may not be secure, and even if she doesn't spill, her reaction might give the game away. It just seems like it's safer to keep this between us for now."

"I see your point, but…how do you envision the two of us handling a conspiracy on this scale?"

Raff made a face that she couldn't interpret. "I don't

have it all worked out yet, but the first order of business is tracking the rogue Eldritch who were working with the ones that tried to off us in the tunnel. They had the stink of camphor on them, not a lot, just a little, but if the others do too, I can hunt them down."

Thalia nodded. Never could she have imagined how helpful it would be to partner up with a wolf. In the woods, Raff would be relentless; it would take a miracle for their quarry to elude them.

"All right, I'm in. I'll hold off calling Ferith for now." She pulled on her coat and geared up as best she could, though her outerwear was sadly insufficient for the weather. "What should we do if the numbers are too great?"

Raff only grinned. "Unless they've got a CTAK, don't worry about it, princess. You've got me with you, after all."

That should've sounded like pure bravado, but she had seen him fight. "Leave one alive for questioning, if possible."

"No promises, but I'll try. Guess there's no point in getting dressed, then. Will you take my stuff?"

"Of course."

As she gathered his belongings and stuffed them in her pack, he shifted from man to wolf, a process that never stopped fascinating her. She wondered how it felt, if it hurt.

This plan was…well, reckless. Thalia acknowledged as much as she followed the black wolf out of the cabin. Normally, she didn't do battle without considering all potential outcomes first, running various simulations and weighing all factors. Now, because a roguish wolf said, "Trust me", she was setting out on what might be a suicide mission.

I'm okay with that.

He set a pace she could match, though he occasionally

raced off to check something and then he circled back, surefooted on the icy ground. Their path led away from Daruvar, west of the tunnel—she thought—but it was hard to be sure. She had far more experience tracking a target using technology, watching signals on a screen and giving orders to troops via wireless. At Ash Valley, that was the first time she'd fought like a soldier, shooting from the walls. Since then, her combat experience had really ramped up.

Unsurprisingly Raff noticed the change before she did. Mostly Thalia kept a close eye on him and reflected on how cold and miserable she was. In all her elaborate rise-to-power fantasies back at Riverwind, she'd never realized leadership could be so uncomfortable. When the black wolf stilled, she did too.

Listening.

Then she understood. There were no noises at all, not a peep from the other creatures of the forest. Before, a few winter birds hopped about, chirping overhead, and squirrels chattered as they gathered nuts. Now, it was all silence.

That means there are enemies close, in numbers large enough to alarm the wildlife.

Raff glanced up at her; she was getting better at reading his canine expressions. The head cock seemed to be interrogative. In answer, she raised a finger to her lips and held it there as a sign that she understood that she needed to keep quiet.

The black wolf nodded, then picked a silent path across the ice. Dark branches snatched at her clothing, but Thalia did her best to leave no trace. While she hadn't completed Noxblade training, she had enough stealth that she shouldn't give them away before they were ready to attack.

She heard the voices and smelled the smoke around the same time. *Looks like they made camp.* Drawing in a long breath, she calmed herself as she drew her blades. It would've been nice if she could've recharged her bracers, but they were at half power, good for five more shots each. Dropping into a crouch, she stayed close to Raff, moving as he moved.

Easier said than done since he was on four legs and she had two.

Until this moment, she'd never wished she could shift, but the more time she spent with the Animari, the more she found to admire. Thalia could see herself as a sleek silver fox, perhaps, or an ice wolf—

They broke from cover silently, cutting her train of thought. Swiftly she counted eight adversaries, all Eldritch. They were bivouacked well, a fine fire burning, and their white thermal tents blended in with the environment. From the smell, they were roasting vegetables in the fire, like this was a fucking school trip.

"Haven't heard back from Ruark yet," one of them said.

"Nothing from Penn and Maris, either. You think something went wrong?"

"We have our orders. You don't get paid extra to fret, do you? Just sit tight. The Talfayen bitch will be dead one way or another, soon enough."

RAFF SNAPPED.

In an instant, he lunged at the nearest scout, knocking him to the ground. Rage was his fuel, and he had plenty to burn. He had been tolerant and patient for too long. Finally, he had a chance to show these assholes a little Pine Ridge style. As the rest scrambled for cover, he bit down on the Eldritch's skull, glorying in the crunch of bone. Blood trickled into his mouth; he sprang away as bullets peppered the ground, dodging behind a tree.

The others armored up and grabbed their weapons, scattering at a bolt of Thalia's lightning. She missed her first shot, left the trunk charred and smoking. *I don't need to worry about her. Time for a killer fucking game of hide and seek.*

Raff rushed, skidding on the icy ground, toward the Eldritch to the left. Rebounding off the tree, he pounced on the scout and used the momentum to drag him across the ground, digging his claws into the enemy's gut. The fallen scout slashed with a knife and Raff bit down, until he tasted more Eldritch blood and the blade slipped from the bastard's hands. Bullets whizzed past, most slammed into the trees behind, but one grazed his flank. Crimson stained the white ground, his and the Eldritch whose arm he'd almost bitten off.

"Raff, behind you!" Thalia called.

Bolts of lightning shot from Thalia's bracers, a beautiful blue arc that slammed into the one taking aim. The Eldritch shuddered from the volts and smoke swirled around his corpse as it fell. She laid down cover fire, giving him the space to charge, where three of them had clustered in the same tangle of icy brush. He tore the throat out of one before the female could get her knife up, and he spat out the taste of her wine-sweet blood.

Two of them were backing away, poised to run; that couldn't happen. If a single one made it out to report that Thalia was alive, their entire plan, flimsy as it was, would fall to shit. When the first broke and tried to run, Raff hamstrung him with a vicious bite. Thalia took the other with a shot to the back, lightning cycling over the corpse in bright sparks.

The surviving scouts sprayed bullets, filling the clearing with the stink of cordite. A couple stray ones hit the mark, one in his rear flank, the other in his side.

Raff snarled and let pain-adrenaline drive him to greater fury. He snatched up the nearest Eldritch, closed his jaws on his thigh, and used him as a shield while the other two filled him with bullets. As they ran out of ammo and scrambled to reload, he flung the Eldritch shield away and dove for the one on the right and ripped his chest open, not stopping until entrails unspooled like a slick and bloody rope and steam rose from where the hot mess hit the frosty ground.

Two left—one male, one female.

The male Eldritch took aim at him, and Raff held, ignoring the pain. Because he saw Thalia, silently signaling with her eyes. *Don't move.* She struck from the shadows, slamming both of her knives into the traitor's temples. *This woman is glorious.* In a graceful motion, she pulled her blades free and swiped them clean on the ground. Raff offered a nod before turning toward the last one standing. She'd apparently decided there was no point in trying to flee.

"None of us will ever talk," the woman said with a sneer. "Lord Gilbraith has eyes everywhere and—"

Thalia ended the budding monologue with a final shot from her sputtering bracer. The power light flickered and died; that must mean she was out of juice. On the ground, one of the Eldritch was still squirming, rolling and screaming as blood gushed from his mangled arm. Raff loped over and growled, an unmistakable warning.

Thalia joined him, staring at the survivor with a grim expression. "Good, you left one capable of talking. Now then, let's ask our new friend some questions."

"Ruark Gilbraith is the one true king. Burn in hell, pretender!"

Raff got the feeling the asshole would have spat, but he didn't have the breath. His color suggested that he was going into shock. Between blood loss and cold, it would be surprising if he survived long enough for a lengthy interrogation. He'd already confirmed one fact without meaning to—he most likely came from House Gilbraith, as it seemed unlikely that a spy from another demesne would be so fanatically loyal to a mere ally.

"Who is the agent hidden in my hold? Tell me what you know, or things will get worse." Her voice was so calm and gentle that Raff almost didn't discern the threat at first.

"Like...hell," the scout gurgled.

His jaw clenched then, but blood bubbled at the corners of his mouth, swiftly followed by white foam. He convulsed in a torturous arc, limbs twisting in one of the most spectacularly painful deaths Raff had ever witnessed. *Bastard suicided to keep us from learning anything else.* The froth smelled faintly familiar, one of the poisons that had killed Lileth at their wedding feast.

Thalia swore. "It seems he was afraid of my methods. I might've gotten a name, given time." Then she seemed to notice his condition, crouching with worried eyes. "How bad is it? I can see that you're hurt, but I can't tell if it's serious."

I've been shot in the leg I broke in the tunnel, got another bullet in my side and a bleeding shoulder from the grazing shot.

If he shifted to tell her that, it would be harder to get back to the cabin. That was their best hope. They couldn't stay here in case the other houses sent reinforcements, and he was in no shape to make the trek back to Daruvar. Time and food would probably be enough to patch him up enough to get there under his own steam. His recovery period would also reinforce the traitor's conviction that Thalia was gone for good…and that conviction would be enough rope to hang himself.

"What should I do?" she was asking.

Thalia wrung her hands, tears standing in her eyes— well, that felt pretty good. There was no sign of her customary poise, and it didn't seem like she had her planning cap on either. His blood on her hands as she checked his wounds had evidently disconnected some key wires in her brain.

Looks like I'm in charge right now.

He padded over to inspect the supplies their enemies had left—nuts, dried fruit and protein bars. The only fresh food was wrapped in foil and had been placed in the fire to roast, now despoiled with spattered blood. Raff pawed the packs, telling her with his eyes to gather up anything useful. She caught on swiftly and loaded up on food and first aid items, then he limped out of the clearing, back toward the cabin.

Oddly, she didn't question their direction. This wasn't the way to Daruvar, though maybe she didn't realize. She just followed, carrying everything he couldn't. It was getting harder to breathe, which meant the bullet inside him was doing bad things to his innards. Thalia probably wouldn't like it when he shifted and asked her to perform surgery.

Just keep moving. We're almost there.

The blood trail he was dropping was a fucking mess, but the wounds coagulated or froze at some point. It was so fucking cold, colder than it should be. The trees looked dark and strange too, stretching and shrinking around him when he blinked. *Guess I've lost more blood than I realized.* He held on because Thalia was behind him, and he didn't think she could find shelter on her own. Raff understood too that she wouldn't leave him to find help. Whether they lived or died out here, they'd do it together.

At last, he broke from the trees and saw the cabin. His three working legs wouldn't carry him any farther. Raff stumbled and went down as the world dimmed to black.

18.

"RAFF!" THALIA SHOOK him, but he was out, a limp wolf sprawled on a patch of ice. *Get him inside. That's my top priority.* With effort, she locked down the panic battering at her mind. He'd helped her keep it together long enough for them to reach the cabin. The rest was up to her. She huffed, wrapping both arms around him and towed with all her strength. He was a large wolf, much bigger than nature allowed, and he was impossibly dense with muscle. Thalia fell twice, scrambling in the slush and mud. Her breath came in ragged bursts, and she had to rest before resuming the struggle.

Finally, she got him to the doorway and she cradled him against her chest, fighting helpless tears. The logical thing to do would be to power up her phone and ring for help, but that would ruin their plan to expose the traitor and it might expose Raff to greater risk. There was no guarantee that those who responded would deliver benevolent assistance. Her enemies might strike while she was vulnerable, especially with Raff too weak to fight.

Putting him down gently, she let out a breath and made the decision. For good or ill, she would look after him and stick to the plan. Her mind made up, she opened her phone and took out the battery, as there was a faint chance that her location could be tracked that way. Now she had an unconscious wolf to deal with. As she hauled him into the cabin, they left red streaks on the ice, on the rough wood floor. His black fur made it difficult to tell exactly where the injuries were, and she didn't have the tools to shave him.

I have to do this. Sorry, Raff.

Deliberately, she pressed down on his injured leg and he roused with a snarl, snapping at her with ferocious teeth. She barely pulled her hand back fast enough to avoid a vicious bite.

"It's me, Thalia. We're at the cabin. I need you to shift." His eyes went fuzzy and vague and she shook him, gentler this time. "Don't pass out. You've done so much, saved me so many times. This is the last thing, Raff. I can handle the rest."

She hoped. As promises went, she didn't feel 100% confident, but he didn't need to know that.

A shudder ran through him and then his body blurred and elongated. It was the strangest thing; even as she looked at him, her mind couldn't quite process how it happened, like a mental skip. One second he was a wolf, and in the next blink, he was a naked man, lolling in her arms.

Now, now she could see how bad it was. The graze on his shoulder had sealed to a scab and it seemed to be healing well, no signs of infection. Likewise, the bullet had gone straight through his bad leg. It was mostly sealed, just a sluggish trickle of blood from her meddling with it. The wound in his side troubled her because there was no exit hole in his back; that meant the bullet was still inside him. Raff's body would heal around it, but leaving metal inside couldn't be good, even with Animari recovery rates.

He clutched her hands with bloody fingers. "You have to take it out."

It's like he can read my mind.

Thalia's first instinct was to argue; she wanted to say, 'I'm not a surgeon, I'm not even a doctor', but in fact, there was nobody else. They couldn't risk exposing his weakness right now. Better to hunker down and let their enemies come out into the open, then once they regained their strength, strike from the shadows and finish this damned game of cat and mouse.

They'll be surprised who has the fiercest claws.

Squaring her shoulders, she nodded. "I'll take care of it."

She found a blanket folded in the rough-built cupboards and spread it on the floor. There was only one bed, one set of linens, and if she ruined them, they wouldn't have anywhere to sleep once she finished Raff's treatment. He rolled onto the coverlet, shivering from such minor exertion.

This is not good.

His breathing was labored, and there was a sickly tinge to his normally brown and glowing skin. *Don't think about what could go wrong. Just do what you must.*

The pep talk carried her through various preparations, like boiling some water and sterilizing her knives, but her hands trembled when she brought the blade to his side, which had already sealed. *I have to cut him. Oh, All-Mother, I can't do this—*

"I trust you, princess."

Those rasped words gave her the confidence to open the wound, but she died a little when he bucked and screamed. Pain sweat beaded on his brow, and he fisted both hands in the rough blanket.

"Fuck me, that hurts."

"I don't have anything strong enough to put you out. Eldritch medicines don't seem to be efficacious for the Animari."

"Different metabolic rate," he grunted. "Just…get it done. Fast is better than slow."

"I know that, but I'm trying to avoid butchering you."

She tried not to show how scared she was or how utterly unsettling it was to be feeling around beneath the skin, layers of muscle and connective tissue with such a terrifying lack of expertise. *Deeper, oh, there.* It took three tries, but she finally got the bullet out, lodged against his ribs. She tried not to fret about bone chips or all the ways he could die as she removed the slug.

"You done?" Raff whispered.

She wished he would pass out, so he'd be spared some of the pain, but he had been with her, ever since she woke him so cruelly. "Just clean up left, now."

Though the cabin was cold, Thalia was covered in sweat as she washed her hands. *One step at a time.* Using her knife, she cut strips off the clean end of the blanket. The first she used to wipe the blood up as best she could. It looked as if Raff had been baptized in it, so it took several rinses to get him clean. Then she applied antibacterial spray and wrapped his side as best she could.

"There," she said finally. "I wish we had pain meds or antibiotics. But this is all I can do for you."

"It should be fine," he mumbled.

"Right. You're unkillable, I remember."

Even in this circumstance, he managed a crooked smile, tugging at her heartstrings. "Many have tried, none have succeeded."

"It only takes one success," she snapped, then reined in her temper.

Why am I mad at him? She wasn't, exactly, except that it didn't seem as if he treasured his life. Not like he should, anyway.

"Don't fret, Lady Silver. I just need food and sleep."

"You need an actual doctor who knows what he's doing and possibly a blood transfusion. Since you've been with me, you've been shot multiple times, poisoned, nearly crushed to death—"

"Don't cry." He raised unsteady hands to brush her cheek.

That was when Thalia realized she *was* crying. *What the hell is wrong with me? I'm the ice queen, unbreakable, immovable.*

"I'm just tired." Her voice came out soft and small, utterly unlike her. "Let's get you in bed."

"That's your game," he teased. "Weaken me until I can't flee from your fearsome appetites. Alas, I cannot escape, so I'll submit."

She swiped at her eyes. "Idiot. Try not to open any of your wounds."

While he was still acting like a lighthearted fool, she'd seen far too much of his courage and determination to dismiss him any longer. Raff Pineda was a worthy partner by anyone's standards.

Thalia used her full strength to lever him off the floor and onto the mattress. Raff inched upward until he was fully ensconced in bed—and it was clear that much effort had exhausted him. He closed his eyes and just let her tuck him in, as if he was a child. Thalia doubted many people had seen the wolf lord this way. His trust felt like the greatest honor she'd ever received. She bent and pressed a kiss to his forehead.

"Sleep now," she whispered. "I'll stand watch and keep you from harm."

IT WAS NIGHT when Raff woke. He wasn't sure what day it was, and he felt weak as hell. Thalia was beside him, asleep sitting up with one hand on his head. She had never looked exactly robust, and now she seemed dangerously fragile, thinner than before, deep purple shadows beneath her eyes. He managed to struggle upright, though his entire body ached. The last time he felt this shitty, his father had beaten him half to death, right after his older brother died.

His movement roused her, and she snapped to consciousness like a soldier who'd fallen asleep on sentry duty, a complex commingling of guilt and remorse.

"Raff? You're awake?" The desperate joy and gratitude shone from her, reinforced when she carried his hands to her mouth and kissed his knuckles one by one.

"You're starting to alarm me, Lady Silver."

"It's been four days," she whispered, touching his hair, his cheek, his beard. Soft, pleasant tingles followed wherever her hands roved. He'd never felt like precious treasure before, but her fingers brushing lightly over his hair nearly made him groan aloud.

"Has it?" he asked, quietly shaken.

Swallowing audibly, she nodded. "The wound in your side was infected. I had to open it up twice and drain the site." From the way her face looked, he could well imagine she'd gone through hell for him and come back again.

"Thank you."

"For what? My poor care nearly killed you." Tears trembled in her thick lashes, spilled down pale cheeks.

He reached for her with arms that wobbled. *Still not recovered, but I'm on the uptick.* Raff was clearheaded at least. Of the last few days, he had only jumbled impressions, mostly Thalia's face and her soft hands interspersed with what must've been nightmares.

She curled into his arms, not a queen, just a tired woman pushed beyond her limits. The way she trembled against him roused every ferociously protective instinct. Somewhere, there were assholes who wanted to slaughter this bright, lovely creature. Then and there, Raff decided they all had to die, no mercy, no exceptions.

"That's a negative outlook. I mean, I'm still alive." He touched his own cheek. "Don't think I've got a fever and I'm still breathing, so that means you saved me."

"You're impossible. Are you hungry? I haven't been able to get much food in you."

His stomach rumbled as if she'd activated it. "Apparently I'm starved."

"Then let's start slow. I made porridge out of the protein bars and dried fruit, but you wouldn't eat any this morning. You kept calling for someone named Catrin."

Raff considered messing with her, despite the heat that rose in his cheeks. He could probably make her think that was an old lover, but that seemed unjust, considering how hard she'd worked to keep his body and soul together.

"That's the woman who raised me," he explained. "Catrin is my mother's cousin, and she looked after me from the beginning. She's the only one who ever nursed me. Well, until you, that is."

"Ah. Is she..." Thalia appeared to reconsider the question, moving away from him to check the pot warming near the fireplace.

"It's all right. There's no sad story. Catrin's alive and well, back in Pine Ridge. You'll meet her, provided we survive our tenure in your territory."

"I'd like that. I'll ask her for all the embarrassing stories from your childhood." She spooned brown mush into a tin bowl, then carried it to him.

That…did not smell appetizing, but judging by his physical weakness, he didn't have the fortitude to shift and hunt for something delicious. Raff forced himself to eat every bite, though it tasted even worse than it smelled. Cooking clearly wasn't her strong point.

"I know it's bad," she said defensively. "But *you* try making a wonderful meal out of basic protein bars and dehydrated fruit."

Masking a grimace, he swallowed several more bites, then replied, "I'm not complaining. You have some too, though."

She shook her head. "I've been eating the nuts. I tried putting them in the porridge, but they wouldn't boil down and they made you choke."

"You should have chewed them and fed them to me like a baby bird." Raff couldn't keep a straight face when he registered her horrified expression.

"You're awful," she said, apparently realizing that he was messing with her.

"That's the rumor. Will I have any new scars from this adventure?"

Really, he just wanted her close again. She'd kept the fire burning, and the room was warm enough to be bearable, but it wasn't the same as feeling her tender heat next to him. Thalia rose to the bait, setting aside the empty bowl and returning to his side to check his injuries.

"I can barely see the mark on your shoulder now...raise your leg?" She bent close, peering at his calf. "This one is almost healed as well. Turn onto your other side, please."

So sweet and prim, that tone, like she hadn't been in charge of his naked body for days. Raff complied, rolling away, so she could check his ribs. That spot did still hurt a bit, so he could well believe she'd been forced to dig at it repeatedly. The work must've been so fucking repugnant that he wished he could wipe the memory from her head, so she wouldn't associate him with oozing pus and necrotic tissue.

Talk about ruining the mood.

"I can't tell yet. You might have a faint scar here. It's still purple."

"Scars make me special," he said. "You know how hard it is for an Animari to get battle marks? I already have two, so let's go for the trifecta."

"I'm not cutting you again. And I'm not trying to alarm you, but we're just about out of food. I don't eat much, but I think you need more...?"

"Finish whatever we have. I'll go hunting tomorrow and stock up on protein."

Her face paled, green beneath the alabaster. "Sorry, can I..."

"I don't expect you to participate. You're pescatarian, I get that."

"All right. Once you've eaten well, we'll head for Daruvar?"

"I think the porridge and a good night's sleep will set me up well enough to shift, and then, if I do well hunting, I should be strong enough to fight an army."

"Your self-assessment is absurd," she snapped. "Right now, you can't even put your pants on without help."

"I'm taking it as a compliment that you can't stop thinking about my pants—or lack thereof—even when I'm sick." He grinned up at her, delighted by her narrow-eyed agitation.

It's so easy to get her riled up. And so fucking fun, too. Even more so because she had a reputation for being unflappable.

"I'm starting to regret all those sleepless nights, mopping up your fever sweat and listening to your delirious ramblings."

Uh oh. I shouldn't ask. That curiosity gives her too much power.

Fuck it, it was impossible to resist the question. "What did I say, exactly?"

Her smug smile drove him crazy. "I guess you *would* wonder. Too bad I'm not telling, but your comments were certainly…enlightening."

Raff might have pursued the issue, but just then, the door slammed open, a gust of bitter wind blowing through the cabin. A huge male stood shadowed in the doorway, half a head taller than Raff, cat by the smell of him. He recognized the scent from when they'd first arrived; this was the cabin's last resident, returned at the worst possible time.

I'm not strong enough to fight, and she's tired. Don't know if her bracers have any charge left, and I don't give her good odds in hand to hand.

Those calculations took only a few seconds as Raff straightened slowly. *Have to make sure this doesn't turn hostile.* Beside him, Thalia was frozen, eyes wide. She seemed to be gauging the distance between her and their discarded weapons.

No sudden moves, princess. Be smart.

"Well," said the stranger. "I guess I'd like to know who the hell you two are and what the fuck you're doing in my bed."

19.

T HALIA TOOK THE man's measure in a single glance and
decided words would have to suffice. This Animari
was massive, on par with the war priest who led the bear
clan and he looked exceedingly pissed off. Not that she
blamed him. They *were* intruding on his territory and it
might not matter if they had a good reason. She was
uncomfortably conscious of her own grime and dishevelment.

*If I tell him that I'm the leader of House Talfayen and that
Raff's the packmaster of Pine Ridge, he'll probably laugh.* Then
again, it might be worse if he believed them. He might hold
them for ransom. After all, it didn't seem likely that a
solitary great cat had a *good* reason for hiding out so close to
the Eldritch border.

"I'm sorry," she said, when it became apparent that the
large man was losing patience. "There was a storm and we
couldn't find shelter anywhere else."

"That, I understand. But from what I saw of the trail
signs, you rested here, went out and fought some, then *came
back.* And you're still here. I guess you know how it goes in
the old stories, when the intruder's still sleeping in the bed

they stole from its rightful owner."

She didn't. Thalia's childhood education had included history and philosophy, botany and strategy, statecraft and diplomacy. Nobody had ever read to her from storybooks. She had been left to pore over old tomes and interpret them as best she could, sometimes with Lileth's guidance, more often not. While the old woman had been vigilant, she had never been precisely…warm.

"I'm getting up," Raff said. "If I could, I'd pay for the supplies we used, but…" The wolf lord shrugged. "Circumstances being what they are, we'll have to owe you."

It would've been polite if the man had turned his back as Raff fumbled to get dressed; Thalia had to help him while their witness observed their every move with relentless precision. He didn't stir except to close the door behind him. Once Raff was out of bed, the cabin owner stomped across the floor and glared at the hearth.

"You used almost all of my firewood. I don't suppose you bothered to collect more?"

She wasn't used to being in this position—with nothing sensible to say in her own defense. The truth was just so fucking messy and complicated and—

"I'm sorry. You were right when you said we were in a fight. I was tending to my husband, so I didn't have a chance to replenish the fuel." Her tone was as humble as it ever had been. Her loyal Noxblades—Gavriel especially—would be horrified.

That finally roused a reaction from their unwilling host. A flicker of something softened his craggy features as he knelt to feed a block of wood to the waning flames. Thalia wasn't good at gauging Animari faces, but he looked to be around Raff's age. Quite young to have chosen life as a hermit, she reckoned.

"Husband," he repeated, sounding thoughtful.

Was that a mistake?

If he was some mad purist, he might attack them for embarking on a mixed marriage. She tensed and from the way Raff's arm tightened beneath her hand, he was ready for this to encounter to spin from bad to worse. *He's in no shape to fight. Dammit, we only needed one more day to rest.* It wasn't fair, and she knew it, but she wished the owner could've delayed his return a little longer.

"That's me," Raff said deliberately. He also took half a step forward, putting himself between her and the other Animari.

"Let me guess, you eloped, and her folk didn't take kindly to it. Things went bad in the woods and he almost died. Now you're hiding out, wondering if you made a terrible mistake."

It was a reasonable guess, based on what he'd observed, but Thalia wasn't sure if the truth would make things better or worse. Before she could reply, Raff said, "I'm not wondering that. If I could do it all over again, I'd still marry this woman."

Even though you've been in constant jeopardy, constant pain, because of me? In front of the other Animari, she couldn't ask. She wanted to. Desperately.

"Those are the magic words. I can't resist a star-crossed romance." The man's tone was oddly wistful, belying his stern appearance.

"Does that mean we can stay the night?" Thalia asked.

"Dear mercy, I was never going to shove you out in the dark. I just wanted to take your measure some. You aren't the first trespassers who've stumbled in. Won't be the last either, I expect."

She let out a long, slow breath, relief making her sound like a deflating balloon. Raff wrapped an arm around her and to their host, it might look like he was being protective, but in truth, he was leaning on her, hard. *Yeah, not nearly ready to march on Daruvar.*

"Introductions seem to be in order. I'm Thalia. This is Raff."

The wolf lord managed a credible bow by clinging to her arm as he dipped at the waist. A scowl creased the other Animari's brow.

"Titus. Don't ask me any personal questions, don't bother me with polite nonsense, and we'll get along fine."

"Thank you," Thalia said. "It's generous of you to let us stay."

"It's clear your man can't move on. If he gets ambushed by your people again, he won't make it out of these woods alive."

"True enough," she said softly.

He wasn't entirely wrong. *If I was the kind of leader who inspired instinctive loyalty, Ruark wouldn't have gained such a following.* The other houses would've fallen in behind Thalia, despite the long shadow her father cast.

Sighing, Titus set down his pack. "I'm bone-tired, so I get the bed, and tomorrow, I expect Miss Thalia to wash everything you've dirtied in my absence."

That...covered a lot of ground. She'd cut up the spare blanket, used it for rags and bandages. The floor was smeared with blood and the sheets...well, she'd never in her life washed anything like that, but if she was pretending to be a normal woman, who'd run away with the love of her life, so be it. Raff started to argue; she shook her head silently.

"I'll take care of it," she promised.

"Good. Of course, freeloaders can't be choosy, but here, you two can huddle up in the sleeping bag I used on the road."

Raff caught the cloth bundle he tossed, and it smelled none too fresh, even to Thalia's reckoning. To another Animari, the damn thing must reek. Still, it was better than lying on the cold wood floor. Since Titus was blowing out candles and dimming the lantern, she guessed it was time for bed, like it or not.

There was no chance for a private conversation. Anything Raff whispered to her, Titus would hear perfectly. The wolf lord conveyed that with a single sideways look and she inclined her head as she laid out their makeshift mattress. At least the slick fabric should be warm, even if it smelled like smoke and...Titus. Raff made a sound deep in his throat when she laid down. Some territorial Animari thing, probably.

Then he appeared to get over it and settled behind her, again putting his body between her and Titus. This sort of thing didn't really happen among the Eldritch. She had no words for how it made her feel, sort of warm and melting and puzzled. Despite how she looked, people rarely treated her as if she was truly...precious. The loyalty she received from her followers felt different than what she got from Raff. Silently he zipped the sleep sack and spooned up behind her, a physical wall between her and any harm that might creep up in the night.

He'd also made sure that she would sleep next to the fire, and Thalia had no fucking idea what she'd do if he crept any closer. To someone who had lived such a chill and lonely life, the sudden warmth blazed too hot and strong, a fire that might burn her to death, if she wasn't careful.

It's so hard to be careful.

FOR THE NEXT two days, Raff watched while Thalia played housemaid. She swept and scrubbed the floor, washed the linens by hand, and tried to cook a soup that he saved from burning while she was dusting the furniture. She wasn't good at any of it, and the effort exhausted her, but she wouldn't let him help. Every time he tried, she scowled and ordered him to sit down, like he was a delicate porcelain figurine. She really didn't seem to understand how fast the Animari healed or how tired he was of lazing around.

Today, he followed her out to the clearing where she'd hung the rug and was using a stick to beat the dust out of it. He plucked the wood from her fingers and took over the task. The fact that she finally *let* him spoke volumes about how tired she was. Marriage to him hadn't done her any favors; she was rail thin and her delicate hands were chapped and blistered, red across the knuckles from all the unaccustomed scrubbing.

Raff glanced at the bracers that she'd left out in the wan sunlight, hoping to catch a partial charge. The solar panels weren't powerful, so it would be better if she could plug in. She should be fighting for her people, not coddling him.

He took his aggravation out on the carpet, until Thalia said, "You'll beat that thing to death. The tiger won't thank you for ruining his rug."

With a snarled curse, he tossed the stick aside and drew her against him. She flattened her hands against his chest, but she didn't push, eyes wide. "What's wrong?"

"Everything. I'm tired of being strategic. I want to go kill everyone who opposes you." He had the urge to kiss her, smooth her fair hair, and rub cream on her damaged hands. This woman would probably stick a knife in him and twist if he tried any of that. She didn't want his protection, and he didn't have much else to offer.

What more can the big bad wolf do?

Thalia laughed softly. "That's sweet, but you're not up to it."

Raff tried to show her how well his leg had healed. "Look, it's better. I can put full weight on it, and the scar on my side is nearly gone."

She shooed him toward the cabin. "Nice try, but I remember clearly how hard I worked to take care of you. I won't risk your recovery. If you're bored, see if there's tea. I'll want a hot drink when I finish out here."

He stomped inside, scowling, and rummaged in the cupboard. *She wants tea.* Never in his life had he been relegated to a role like maker-of-tea. Korin would laugh her ass off, if she could see him now.

Titus snickered, appearing to find it all extremely amusing. "Are you ever going to tell her that you're fine, wolf?"

Briefly, he considered punching their host. *Better not.*

"Does it look like she'd listen?" he snapped, putting the kettle on.

The great cat laughed and shook his head. "Maybe not. Her willingness to ruin those pretty hands speaks to how much she treasures you, though."

Raff sighed. If that were true, maybe he wouldn't mind so much, but it felt more like he was accruing a debt to her that he had no way to pay. "We'll be moving on this afternoon. I'm sorry to have troubled you this long."

"Is that so? Do you have a plan, at least?"

The tenor of the question raised his hackles; something about the other Animari's expression made Raff think he knew more than he'd let on, possibly since the beginning. "What are you getting at?"

"You can't be planning to stroll back to Daruvar. If your enemies have taken the fortress, returning without a sound strategy would be suicide."

Raff stared. "You know who we are?"

"Please. Everyone knows that the packmaster of Pine Ridge recently married the Eldritch princess, against counsel from advisors on both sides. Does it make sense that there would be some other mixed couple wandering the wood near the Eldritch stronghold?"

"Why did you mislead us with that silly story about star-crossed lovers?" Thalia stood in the doorway, wearing an expression of coldest fury.

"How else could I make you work for your keep?" Titus smirked, seeming pleased with himself.

"Hilarious," Thalia bit out.

"It would be wrong of me to let you wander off without telling what else I've heard." The levity evaporated from the great cat's aspect.

Raff wasn't sure if they could trust their benefactor, especially considering he'd already tricked them once. Then again, making Thalia do housework didn't exactly rate among the top evil conspiracies of all time, more childish than malevolent. He swapped looks with his wife, and then said, "We're listening."

"Seems the fortress was in quite a flutter when you first disappeared. Search parties, lots of movement. But soon, there was an internal shuffle. Now we're seeing a lot of external movement, troops coming freely from the other houses."

"Shit," Raff said.

If they'd missed the window of opportunity, the traitor might have already seized control of Daruvar. If that was the case, they might have executed Janek and Sky. An icy hand clutched at his heart.

"How do you know all this?" Thalia demanded. "Who the hell *are* you?"

Titus sighed, motioning them both to take a seat. The only place they could all sit was at the rustic table, which had four rough chairs. Reluctantly Thalia closed the door and moved to comply, so Raff went along. There was no point in escalating this situation, if it could be resolved otherwise. He didn't like the idea of fighting the man who had given them shelter, even if he'd been miserly with the truth.

The water was boiling, so he made the tea she'd requested earlier. It might be faintly ridiculous to drink it now, but she was still cold, whatever else might happen. Titus gave him a look as he served the drinks. He responded with a shrug, setting out powdered milk and sugar. While the cabin might be equipped with basic supplies, he'd enjoy returning to civilization, where he could get a proper hot toddy with fresh lemon and fine aged whiskey.

Assuming that this asshole doesn't throw down with us here and now. That didn't seem likely, but the boundaries demarcating who they could trust blurred by the minute. Titus might have backup he could call in—

"Raff probably already knows that this cabin is a meeting point. There's no erasing scent trails."

He *had* smelled a variety of people, converging here—

Titus was just the most recent—he hadn't realized that meant that this was more than a hunting retreat. Raff decided to keep quiet on that point and only offered a silent nod. Best for the great cat not to figure out that Thalia was the true bright spark between them.

"What about it?" he asked.

"We're all outsiders for one reason or another. Left our prides and packs years ago, but that doesn't mean we have no interest in the world."

"You're wise to be worried," Thalia said softly. "If Ruark Gilbraith finishes my father's work and solidifies an alliance with Tycho Vega of the Golgoth, nobody will be left to live as they wish."

"That is the absolute truth. I went on a supply run and was trying to figure out what to do with that information when I found you two here. If you don't mind my saying, it seems like providence."

"What does?" Raff asked.

"Well, instead of passing the word along, as I was planning to, I believe I'm meant to take a more active role this time."

Thalia cocked her head. To his watchful eye, it looked as if some of her aggravation had dissipated, or at least cooled to a calmer curiosity. "It sounds like you have an idea."

With a nod, Titus said, "Of course I do. Listen up, and if you approve, we'll get started before this tea cools."

20.

PLAYING DEAD WAS never among Thalia's top strategies, and it was fucking humiliating, but she cared about results, not elegance. Her dignity could get fucked permanently, if it meant resolving the standoff at Daruvar. The wolves were in position, as Korin had come in response to an SOS from Janek, abruptly cut off twelve hours before.

The idea that it might be too late, well, she wouldn't think about that.

The filth and animal blood that Titus had rubbed on her to transform her into a compelling corpse reeked, and it must be ten times worse for Raff. He lay like a truly dead person beneath her, not reacting even a trifle to the ruts in the rocky forest path. Titus was hauling the cart like a mule, and she wondered, not for the first time, if they could truly trust him. He'd proposed returning their 'bodies' for the bounty Ruark had posted, and once they were inside, the wolves would strike, helping them liberate the fortress and root out the traitors.

It was a sound plan, but one that hinged on a stranger not betraying them at the worst possible moment. For all she knew, Titus's real intention could be to sell them to their enemies, and here they were, quietly going along with the capture. Raff had said he didn't smell deceit on the great cat, but she'd heard of gifted conmen who could lie without a single physiological sign.

Worrying is pointless. Even if Titus turns on us, Korin is here.

The journey seemed to take forever, and periodically, Titus had to lift the cart physically over a large stone or tangle of roots, jolting them around with absolute unconcern. That was for the benefit of those who were undoubtedly tracking his progress. It didn't make sense that whoever had taken control of Daruvar in Ruark's name wouldn't have posted scouts or sentries.

No, they know he's coming. He's passed the preliminary inspection.

With her eyes closed, it was tough to gauge their progress, but maybe she'd been in the wild long enough for her senses to sharpen because she noticed when the scents around her changed. Most of what she smelled was old blood and Raff, but instead of the crisp verdant scent, she also detected hints of smoke, likely from the hearths burning inside Daruvar.

Not far now.

Thalia wished she could get a final word of encouragement from Raff, but their success depended on selling this ruse, so she didn't move or speak; she barely breathed as Titus dragged the cart up a small incline. She let her body tilt like a dead person would, completely at the mercy of gravity's pull.

"Who are you?" an unfamiliar male voice called.

"I'm a hunter," Titus replied. "Bodies I found in the woods match the description I got from another tracker. Word is, there's a reward offered. It'd set me up nicely for the winter if I could get paid."

Moment of truth.

If she or Raff moved before the gates opened, they'd unload from the walls. Titus still hadn't broken character; that was a good sign. She held her body so rigid while they waited that it was a wonder she didn't vibrate with tension. Then Raff's fingers brushed hers, too slight of a movement to be visible and covered by her hair as well. That was another sign that she must be dead.

The long delay made her itch, but finally, a female voice called, "Open the gates!"

And her heart died a little. She recognized it—how could she not? Tirael was one of the three Noxblades who had survived the battle of Hallowell and returned to her side with Ferith and Gavriel. The latter was gone on a mission with Magda, Ferith might have died in the cave-in, and she would have said that Tirael was loyal for sure.

Until just now.

She belongs to Ruark? Since when?

No time for further questions. As soon as the gates ground apart, Titus moved, pulling them swiftly toward the doors. "Now!"

On cue, she and Raff bounded out of the cart, shielded from sight by the framework of the walls. Korin and her people poured out of the surrounding forest, charging the hill with a surety and speed that Thalia admired. Raff was wedging the doors open, as previously agreed, while she followed Titus, who shifted before her eyes into a sleek and powerful tiger. He was too fast for her to follow, drawing fire that could've killed her.

Thalia whirled out of the gateway with blades in hand, lightning firing from each of her bracers. Half the soldiers dropped their weapons, some sobbing openly in relief. The rest must belong to Ruark and would have to be put down. She acknowledged the mass surrender with a nod, taking it as a pledge of fealty. She couldn't blame these people for not fighting to the death when word of her demise reached the fortress. Trying to survive wasn't a crime.

"Don't just kneel," she called. "Help me defeat the traitors!"

In response, the guards who had dropped their weapons took them up again and turned on those still fighting. Much as she hated hurting her own people, this had to happen. Paring away hesitation and mercy, she fired again and again, cutting the throats of those who fell. Korin's forces surged everywhere, led by a massive black wolf. Raff's ferocity would have chilled her blood, had it not been unleashed in her defense.

"Tirael is mine!" she shouted. "If you find her first, bring her to me."

Animari forces nearby responded with growls that she took as affirmative. The remaining Eldritch soldiers fell in behind her, according her the respect of leading the charge across the courtyard. There were bodies everywhere, blood freezing on the paving stones. Her breath smoked as she let out a sigh, adding to the infernal atmosphere.

This day's work didn't feel good, as she'd led outsiders to slaughter her own people. *Necessary,* she told herself. *And we have an alliance.* It wasn't like she could allow the Eldritch to follow Ruark into Tycho's madness. Certain policies could sound reasonable, even favorable, but on closer examination, it was all bigotry, racial purity, and hatred. The Eldritch would walk that dark road over her dead body.

Some might say she was no better, choosing to butcher

her own people so.

Thalia ignored the sickness roiling in her stomach. *I will not count the cost. This is right. This is—*

A black wolf lunged in front of her, taking the shot that came down from the walls. He stumbled, shook himself, and snarled. *Still alive.* Her heart nearly stopped, but Thalia couldn't. She rushed from the courtyard, removing herself as a target. In Daruvar's halls, the fighting was tight and fierce, impossible to tell friend from foe until they attacked. She responded with lethal force.

The enemies died swiftly, until she'd nearly drained the batteries on her bracers—she always kept one final shot in reserve for emergencies—then the fighting got bloodier, blades against knives. Their hot blood spattered her skin, her face, and she fought on, grimly relentless. Thalia battled all the way to the cells, hoping that they wouldn't have executed all resistance yet. Sounds from the struggle elsewhere reached her, through the thick stone walls: shouts and cries of pain, the clang of weapons, distant gunfire. She squared her shoulders and stepped forward, peering through the bars on the small access window set in the heavy steel door.

Ferith, injured but alive. Sky, the little wolf beside her. Both injured, but alive. Her heart sank when she didn't spot Janek. "Open the door!" she ordered.

One of the guards found the keys and released the prisoners, not nearly fast enough. Thalia rushed inside, knelt beside the women. In here, the smell increased, a grotesque combination of the waste bucket in the corner and their infected wounds. Ferith tried to stand, but her leg wouldn't hold, and Sky was too weak to lift more than a hand in a greeting. Neither woman could speak.

"Janek?" she whispered.

Sky closed her eyes and shook her head. "He wouldn't yield."

Ferith sounded like death, her voice cracked and scraping like dry bones. "Fought to the death, took ten of Tirael's men with him."

"I'm sorry," Thalia whispered. Then she straightened, eyes burning with unshed tears. "Get them to Dr. Wyeth, if he's still alive and loyal. It's time to end this."

Finally.

RAFF HAD NO reason to hold back, and he left a wicked trail of bodies behind him. *No quarter. No survivors.* He'd wanted to wreck this place since the first attempt on Thalia's life, since her foster mother died. Now he gave everything to vengeance, lost to the primal thrill of executing his enemies.

The Eldritch were fucking soft, reliant on weapons or gifts. Their soldiers couldn't stand against Pine Ridge elite wolves, concentrated in assault mode. Korin had his back, and she kept them off him as he pushed to clear the walls. Blood smeared the stones as he snarled and slashed his way up the stairs. *Hamstring, hamstring, throat.* Crimson soaked his fur in a hot, coppery spray, and he leapt over the falling corpse to press the advance.

Where are you, Tirael?

Raff had a lot of hard fucking questions for when he found her. She was one of Thalia's closest associates, the Noxblade second in command. This had to cut deep. *Only way it could be worse is if it was Ferith.* He could almost feel sorry for the grunts he chewed through on the way to the top of the stairs.

It would've been faster, but he had a fresh bullet in his
back in addition to all his recent wounds. This should go on
record as the most dangerous honeymoon of all time, and
he gave a canine smile, showing teeth as he topped the
stairs. Korin snarled a question from behind, but he shook
his head.

Later, he growled.

Once the fighting stopped, she'd need a briefing. Right
now, though, she just needed to keep killing. Too bad she
didn't have the bear clan war machine she'd piloted during
the Battle of Hallowell; she could unleash death from above
on their enemies, but to Raff, that seemed like a cheap way
to fight, out of your enemy's reach. It was better to
overwhelm them with your strength and taste their death
with all senses.

Raff rushed, bursting from the tower to flatten the
closest Eldritch before he raised his gun. *Not used to fighting
wolves, you son of a bitch?* The Eldritch lacked muscular
density; they were fast and quiet, but not strong. If this was
a cloak and dagger dustup in the woods, they might have a
chance, but not here on the open walls. The merciless
winter sun wouldn't let them hide, unless that was their gift,
and few of them seemed—

A high, shrill note pierced the air, like the mourning
pipes that marked Lileth's funeral. Raff's muscles locked.

His brain screamed at him to move—to launch himself
at the golden-haired woman playing that hideous melody.
This effect had to be part of some fucking Eldritch gift but
knowing that didn't help him break free. *Fucking Tirael.* He
recognized her now, as the Eldritch beside her raised a
weapon, a gun big enough to explode his skull.

Sudden death, catastrophic damage.

That was the quickest way to kill an Animari, but it wasn't easy to inflict. The caliber of that boomstick would do the job, and he *couldn't fucking move*. Not even to glance back to see if the rest of his troops were affected with the same paralysis. The pitch of Titus's snarl-scream somewhere nearby said that he was locked down and pissed as hell.

It's something that impacts Animari.

Raff glared defiance at the bitch who was about to end him, rage to the end. He couldn't even close his eyes, but he wouldn't have, if he could. Good thing, as he would've missed the arc of blue lightning that arced through her. As she dropped, the flute fell, and he sprang into motion. The shot blasted the parapet behind him, singeing his fur, but thanks to a certain Eldritch queen, he was still alive and breathing. Thalia locked eyes with him for only a few seconds from the other end of the wall, but it was enough.

Warmth surged through him as he savaged the shit out of the asshole who'd thought he could end Raff Pineda. Sure, he'd lived through no ability of his own, but picking the right mate, that was a fucking skill, too. Euphoria sang in his veins, so the killing became a kind of glorious symphony, with screams and howls in place of cymbal and drums. Terrified Eldritch hearts racing became his private song and their pleas for mercy as Raff cut them down, well, he savored those too.

He would've stopped if Thalia had asked him to, but she was beside him on the walls, reaping like the angel of death with her shining twin blades. Her braces must be dark now; she'd probably saved one shot, just in case, and she'd saved his life. Again. While she seemed to think she was in his debt, he'd lost count of how many times they'd saved each other. All he knew now was that she'd be there if he needed her.

Maybe it was too soon for that conviction, but as they bathed Daruvar in blood, the conviction grew. *Korin, still alive. Fighting on.* He exhaled and finished a wounded Eldritch who was sobbing, pleading for clemency. *Not my call.* Thalia knew best what needed to happen here. He'd fight until she called him off. Some might say that made him the Eldritch queen's hound, but they could go fuck themselves.

At last, the keep was theirs, bodies piled in the court-yard, and Tirael was chained hand and foot. Thalia dragged her personally, kicking her down the stairs when the other woman balked. Hatred sparked from Tirael's eyes, so shockingly clear that Raff could hardly believe she'd hidden it all this time. Thalia shoved her onto the filthy stones, beside the carcass of her failed rebellion.

The wolves circled behind Raff, still shifted, and ready to face a fresh incursion, if Ruark happened to get word of the massacre. Not bloody likely, they hadn't left any survivors to spread the news. He couldn't speak to Tirael, but that wasn't his place anyway. He settled on his haunches, content to let his mate finish things as she saw fit. Korin sat next to him, Titus on the other side, bloody, but whole. Hard to say if any of that red belonged to the tiger.

The surviving Eldritch took to their knees, hands sealed over their hearts in a gesture that he presumed represented fealty. Overhead, the sky was palest blue, clear as a winter's day ever was, but still cold enough that he saw Thalia's breath when she spoke.

"Why?" The word was an icy blade, cold as condemna-tion.

Tirael glared, eyes sparking with fury. She spat blood

before answering. "You dare to ask me that?"

"This is your only chance to speak some last words, but if you prefer not to offer anything to posterity, that's fine with me. Your execution will provide me great satisfaction."

"I suppose it would," Tirael said. "But then, you'll also have to live with knowing that you murdered your closest kin. Sister."

Raff sucked in a breath as Thalia staggered. That was the only sign of her shock and she recovered swiftly. "Lies."

"But it's not, dear sister. Run the necessary lineage tests, if you wish. Our father betrayed you, installed me at your side and called me 'cousin' when the truth is, my mother poisoned yours and afterward, once she was caught, I had to see her head on a pike for countless weeks, watch as the birds ate her pretty face and pecked out her eyes."

"Then—"

"Everything you believe about yourself is a lie. You're not better suited to be queen, not more destined. Certainly not more royal or more worthy. You're just *lucky,* princess. Even now, you have animals at your back, willing to kill on your command. And this, the Eldritch will remember. I promise, your reign will not be peaceful...or long."

21.

THERE WAS NO immediate way to know if Tirael's claim was true, as DNA testing would take a couple of hours. Even if it was, Thalia would execute her half-sister the same as any traitor. Instead of responding to the furious taunt, she ripped the woman's filthy sleeve and gagged her with it.

This victory was too hard-won for Thalia to allow it to be tainted. She hoped that most surviving soldiers hadn't overheard about Tirael and Thalia's kinship, and now they never would. For a moment, Thalia knelt beside the woman who'd claimed to be her sister, trying *not* to remember confiding in Tirael and asking for her help, like after they discovered the poisoned wine at the wedding feast.

Would Lileth have lived if someone else had summoned help? Eliciting that truth from Dr. Wyeth might push Thalia over the edge, so she decided to staunch that awful curiosity. It required complete self-restraint not to choke the life out of this treacherous bitch at once.

Thalia whispered, "You're in no position to make threats or promises. The victor decides on their version of the truth, and in *my* story, you're nobody, a failure just like your mother. But don't worry. You'll see her soon."

Tirael's eyes blazed with liquid loathing, but she was bound too tightly to react otherwise. Straightening, Thalia scowled at Ferith, who had struggled to the top of the walls despite a grievously injured leg. "You're supposed to be with Dr. Wyeth," she snapped.

The Noxblade shook her head. "Later, once this is finished."

Thalia knew better than to argue. Even if Ferith was bleeding out, she wouldn't stand for being locked out of dealing with a traitor. It had to cut deep, as Tirael had been her second-in-command, secretly scheming against them both. Accepting the inevitable, she said, "Send someone for my father's sword."

Largely ceremonial, the blade was too long for Thalia to use in battle. She'd trained on twin knives, perfectly balanced, but for some occasions, there was no substitute for the enormous weapon known as Lawbringer. The longsword had been in her family for almost a thousand years, the metal dull with age, its engravings stained with blood. By the way Tirael trembled, it seemed she understood what was to come.

When a young Eldritch rushed up with Lawbringer, he also had a wooden block, saving her the trouble of asking for one. Ferith came forward on her own and slammed Tirael's head onto the square. Thalia raised the sword with both arms, conscious that she would need *all* her strength to make a clean cut. Though Lawbringer was preternaturally sharp, it still wasn't easy to sever a neck clean through.

"For the capital crime of treason, you are sentenced to death. You've spoken your final remarks, so we only need to carry out that judgment now."

Thalia sucked in a deep brace, raised the sword, and struck with all her might. Tirael's head bounced away in a spray of red, and she fought against rising queasiness. *So much blood.* Daruvar might never be clean again. A ragged cheer rose from the Eldritch nearby, a keen, sharp victory call that spread among the survivors until the stones echoed with the chant. Her entire body ached, but Thalia responded, striding to the edge of the wall and raising Lawbringer overhead in a triumphant gesture.

She let the roaring go on for long, loud moments, then she signaled for silence. "Today, we won an important battle, but we also lost brothers and sisters who lost sight of our goals. Unity. Friendship. Life without prejudice. I'll renew treaties with the Animari and the Golgoth, after we settle Ruark Gilbraith. Once I take his head, the other houses will follow me, and I hope we can move forward without more senseless bloodshed. There will be peace and prosperity ahead, if we fight for it."

"My queen!" someone shouted.

At first, it was a lone voice in the crowd, but others took up the proclamation. "For our queen!" Until the fortress thundered with Eldritch approbation. Thalia hardly knew how to respond, but she lowered Lawbringer and acknowledged the clamor by posing with both hands on the longsword, bowing her head for a moment.

She couldn't rest on her laurels, though. There was too much left to do. "All right, people. If you're injured, prioritize amongst yourselves and see Dr. Wyeth. Those who are healthy, I need the bodies of our fallen in the courtyard. The traitors will be buried, not burned. Divide into teams and get order restored. Now!"

That broke the spell, sending the Eldritch scurrying.

Thalia stepped back from the edge of the parapet and turned to Ferith. "Will you get treated, or must I threaten you?"

"No need. I'm not needed on corpse watch."

To her surprise, the young wolf, Sky, stepped forward, offering her shoulder, and Ferith accepted the near embrace without hesitation. There was a certain air between them, as if they'd bonded during their captivity. It gave her a sweet feeling to see Ferith's head nestled next to Sky's. The two descended the winding tower stairs together, completely in sync.

One by one, Raff's wolves shifted back and since it was cold as hell, they went to don their winter gear. Only he lingered in the icy wind, but before he could speak, she dug into her dirty pack and found the clothes she'd been holding for him. "Here, get dressed first."

The fact that he did it on the wall, casual as anything, well, it was endearing. Maybe she was reading the situation wrong, but it *felt* like he didn't want to leave her side long enough to tend to his own needs. Not because he was obligated, either. Nothing in their marriage contract stipulated that he had to *care*.

"You all right?" he asked, tugging the sweater over his head.

He was a mess of fresh wounds, smeared with blood, and she didn't mind. When he opened his arms in a silent offer of solace, she curled into him like they were magnets holding an opposite charge. Thalia nestled her head against his bearded chin, relishing the scrape of his hair against hers. Raff stroked her back quietly for a few seconds.

"I'm not well," she finally answered. "But I'm still here."

"Sometimes that's all we can do. Think it's true? What she said."

She shrugged. "It's possible. My father had so many secrets. Just when I think I can't hate him more…"

"I'm sorry, princess."

"To him, I was never even a person, just a tool to be used in his grand design. When I began to think for myself, I enraged him, but he couldn't bring himself to get rid of me. Not when I was an emblem of his virility, sired from his loins."

Raff stirred against her, and Thalia thought he was probably disgusted by these revelations, family secrets that she'd hidden until she was sick with their keeping. "I'm sorry. I shouldn't—"

"No, it's good," he cut in. "Well, the shit you're saying, it's terrible. No disputing that. But it's fucking lovely that you trust me with it. I'll be your vault, I swear. Nobody will pry your confidences from me, even with a hammer and chisel."

"Thank you," she whispered.

Sometimes, before, the pressure built until she had to find a place to hide, where she could scream until the throbbing stopped. Now, hearing his words, it drained away on its own, like he'd physically taken it from her head. Thalia leaned against him harder, marveling at how easily he took her weight. Like it was natural.

I can't be without him now.

And it was such a terrifying revelation, completely unprecedented, and certainly not covered in the contract they'd written up. Raff hadn't promised her emotional support in those documents, so this could stop at any time. Her heart skittered, racing in anticipation of that loss, and she pulled away.

"What's wrong? You're scared?"

She hated that he knew, that he could sense things about her so easily, when she was meant to be a glacier of a woman: immense, icy, and immovable. Mechanically Thalia shook her head. "Just...reaction setting in, I suppose. So much has happened."

"Right."

There was one important task left, anyway—something she'd sworn before she knew who the traitor was. Without hesitation, Thalia snatched up Tirael's head by the streaming hair and impaled it on a spike jutting from the front ramparts, a message to the enemies who were surely watching.

You're next.

RAFF HAD RARELY wanted a hot shower so badly, but he had to see to his fallen first. None of Korin's people had been lost in the taking of Daruvar, but Sky had just informed him of Janek's death. His knees nearly buckled when she led him to the old wolf's corpse, carelessly stashed in a storage room like Janek was a sack of rice.

"He wouldn't kneel," Sky whispered from somewhere behind him. "I did. I'm sorry."

Tears thickened her voice, and he turned, wrapping an arm about the little wolf as she broke down. He whispered words that were meant to comfort but not quell. She shouldn't feel guilty about surviving, but he understood why she did.

"You did nothing wrong, pup."

"They were going to ask for ransom from Korin, more drones and mines," she went on. "I didn't expect her to pay, not for someone like me, but...I didn't want to die. I'm sorry."

"Stop. I only wish Janek had bent with you. There's no shame in bowing your head, if it meant your life, and I know damn well that your heart never strayed from Pine Ridge."

From her fresh injuries, it looked as if Sky had been tortured repeatedly. Animari healed so fast that the last session couldn't have been long ago, as she still carried stripes on her back and fresh bruises on her face. *What the hell was that awful bitch trying to learn?* Sky had no access to the inner workings of Pine Ridge security. If Tirael had known that and still hurt the little one, then the quick end she got with Thalia's sword was too fucking good for her. Janek had known more, and maybe that was why he'd chosen to die as he did, no risk of betraying the pack.

He knelt and closed Janek's eyes. The old wolf had been left to stare at the cold ceiling in death, and that gnawed at him. Ignoring the bullet in his back, he swung Janek up in his arms and carried him out of the dark. Korin was waiting for him in the courtyard, their vehicles newly parked beside the mound of Eldritch. These had to be the traitors who would be buried without ceremony, no burning to ease their passage to the next world, no songs or candles to guide the way.

"The cavalry came just in time," he said to his second.

Korin might have smiled, except her gaze locked on Janek. "Not soon enough for some. Seems like you've seen some shit, packmaster."

"Don't call me that. We run this joint fifty-fifty."

"So you keep telling me. Give Janek to me. I have to get back to Pine Ridge and kick some Golgoth ass."

Raff froze. "There's been an incursion?"

"Nothing serious. Yet. They're testing our defenses. Mines took out an entire platoon, and I don't think there are many more nearby, but I should be there since you can't be."

So much shit had happened so fast, he didn't even know how much longer he'd promised to remain in Eldritch territory. *Two months, maybe?* Whatever, Korin was right; she had to defend the pack holding in his stead. And he completely trusted her to do it.

In response, he carried Janek's body to Korin's personal vehicle. "Get me some blankets. He's been cold long enough."

Fucking irrational, but those measures might restore some of the respect that the old wolf had earned through a long and worthy life. With reverent hands, Raff wrapped him up, head to toe. He'd probably never be able to forget the awful angle of his head or the color of Janek's throat. *They broke his neck and kept twisting.* With Animari healing, it must have taken ages to die, and it would've been excruciating.

I'm sorry, old friend. I failed you.

Part of him wanted to ask Sky exactly *when* but knowing wouldn't help or reduce his complicity. It wasn't like he could go back and save him, so he stepped back and closed the Rover's rear doors. He faced Korin with a neutral expression, he hoped.

"Give him full warrior honors at the service. I wish I could be there, but I'll have to settle for visiting his ossuary when we come home."

"We," Korin repeated. Her eyes held questions that he couldn't answer.

Raff resorted to an obvious truth. "It's in the marital

agreement. Thalia will spend three months at Pine Ridge once we finish here."

Thankfully, Korin didn't pursue whatever curiosity she might be nursing, and she was *way* too smart not to realize this wasn't the time to roast him. "We'll be waiting. Unless you need me to stick around, I'm taking most of the troops back with me. Do you have enough forces with the quarter I'm leaving and the Eldritch still loyal to Thalia?"

"It should be. If a full unit comes at us, the mines will decimate them. You only got to the fortress because you know where they're placed."

"True," Korin said. "Take care of yourself."

He glanced at Sky, hovering like a shadow near the walls. "I'm not sure what to do with her. She's not all right."

Korin sighed. "If I take her home now, she'll read it as a vote of no confidence. I'm not sure she'll recover from that."

"Then she stays. I'll ask her to read up on Eldritch customs, so she can take Janek's place as my closest personal advisor."

For a second, surprise flashed in his second's expression, revealed in the arch of her brows and the tilt of her head. "That's...unexpectedly wise. And thoughtful."

He made an obscene gesture. "What, like I never came up with a good idea before?"

"You want an honest answer here, Raff?"

"I don't know, do I?"

"Well, I'm giving one. It's not that you *couldn't* come up with good solutions before, more that you didn't try. I'm not sure if it was because your old man brainwashed you into believing your head's full of sawdust, but before you came to Daruvar, you seemed content to let me do the thinking, so you could keep drinking."

"Ouch." He wasn't even pretending; that fucking *did* sting.

"Don't look at me like that. It's a compliment, I'm saying you've changed. You're stepping up…and I like it. Responsibility looks good on you, wolf lord."

Raff mumbled something, stepping away from the Rover. "Get clear of the woods before nightfall. The mines can only protect you so far, so I'll have a drone keeping watch until you get back to Pine Ridge."

"Understood. Take care of yourself…and your new wife. I haven't spent much time with her, but I can tell she's a force to be reckoned with by the way she swings a sword."

At Korin's signal, the bulk of the wolf forces mounted up. The gates slammed shut behind the convoy, and he kept watch from the walls until the vehicles vanished from sight. Sky stood behind him silently, probably still stewing in her guilt.

"I have a new assignment for you," he said.

Surprise lit her delicate features before she nodded. "Anything. I'm ready."

As soon she heard, Sky headed to the library, where she should be safely immersed in Eldritch lore. Weariness set in, making Raff aware of all his aches and pains. He still wanted that shower, but he needed to talk to Titus, see what the great cat had in mind. If he didn't have any plans, Raff had an idea there, too. Seemed like maybe Korin was right, and he was suddenly full of plans and schemes.

It's because of Lady Silver. I'm trying to keep up.

If Raff was completely honest, he was trying to please her and make her proud, and *never* fucking give a reason to regret choosing him.

22.

THALIA FOUND RAFF in the makeshift field hospital, having Dr. Wyeth cut yet another bullet out of him. She flinched as the scalpel dug into him, as the red trickled out. The wolf lord didn't know she was watching, but he still refused all anesthetic, though he did accept a unit of Eldritch universal donor blood. Who knew how *that* would turn out? Most of what they did together was unprecedented.

When he finally noticed her, he pinned a smile on immediately, no matter how unconvincing. She returned it, trying not to think of that terrible moment on the wall. *He almost died. Again. If I'd been even a second later—*

No. There was no gain to be had by obsessing over tragedies that didn't happen. Still, her insides churned with fear and adrenaline. It took all her self-control not to run to him and pull his messy head to her chest and slap the doctor's hands away. Those impulses were both fierce and foreign, giving her no inner peace.

"Seems like you survived," she said then.

"Not trying to brag, but I'm bloody good at it."

Frustration rose like a stormy wave, but she quelled it.

He wouldn't appreciate being chided in front of the physician. Thalia wrapped that concern up and packed it tight and deep, along with her sorrow over Tirael. Layers of sadness and grief, hardly acknowledged, trembled within her, along with feelings she could scarcely name. The other Eldritch couldn't see her weakness or uncertainty, however. They followed an icy, confident woman, one worthy to be queen.

Rather than quarrel with Raff, she turned to the doctor. "Is his treatment finished?"

"For now. He needs rest, though, and to stop taking terrible wounds."

"Understood. I'll try to keep him out of trouble," she said.

"I'd appreciate it if you could extend that claim to the rest of us. Daruvar has seen sufficient excitement."

It wasn't quite a reproach—Wyeth wouldn't dare—but the words held a similar shape. Thalia inclined her head. "I'll do my best."

Raff stood on his own. "I've been fantasizing about warm food and a hot shower, or vice versa, for what feels like forever. Any chance that a war hero could get some recognition around here?"

"A war hero? Really?" But she took the hand he held out to her. "Thank you, doctor. We'll get out of your way now."

She had no idea who to ask in the current hierarchy, who had been just below Lileth, so she stopped a random Eldritch staffer in the hallway. "Who's been running the keep since..." There was no way to finish the question, not physically possible.

The woman knew, though, her eyes soft and kind.

"Madam Isoline. Do you need her for something?"

"Not right now. We only require some food, as fast as you can prepare it."

The worker nodded, glancing between her and the dirty wolf warrior at her side. *I probably don't look much better.*

"Right away, Your Highness."

"Oh, and if there's venison left from Raff's hunt, please give him a generous portion." She suspected that the additional protein would help mend his injuries faster, though she was no expert in Animari care.

I need to become one.

As the staffer left, Raff brushed Thalia's tangled hair away from her face. "Let's take a break, shall we? It's been rough."

"Agreed."

At her urging, he took the first shower and while he was safely out of earshot, she cried. For Tirael, the secrets she'd kept, hatred nursed furtively and kept alive through years of conspiracy and secret violence. She must have wanted vengeance for her mother and to stand proudly at their father's side. Now she shared her mother's ill-starred fate, a head on a pike, hair streaming in the bitter wind.

Thalia wiped her face as Raff stepped out of the bath in a whorl of steam. She'd hoped he take long enough in luxuriant scrubbing that he wouldn't catch her, but he zeroed in on her tears straight away. Wearing only a towel—and that in the most cursory fashion—he dropped down beside her, water still beaded on his chest and shoulders.

"I'm fine," she said.

"You're not. Come here."

When he opened his arms, she went. Before she met

Raff, before Lil died, Thalia had always cried alone. *Always.* Lileth had hammered it into her head almost from birth that she couldn't trust anyone with her vulnerable moments; she had to hide them, deny them, pretend she was nothing but a suit of armor filled with endless courage.

She'd meant to stop, dam up the waterworks, but with his arms around her, the tears fell faster, and her sobs came loud and harsh, until she feared she might choke or pass out. He took it all while stroking her back and whispering nonsense words into the tangled mass of her grungy hair. Thalia didn't even know why he would; none of this was covered in their agreement, but she held onto him with all her strength, her face against his warm, hairy chest. Unexpectedly comforting.

Who knew what else she might have said or done, if a knock hadn't sounded. Raff released her gently and stood. "That'll be our dinner. I'll take care of it. You get cleaned up."

Thalia retreated to the bathroom, conscious that he was shielding her. The room was still steamy, and the mirror blurred, but that made it easier to strip without minding how much weakness she'd revealed. Trust didn't come easily to her, but he'd had so many chances to betray her that she couldn't imagine him turning now. No matter why, Raff continued to honor their agreement and offer perplexing extra services.

Like holding me while I wept.

He'd probably object if she told him that the three words that sprang to her mind to describe him were sweet, generous, and gentle. Smiling, she stepped into the hot trickle of water that was the best Daruvar's ancient pipes could provide. Because of the low pressure, it took a long

time to scrub herself clean and rinse her hair properly, a
delay sufficient to get her emotions in order, as Raff had
doubtless known. She put her hair up in a towel and
wrapped another around her body. For Thalia, that wasn't
an oversight but an intentional choice to respond to the
intimacy of his dishevelment in kind.

When she stepped out of the bathroom, he had the food
laid out on a low table, the fire built up in the hearth just
beyond. "We dine by firelight?"

That, too, was kind, as the flickering shadows were
forgiving of her red and swollen eyes.

Raff beckoned, patting the place next to him. "You have
bread and a bubbling vegetable soup. I have a slab of
venison in gravy over a bed of roasted potatoes."

"Have you been charming the kitchen staff again?"

"Guilty," he said, taking up his spoon.

Their meal was mostly silent, punctuated by the crackle
of the fire. The flames gilded his skin and lent him a startling
allure, so much that she kept sneaking looks, veiled through
her lashes. One wasn't enough, so her gaze returned to him
repeatedly while she tried to decide when he'd become so
beautiful. It wasn't any single feature, but she loved the long
spill of his dark curls now, and the breadth of his shoulders,
the tight-coiled springs of his beard, and the crinkles at the
corners of his eyes when he smiled.

As he was doing now. At her.

"What?" she mumbled.

"You're staring. Do I have stew on my face?"

"No." It was an awkward wedge of an answer, stuck in
the intangible door between them, but her sudden curtness
didn't dim the twinkle in his night-dark eyes. They were
beautiful too, the deepest brown, fringed in ridiculous lashes

and topped with thick, slightly intimidating brows.

"Hardly."

Using the edge of his spoon, he scraped his bowl clean, seeming untroubled by Thalia's scrutiny. "Then what is it? And if you can't tell me this, tell me something else, a secret nobody else knows."

RAFF DIDN'T THINK Thalia would respond with a real answer. He expected a joke or a quick dismissal, but to his surprise, she bit her lip, deeply pensive. Then she scooted closer, as if the walls might seriously have ears. In this place, maybe he shouldn't rule out the idea.

Eldritch politics were a lot deadlier and more convoluted than he'd bargained for. Raff still hadn't completely wrapped his head around the fact that her half-sister had been hiding in plain sight and plotting Thalia's downfall for *how many* years? Unheard of among the Animari—tempers ran too hot for that sort of treachery. In Pine Ridge, if you pissed someone off, the two of you fought it out and let it go.

"I've been wanting to tell you this anyway," she whispered. "But I couldn't figure out how...and maybe it won't matter to you—"

"Just spill it," he cut in.

Must be something major if she's this nervous.

"I don't have a gift," she said, low.

Holy shit.

From what he'd gathered about Eldritch culture, this would be akin to revealing that she was Latent. Raff knew that gifts developed in early adulthood and that using the preternatural ability too much equated to burning life force.

Korin had briefed him about the Eldritch Noxblade, Zan, who sacrificed himself for the Golgoth Prince during the Battle of Hallowell. His mind raced, weighing the implications. If her people knew, would they still support her push for the throne?

"That's why you use the bracers," he guessed.

She nodded, staring pointedly away from him into the fire. "I do have a certain mechanical aptitude that lets me design and build unusual things, but no innate power."

"Did Lileth know?"

"She was the only one, until you."

"Why'd you tell me?" Raff had asked for a secret, but he never could've predicted she'd share something so momentous.

The level of trust it indicated stole his breath. Right then and there, he decided it didn't matter whether her people would still back her; they'd never hear of it from him. Plus, if she'd come all this way on sheer determination and charisma, then in his book, she'd more than earned the dubious benefit of an antiquated Eldritch title.

"You asked."

"That's an excuse, Lady Silver. You could've shared something else, like a little story about stealing cookies as a kid."

A fleeting, wistful smile flickered at the edges of her mouth. "Lileth never let me get away with anything like that."

"Sounds like she ruled your childhood with an iron fist."

Thalia nodded. "There was no other choice. I would've been crushed if she hadn't kept me safe, taught me all the skills I needed to survive my father's court."

She made it sound onerous...and unbearably lonely, a

truth reinforced by the deep blue of her eyes. Sometimes they looked purple, but now, wrapped in that white towel, they were like the sea just before dusk, open and empty, as she gazed inward, across an icy tundra of desolate years. There had likely been no friendships, no roughhousing like he'd gotten from packmates, no solace from roving the hills.

He pictured her holed up in the library, endlessly reading. Given her prowess with the blades, he added to that mental image, placing her in Noxblade training from a young age, drilling alongside those who had to see her as better, stronger, and smarter, no matter what. If she fell, she had to get up twice as fast, if she took a wound, she had to pretend it didn't hurt and examine the damage alone—while her mad father plotted to restore the glory of the old days, when the Eldritch ruled over the rest of the Numina.

How did she come out whole from that special hell?

It was beyond Raff *not* to reach for her, slowly, in case she wanted to be left alone. When she curled into him a second time, just as eagerly as when she was crying, his heart lurched in his chest, clenched and tightened. She felt so delicate and small, fragile compared to an Animari lover, but he already knew she was stronger than she seemed. Her heart raced against his, more proof that his touch did things to her, and her scent warmed, ripened, sheer chemical enticement.

"You like it when I touch you."

It wasn't a question, only an observation, and not even a surprising one. Raff was good at giving pleasure, but it rarely meant anything, and close skinship had never filled him with such euphoria before. She let him approach when no others were allowed the same privilege. Only *he* saw her softness and her faltering moments, and it was a kind of compliment that he couldn't have envisioned receiving, before.

"Why state the obvious?" she muttered.

"Don't sulk, I like it too. Your hair especially. Shall I fix it for you? Summoning your dresser would ruin the mood."

Before she could protest, he got a comb from her night table and unwrapped the towel. Her hair spilled out, liquid silver in the firelight, so light and fine that it practically floated with static, half-damp and wild. With a little primitive thrill, he decided he would most likely kill anyone else who saw her like this.

"What are you doing?"

"Soothing you." He didn't say anything else about her lack of a gift. This was his way of comforting her and affirming their closeness. "I'll be careful."

Easier said than done, as there were lots of knots and snarls from their time in the wild, but she relaxed beneath his touch, eyes dropping half-closed as he worked on the tangles. He savored these moments with an intensity that skated so far past liking that the feeling must end some-where in the hills of adoration. Eventually, the comb slid through her hair smoothly. Raff suppressed a quiver of a disappointment that he had no more reason to touch her.

"Is grooming normally part of the mate relationship in your pack?" she asked softly, as his hands fell away from her hair.

An interesting question, not one he'd considered before at length. "We don't have a manual for such things. Each couple decides privately what works and suits them best."

"Maybe it's because of our long lifespans, but romantic pairings aren't like this among my people," she said.

"No?" That was an invitation to elaborate.

Thankfully, she took it. "Even sex and love are a game with power at stake. The one who cares more, gives more, loses more. Thus we strive not to reveal the true level of our desire or the real tenor of our yearning."

"If you don't ask for anything, you can never be denied." That was one of the main reasons he'd never shown any sign how much it would mean to get his father's, that crazy old wolf, approval for one of his own ideas, not one that came from Korin.

"Precisely. And if you make your lover beg, you win again."

"Sounds terrible," Raff said. "I hope you don't intend to play those games with me."

"There's no point. I threw out the scorecard some time ago, even if I was initially inclined in that direction."

"Why is that?"

"Because I can't measure you, and I don't want to." There was no mistaking her honesty, evident in her soft voice and the clarity of her eyes, raised slowly to meet his.

"Well, my good wife, you'll never need to plead with me for anything, except maybe an orgasm. I do like the pretty way you gasp and quiver when I'm holding you at the edge."

She raised a pale hand to his face, her fingers light and cool on his cheeks, his brows, but the touch set him alight, no matter its delicacy. "Will you take me to bed now, husband? I'm not *begging*, mind. Only asking."

23.

THALIA DIDN'T WAIT long for Raff's answer. He was a man of action, as she'd already surmised, and he swept her into his arms, despite the bandage from where the bullet had recently been removed. She held on as he carried her to the bed. Compared to the bedroll they'd shared in Titus's cabin, the soft linens seemed positively decadent. Her towel dropped when she slid under the covers, or more accurate to say she didn't bother with it.

"Now then, we're in bed," Raff said. "What more did you have in mind? A cozy, comforting experience or something sweaty and seductive?"

"Can't I have both? The latter, then the former seems ideal."

"So you'd prefer a solid fucking with snuggles after? I like to be clear."

Thalia smiled, finding the slope of his shoulder in the flickering firelight. His skin was always so warm, as if his body had a core of molten lava. "If you're up to it. I don't want to ask for more than you can readily provide."

He scoffed. "Are you suggesting that these paltry injuries could incapacitate me?"

"More that I don't want you to hurt because of me. Not even a little."

His hard face softened into the sweetest smile she had ever seen, and it did funny things to her heart. "Then I'd say that if that's true, *you* should do the work this time."

Heat pooled low at the idea. "You're giving yourself to me? For whatever I want."

"Without hesitation. Do be gentle, though. As you noted, I'm still recovering."

She could have said so many things, but the time for talking was done. Even through the sheet, she glimpsed his hardening cock; he was halfway there at the simple idea of giving himself to her. *Time to surprise him.*

Currently the sheet covered half of Raff's chest and his lower body; Thalia left the pale fabric in place and started with a soft kiss behind his ear. He was about to learn why her people were said to possess legendary patience. A soft sound slipped out of him as he angled his head to give her better access, but she stayed right there for long moments, behind his ear—kissing, licking, and nuzzling—and when she finally shifted, it was to toy with his earlobe with gentle teeth.

Raff was already squirming, and she'd barely gotten started. He reached for her, but only to stroke her head in silent encouragement. "Who knew that would feel so good?" he whispered.

Smiling, she went for his throat next, but delicate and gentle, sucking lightly so that he arched his neck, and she watched his cock come to full bloom beneath the sheet. Thalia kissed him all over his face, pressing worshipful kisses to his brow, his cheeks, the tip of his nose, until his breath grew labored with the restraint he was exerting.

"Mouth, next?" she teased.

He lifted his bearded chin enough for an affirmative, letting her come the rest of the way to take his lips. She loved how his beard grazed her cheeks and jaw, another layer of sensation to contrast with the heat of his mouth. At first, she kept the contact chaste and fleeting, leaving him with lips parted and likely aching for a deeper taste.

After countless tantalizing moments, she rewarded him with a long kiss, her lips sealing over his, and she gloried in how quickly he opened his mouth and offered his tongue. She swept hers in seductive strokes, delving, thrusting, until they were both gasping and breathless, and his big body trembled against her.

When she pulled away at last, his mouth gleamed wet and a bit red, incredibly hot because she'd done that to him. "How do you feel? No pain?"

"My cock's aching," he confessed. "But I can wait for you to get there. I'm enjoying all the pleasures of your journey."

"Mm. That's good." She kissed a path across his shoulders and then downward, nuzzling her cheek against his chest.

So different from an Eldritch, but she liked the texture of the hair. He seemed to enjoy it when she used her hands on him, caressing his chest, then testing the density of his muscles with her nails. At that, he arched and groaned, and a tiny portion of the sheet draped over the tip of his cock went translucent.

He's leaking, he wants me so badly.

Waiting must be excruciating in that case, but he was still passive and quiet, letting her set the pace. Knowing that made her want to rip the sheet away and accelerate her foreplay. Thalia quelled that impulse. Drawing out his pleasure would yield a stunning orgasm, and she wanted to blow his brains out. Figuratively. That was a conscious desire; since he'd made no secret of having taken lots of lovers, she needed to be memorable, to etch herself into his body and his desires, so that whenever he wanted to get off, he remembered her lips, her hands, her face. Perhaps this wasn't so much pleasure as possession, but she couldn't stop. Not until he came, helplessly groaning her name.

His small, brown nipples were tight. She put her mouth near one, exhaling a slow, hot breath, and his hands came to her head, like he wanted to exert pressure. Somehow he managed not to, only stroking her hair. Thalia sucked his nipple into her mouth at first softly, but she gauged his reaction and sucked harder, using her teeth until he cried out.

Raff liked it rough, with slices of sharpness interspersed with the soft. She loved his nipples with her fingers, her mouth, and his breath went wild, ragged and harsh.

Onward.

He moaned when she peeled the sheet back to reveal his fluttering stomach. His abs were already tight, rippling with anticipation of her touch. The sight of her pale hair spread across his brown skin should be exciting, so she lowered her head and kissed his belly, making no effort to be tidy about it. Sex should be messy and unrestrained.

Maybe he expected her to step up the pace, or hoped, but she kept to her measured exploration, despite the flush kindling all over her body, and the heat making it hard for her to think. Now, she acted on instinct, sinking her teeth into his lower belly, nuzzling at his hipbone and licking the length of his thigh. Raff raised his leg, offering himself to her with wounded, desperate eyes.

"I could do so many interesting things," she whispered. Thalia hardly recognized her own voice, so husky and deep. "Do you have any suggestions?"

"Many. But most of all, just don't stop. I might die."

"I won't," she promised, and flung the sheet away.

His cock stood up, dark and veiny, slick with precome. Her plans evaporated in the white-hot lust that drove her to straddle him, work her aching pussy against that tantalizing shaft. *Oh yes. Fucking perfect.* She moved her hips, grinding, and her entire body shivered at the pleasure of those long, luxurious strokes. Until this moment, she hadn't realized that she was *so* close to coming, and how was that possible, just from teasing him?

"That's it," he urged. "Use me."

She did.

In quick lunges, Thalia chased the feeling, hot and melting, tightening her stomach, sharper when she tightened her thighs. *This wasn't supposed to be about me.* But she couldn't stop herself, and she lost herself in his body, humping so wildly that her movements jolted little sounds from him, moans and groans and words of praise.

Her orgasm hit hard, and her whole body locked as the sensations washed over her, fierce at first, then in slowly quieting waves.

The sweetest of wolves caught her when she fell.

RAFF WOULD BE lying if he said he wasn't frustrated, but it was buried beneath layers of satisfaction. Thalia started out intent on seducing him and ended up like that. No way he didn't take it as the highest of compliments, so he held her against him and stroked her back, idly sifting through her hair with careful fingertips. She stretched in his arms, and he settled her even closer, so that he could revel in her slowing heartbeat.

An asshole might try to claim that bodily harm would result from getting all stirred up and being left unsatisfied, but his penis was like a gun. It would still fire just fine next time, even if he left a bullet in the chamber, so to speak. His cock settled to half-mast while she regained her senses in his arms. As she came down, she still shivered beneath his lightest touch, making it tough to get his own head together.

"You good?" he asked, maybe a skosh smug, already knowing the answer.

"That…was not part of the plan."

Raff swallowed a smile. "It's important to be flexible."

Her eyes snapped open, and the light dimmed, like a shade being drawn. "Is that why it was so easy for you to stop courting Magda?"

Hell.

"I was never doing that," he said.

"Everyone commented on how you chased her in Ash Valley." That tone dared him to deny it, so Raff didn't even try.

Rather, he attempted to explain. "It's more that I was trying to get her to…choose me. Because Mags has high standards, and if she did, that'd mean I was worthy."

"Oh. And you don't need that validation now?"

"Your judgment is impeccable, princess. I have all the approval could ever need." He hugged her for good measure.

She smiled up at him, pure fucking sunshine.

"Then...why don't we sleep for a while?" She did look done, lashes already drifting shut, and she lay like cooked noodles in his arms.

Raff quashed minor disappointment and said, "I was about to suggest that."

"Thank you," she whispered.

Before he could ask what for, she winked out like a light, flattering if slightly disappointing. He firmly closed his mind to all the sex stuff that wouldn't be happening and tried to go to sleep himself. Briefly, he entertained the notion of sneaking to the bathroom and cranking one out, but if she woke up, she might read it as a rejection, instead of a practical move that held no secret subtext.

Better not risk it.

Still, it took him a long time to drift off, not least because she felt amazing, naked in his arms, and he had the bright, hot memory of her mouth and hands roving his skin. *Stop, enough of that. Fuck, this is mission impossible.*

At some point, he must have drifted into a horny, uncomfortable doze because that was when the scorching dream started. Like most dreams, there was no introduction, just suddenly, Thalia's hot mouth was wrapped around his cock, and she was sucking him like she'd starve without his taste. His hips moved—no reason not to savor the fantasy—fucking upward, so that she nearly choked.

I can be selfish in my dreams.

"Deeper," he mumbled. "Suck harder."

She responded instantly, increasing the suction, and it felt so good that his balls tingled. There was no reason to hold back, nobody to impress with his control, so Raff gave himself fully to the pleasure, pushing his cock past her soft lips. Her mouth was wet and hot, her tongue delicate against his sensitive skin, and she was careful with her teeth, grazing now and then, but not enough to hurt.

Fuck, that's good.

He didn't realize he'd said it aloud until her laugh vibrated against his cock. Knotting his hands in her long hair, he pushed her head against him, and she renewed the suction, her mouth moving up and down with such alacrity that if he hadn't been dreaming, he'd need to worry about her comfort, like if her neck and shoulders were tired or if this was a bad angle. This way, he focused only on the feeling and Raff brought his knees up. In this fantasy, there were no limitations. He could have whatever he desired.

It didn't even surprise him when she shifted down, licking his balls with her hot mouth. Her lips and tongue went *everywhere,* even places he'd never dare ask for if he was awake. Raff squirmed against the delicious torment and he only stopped her when his cock spurted precome.

"I'm almost there. Let me finish in your mouth."

"With pleasure," she purred.

What a dream.

This was probably the only time the Eldritch queen would be so obedient to his every whim. Savoring the moment, he still couldn't restrain a groan when she sucked his cock into her soft mouth. While he loved fucking, there was an extra decadence to laying back like a lazy bastard and getting serviced until he came.

Best. Dream. Ever.

Normally, he'd wake up before the best part because his unconscious mind was an asshole, but it showed no signs of interfering this time. Thalia was still everything and everywhere, her scent, her lips, her tongue. Raff went after his delayed satisfaction with complete focus, working in and out of her mouth until he couldn't hold it. His strokes went short and quick, tension in his lower back, and then he went, spurting between her sweet lips in delicious release. In that weird moment between sleeping and waking, he had the awful surety that he'd come in bed, a wet dream the like of which he used to have as a pup, and shit, it would be so embarrassing—

Then his eyes opened, and he registered a few things. Thalia, between his legs, softly sucking. The covers were just gone, just as they were in the dream, tumbled beside the bed, and the room was cool. Thalia, licking his cock clean, his come on her lips. He blinked in utter confusion.

Not...a dream?

"I hope you don't mind," she said. "I woke up feeling peckish."

It took him a minute to find his voice. "Ah, no. I don't. Mind. I gave you permission to do whatever you want, and that includes sucking me off in my sleep."

"You make it sound so dirty when I was just leveling the scales."

Raff shook his head, still reeling. "No reason to do that. You said we're not playing a game, and I'm damn sure not keeping score, so you don't owe me orgasms paid in kind."

"Oh." Her voice flattened, and he had the sense he'd hurt her, but fuck, he was still so dizzy and befuddled.

"Did I say something wrong?"

She sounded timid for once. "No. Maybe I did. Then...would you accept that I just wanted to? Not because I was in debt."

He pulled her up, over his body, and the traces of his orgasm slid between them, her saliva, his semen, and it was all so delicious that he could've fucked her right then.

"That's the best of all possible reasons. It's beautiful that you woke up and you wanted me, so you took me. On my end, it was all sweet and good. I didn't hurt you?"

"No. I liked it."

Raff kissed her then, long and deep, delighting in the taste of himself on her tongue. The moment they stepped out of this room, even if she scrubbed for an hour, every wolf would know how thoroughly she belonged to him. He'd have to find some other method to pass the word to the Eldritch, especially that bastard, Gavriel.

"Do you have the energy for another round?"

"I slept enough," Thalia said.

With a wolfish grin, Raff rolled her beneath him.

24.

I N THE MORNING, Thalia woke first, as tentative fingers of light crept across the window sill.

For a few seconds, she stared at Raff and then she slipped out of bed silently. If Lileth was here, breakfast would already be cooling outside the door. Her absence ached like a bad tooth, too deep for cutting, and she put on her clothes in the dark. She understood grief; they were old, intimate companions, and Lil wouldn't thank her for breaking down. If the older woman wouldn't let her weep over missing her mother, even as a child, then she wouldn't be gentle about this, either. That strict regimentation had kept Thalia alive, so she couldn't resent it.

She stepped out into the chill hallway, listening to the guards and workers hurrying to restore order. The fortress was still recovering from the battle and its aftermath. She mourned for those who had chosen Tirael's side even after Thalia's return, and wished there was a path to victory not so strewn with the bodies of her people. This war would dangerously deplete their numbers, and it might well take four or five generations to recover, given their low birth rates and difficulty with conception.

Making her way to the kitchen, she keenly felt Lileth's lack. By now, the older woman should be by her side, apprising her of all the most important issues. Instead, Thalia hunted up her own breakfast, toasted bread and cheese for her, and a dish of hearty stew for Raff.

A young Eldritch stopped her with eyes wide, head down, though she couldn't stop snatching peeks at Thalia. "Let me carry that for you."

"It's all right, I've got it. What's your name?"

"Belen, Your Highness. Did you need something?"

"No, I just wanted to learn a bit more about you."

The girl shuffled her feet, trying to hide beneath a spill of fair hair. Hers had a golden cast, and it hung past her shoulders in unwashed tangles. "Am I in trouble? Is it because I served Tirael? Nearly everyone did, Your Highness. We had no way of knowing that you were coming back."

Thalia filed that statement away under regrettable truths. "Is there anything else you'd like to tell me while you have my ear?"

"If you'll pardon my candor, since you seem to be in a listening mood, at my level, it doesn't matter who sits on the big chair. We just want to be left alone to live and eat. I guess we're also a bit worried about going to war with the brutes and the beasts, so it'd be good if the high hat could keep us safe from them as well."

Her face felt frozen. Maybe *this* was why Lileth always kept a buffer between her and the rest of the staff. Otherwise, she would've realized how little anyone else cared about her destiny. Just as Tirael had accused, she wasn't chosen, fated to lead their people. The All-Mother wasn't on her side. Perhaps the rest of what Tirael had said was even true; that Thalia was simply a little luckier than most.

"Understood. I'm sure you have other duties. Please tend to them." It was hard to speak with the weight of that disappointment on her chest.

The worker dodged around Ferith as she ran back into the kitchen. Thalia gauged the Noxblade leader's mood by her expression, and it was dark indeed. "You have more bad news, I gather?"

"I suppose it could be read that way."

"Let's talk in the strategy room." She left Raff's breakfast just inside the bedroom and then continued with Ferith, who waited until the door closed behind them.

The chamber smelled musty, a layer of dust on all her maps and books. Lileth would never have permitted such laxness, but she supposed that, overall, she was lucky to be standing here again. Things could have gone the wrong way, and it might be Tirael burning her things while her own head was impaled on a spike above Daruvar, warning others not to reach beyond their grasp.

She sat and gestured Ferith to the opposite chair. "I hope you don't mind if eat?"

"Go ahead. I've had breakfast and I presume you can listen when you chew."

Thalia smiled. "It's one of my many talents. Please, go on."

"There aren't enough parents voluntarily enrolling their children in the Academy. People are frightened, and they aren't sure…" Here, Ferith paused.

"About what?"

"If we're going to win this. They want to wait until the war is over and make sure they're pledging their children to the right cause."

That…was terrible news. She closed her eyes for a few seconds and stifled a wave of impotent outrage. This was almost the same as saying outright that Thalia was a pretender, and that Ruark might do a better job leading in her stead. It put her in a completely untenable position because if she allowed them to delay, it read like a tacit admission that their doubts were warranted, and if she conscripted their little ones, then she became an unreasonable despot who didn't respect parental rights.

"How do we win this?" she asked, not really expecting an answer.

Lileth would have known.

More likely, if Lileth had survived the wedding feast, they never would have lost Daruvar in the first place. She wished she hadn't sent Gavriel away; he had more experience than Ferith, and at the time, his request to be set free had seemed little enough reward for a lifetime of loyal service. Calling him back would only dishonor her current head of the Noxblades, and there was no guarantee Gavriel could get back in time to help.

Ferith let out a tired sigh. "I don't know. To be honest, I haven't slept in days. The prison cell wasn't precisely restful."

Remorse overtook her, and she cringed at how selfish her thoughts had been. "Get some rest. You reported the issue to me. I can take it from here."

While that sounded tremendously capable, inwardly she had no earthly idea how she could resolve the matter without a deep deficit, either of leadership or compassion. She wasn't even dressed for public appearances, still disheveled and unwashed. Little wonder the kitchen worker had stared at her so.

I'm coming to pieces, losing my polish. Soon nobody will want to follow me.

She silenced that malicious inner voice and headed back to the bedroom, where she found Raff awake and eating stew in bed. Of all things, that shouldn't *anger* her, but his insouciance, lolling about the pillows, sparked to life a cranky core she hadn't known she possessed. It wasn't fair, and she knew that; he was already doing more than they'd agreed upon, so how could she want more? Yet she *did*, and there was no altering it.

That made her mad too.

Taking her mood out on him was a terrible idea, though, so she tried to smile. "Did you sleep well?"

"Like a hibernating bear," he said with a luxuriant stretch. "Do we have some new emergency on deck or can you come back to bed for a while?"

The way he said it rubbed her the wrong way, like the constant stream of problems could've been prevented by someone else. Thalia clenched her teeth around a sharp reply, deciding to pick his brain instead. He always claimed he wasn't clever, but she'd seen ample evidence to the contrary.

"Just a small issue." Perching on the edge of the bed, she explained the dilemma and finished by asking, "Do you have any suggestions?"

Now that she took a proper look at his expression, well, she'd call that...appalled. Raff narrowed his eyes and used a napkin to blot away the traces of his meal, a delaying tactic that hinted she wouldn't like what he was about to say.

Never let it be said that I can't accept difficult truths. Let's hear it.

"Did you ever think that maybe it's time to let that kind

of thing go? You claim you want to build a brighter future for your people, but part of what makes us shy away from the Eldritch is all the backstabbing and the assassination protocols and the years devoted to studying the best way to kill from the shadows. I've heard your children start at five, and that's fucking crazy, Thalia. What parent wants his child learning about poison when he should be playing with other kids and learning his multiplication tables?"

WHEN THALIA FLINCHED, Raff figured maybe he should've pulled his punches a little, worked up to the fact that certain aspects of her society were deeply fucked up. She stiffened up like a poker and her face chilled into the polite expression that drove him crazy. Her hands locked behind her, another sign that she was pissed.

"I should've known better than to ask you," she said coldly.

He stilled, getting the first clue that shit might be more serious than he'd suspected. "What's that supposed to mean?"

"Exactly what it seems. You're deeply ignorant of our culture and you've just proven that by measuring our beliefs by your standards. I've tried my best not to be judgmental when your ways seem backward to me. It appears the same tolerance is beyond you."

"I may not be as studied as you, Lady Silver, but that sure sounds like a fancy way of calling me a dumbass."

"Think whatever you wish," she snapped.

She stalked out, still light on her feet, even in a fury. Raff got out of bed with a snarl, and instead of going after her, he took a long shower and nearly scoured his skin off trying to calm down. As he stepped out, he was still smoldering, but the spike of anger couldn't entirely conceal the aching disappointment.

I never thought she'd use that against me.

He'd woken up in such a fantastic mood, too. Good sex helped in pretty much every scenario. While the situation still wasn't ideal, at least they were making progress toward uniting the Eldritch, had retaken Daruvar, and had rooted out the traitor working against Thalia from the inside. Raff had thought they'd gotten to the point where he could be honest, but her reaction proved that she considered him an interloper, one who had no business commenting on Eldritch issues.

His first instinct was to pack his shit and go back to Pine Ridge, but he had to be better than that, even if he was pissed and didn't want to be. The agreement didn't provide for piking off after a quarrel, which meant he had to stay here and be useful. Raff set his jaw and tried to leash his temper. Considering her side might help.

Okay, it's possible I could've been more tactful. She came to me with a problem and I basically told her that her way of life was wrong. I could've eased into that, maybe.

Or not gone there at all?

That was the tougher question, and the deep sort that Raff wasn't used to tackling on his own. He wished Janek or Korin were here to give an opinion. He suspected they'd tell him he was a dumb shit, more bluntly than Thalia. Still, he didn't think he was wrong about kids deserving to have a damn childhood, but he could've handled things better, right?

Yeah, definitely.

Sighing, as Raff got dressed, he privately admitted that

he'd fucked up, but then, he wasn't used to dealing with important shit first thing in the morning. That was Korin's job, or at least, it had been. Which wasn't fair, he acknowledged, since he got all the respect and she did all the hard thinking behind the scenes.

Need to change that.

Well, he'd give Thalia some time to cool off and then see if he could charm her with some sweet words and a sincere apology. For now, he needed to find Titus and put his idea into practice. If the great cat agreed, this was one way he could help Thalia, a concrete contribution to her cause.

It was good that he went looking early, because Titus was already in the courtyard, ready to head out, when Raff caught him. "Hold up a minute. I need to talk to you."

"My job's done here, wolf. Don't get sentimental on me."

"I'm not. This offer is worth your time, though. Will you give me five minutes?"

Titus sighed and tilted his head back, assessing the clouds overhead. "Looks like rain, late in the afternoon. It won't be cold enough to freeze, so pass that along to your troops and any of the patrols."

"You're like a weather wizard," Raff said.

"Buttering me up won't get me to do you any favors."

"Didn't your mother teach you to take a compliment gracefully?" He meant it as a joke, but Titus's face darkened, brows pulling together.

"No. I never met the woman. And you're burning through my patience."

I am not on my game today.

"Well, let's get out of the wind, at least. Will you hear

me out or not?"

After mumbling a few choice complaints, Titus said, "I wanted to take a last look from the walls before I left anyway. Let's go."

The great cat led the way and Raff followed, hoping he could sell this idea. Atop the ramparts, he glimpsed the end of winter. The snow that trapped them in the cabin had melted off, leaving patches of dirty ice and brown ground that would be green again in a month's time. Hard to picture now, but warmer days were coming.

"Before, you mentioned that there's a loose network of nomads who hunt and stay off the grid, no alliances to pack or pride."

"What about it?" Titus sounded belligerent, and when Raff glanced over at him, that impression was reinforced by the big cat's scowl.

"I'd like to hire you. To keep watch, like you did when Daruvar fell. Your intel could be critical in planning defensive measures and keeping tabs on enemy movements."

Titus made a dubious noise in the back of his throat. "You want an independent spy network, wolf? That's damned presumptuous."

"You said it yourself. While you may not want to live in Ash Valley, if the place falls, if Ruark Gilbraith allies with Tycho Vega, you won't like what happens next. I'm not asking you to do anything more than you're already doing."

"Except for the part where we tell you what we know," Titus said.

"Okay, one extra step. Teach me about the trail signs you leave for each other." Raff ignored the other man's surprised look.

Yeah, I know how you communicate out there, and it's a low-

fi failsafe, no chance the info gets hacked.

"That's really all you want? A copy of our code and for us to keep on as we were?" The great cat cocked his head, as if to say, *tell me another one.*

But Raff nodded. "Any edge we can get, we'll use. I can leave caches of goods and supplies in payment for looping me in. I won't ask your people to risk themselves, to fight or otherwise get involved. Do we have a deal?"

Titus hesitated. "I wish I could ask the others, but I can't exactly call them. We only meet up once a year. The rest of the time…"

"It's signs on trees, I got that. Even if you're not the leader, per se, you need to make the call, because you're here, and I could use the help."

A long sigh slid out of the taller man, and he stared off at the horizon as if he saw a much grimmer picture than rolling hills and winter trees. "Fine. I'll stop by the library and write down our signs and the zones where we leave word. Beyond that, it's up to you to find anything of value in the forest."

"Thanks," Raff said.

Before Titus could answer, someone came running out of the tower, a small female that he identified as Sky, before he saw her tear-stained face. Her scent was familiar, reminded him of home, and Titus was already backing toward the doorway. Evidently, he wanted no part of a crying woman.

"I'll keep up my end of the deal," he muttered, "but this is my cue to leave."

Whatever Raff might have said back, he lost track when Sky threw herself into his arms, sobbing like her heart would break.

It was going to be one of those days.

25.

THALIA SPENT MOST of the day avoiding Raff.

At least, she was, right up until she realized she had no idea where he was or what he was doing. She also had some inkling that she wasn't setting a good example or being mature about their quarrel. It was too embarrassing to *ask* anyone where the wolf lord had gotten to, but Daruvar had limited ground to cover.

As the shadows lengthened, she prowled the fortress silently. She might have predicted that he'd be socializing somewhere, but she found him in the library, sitting quietly on a sofa with a sheaf of papers in his hand, books piled up around him. *He hates reading.* Remorse flickered through her. *Is this because I said he was ignorant?* Jabbing at someone's weak point, particularly when they'd trusted you with it, well, regret flowed into the hollow spaces and she resolved to make it right.

Taking a silent step forward, she paused just outside the door, belatedly realizing that he wasn't alone. The little wolf, Sky, was curled against his side, head resting on his chest, and Raff had his arm around her. That—it shouldn't bother her, really shouldn't—because the contract didn't stipulate fidelity. Theirs was a political alliance, and she had no claims on his heart or his body, so there was absolutely no reason why her insides should feel like they were on fire.

None at all.

Thalia didn't even breathe, calling on all her Noxblade training to slip away unseen. Best not to interrupt such an intimate moment. He probably didn't care about their argument anyway. Sex was easy for him, and he was good at making people care. Too good, truly—she blinked away what must be dust in her eyes.

I am not crying.

Thalia found a quiet corner and dropped into a crouch, wrapping her arms about her knees. Her hair veiled her face, so hopefully nobody would recognize her while she got herself together. She swallowed the tears, but she shook as she did it, nails biting into her legs, teeth sinking into her lower lip until the outward pain suffocated the inferno within.

Odd, it feels as if someone I love has died.

That was closer than she liked to the truth than she preferred. But not someone, some*thing*—several things, actually—such as possibility and hope. *Idiot. You knew what he was from the beginning. He never tried to fool you. The wolf's always been a wolf.* It was ridiculous that she'd started to dream of more. Her life had always been solitary. It would always be so.

When she rose, some while later, she was all icy composure, and she went to find Ferith. The Noxblade leader was on a conference call with the parents who had gathered to hear Thalia's decision. As luck would have it, she arrived in time to give the answer herself.

Ferith stepped aside and beckoned her toward the camera, ready to beam her words. Thalia brought up a practiced smile and said, "Our children are so precious. On further reflection, I cannot ask you to send them until I prove my worth and unite our people. We can revisit the matter once I sit upon the silver throne."

With a click, Ferith ended the transmission. "You've decided to be a benevolent ruler, then?"

"I always wanted to be. The old ways are hateful and brutal."

"That they are. What's next for us?"

After Gavriel's departure and Raff's fickleness, it bolstered her to hear the word 'us' from Ferith. "We don't have the foot soldiers for an all-out war with the other houses, and the drones can only stretch so far. Mines will keep them from taking Daruvar without the spy in our ranks, but they won't gain us any ground."

"I'm aware of all that, Your Highness. Or are you thinking aloud?"

Slightly chagrined, Thalia nodded. "I used to do this with Lileth in the room. Does it bother you?"

A smile softened Ferith's lean features, her eyes crinkling at the corners. "No, I don't mind being your sounding board."

"Bribes and gifts will only empty our coffers without guaranteeing allegiance." The more she thought about it, there was only one way to resolve this, quick and clean.

"Allies you buy only stay bought as long as you can afford them," Ferith said.

"True. Which is why we're going to kill Ruark Gilbraith."

The Noxblade laughed. "Is *that* all?"

"I'm not joking. Gear up and tell me anything you

learned from Tirael while she held you captive. I've got an old map of Braithwaite, where Ruark is holed up."

"You're serious? The two of us will end the fighting by assassinating the head of House Gilbraith?"

"There's a historical precedent," she said defensively.

Before she could elaborate on it, Ferith sighed. "I know our history, same as you. It's not the after-effects I'm questioning, but the likelihood of us getting to that point. This seems like a good way to get ourselves killed."

It was difficult to find the right words because her head and heart were such a mess, but she was positive that this was the right move. She just had to convince Ferith. "I spoke to a kitchen worker this morning."

The other woman arched a brow. "You want a cookie for that?"

"No, that's not the point. She said she doesn't care who rules, right to my face. And I'm sure that's probably true for most. Which means I need to take power with a swift, decisive strike, or not at all. The people just want the fighting to stop. They don't really care about my high ideals."

"A rude awakening, I suppose," Ferith observed.

"Perhaps a bit, but a welcome one. I'd rather have the truth, even if it hurts."

Like a husband snuggled up with someone else in the dark. Briefly, she considered asking Ferith what she thought of Sky and Raff. Before, it seemed like Ferith had bonded with the young wolf during their imprisonment, but it didn't seem right to involve anyone else in their private business.

Thalia let out a shuddering breath and banished the memory of that scene from her mind's eye. *I won't think about this anymore.*

"Anyway, if I'm meant to rule, this can be my trial by fire, the start of the legend of Good Queen Thalia, first of her name, restorer of the silver throne."

"Or a footnote about a pretender who died," the Noxblade said in a somber tone.

"That's the other possible outcome."

Ferith stared at her, unspoken questions and doubts in her pale eyes. Thalia thought, *Gavriel would have gone with me without a moment of hesitation.* But that sort of reckless devotion wasn't what she needed; Ferith's caution might even let them complete the mission, however improbable it seemed.

"Very well," she said finally. "Let's do it and let our names be writ large in posterity."

Thalia grinned. "You just want to kill Ruark Gilbraith."

"Guilty. The man's *such* an asshole."

"Then pack your gear and meet me at the front gate. We can take a Rover mini part of the way, at least to our own borders."

"I'll reprogram a drone from the stockpile, get it to run recon for us."

"Good thinking. I'll download all the plans I have for Braithwaite, pack up our best poisons, and see you in an hour. Is that long enough?"

"Any longer and I might come to my senses."

That was a joke. Thalia might not be as emotionally close to Ferith as she had been with Lileth, but the Noxblade was known for keeping her promises. There were stories about impossible kills she'd pulled off for Lord Talfayen while secretly working to further Thalia's interests among the rest of their people, and she knew how many of those tall tales were true. In a guild of killers, Ferith stood head and shoulders above the rest.

She only hoped her lesser skills didn't get them caught, but this wasn't something she could send an assassin to do alone. Truth be told, her excitement was growing by leaps and bounds, fizzing euphoria in her bloodstream.

Thalia packed swiftly and scrawled a note that she tossed onto their unmade bed. Mentally, she shrugged. It wasn't like Raff would be looking for her anyway.

And then she crept out into the night.

SKY WAS CALMER when she woke, much to Raff's relief. She still hadn't explained why she was so upset before passing out; maybe now he could get some sense out of her. Rubbing her eyes, she sat away from him and hung her head, the picture of chagrin.

He waited until she composed herself fully to ask, "Can you talk?"

"Yes. Sorry."

"Did something happen?"

"I'm not sure how to explain it without sounding silly," she hedged.

"Well, you already cried yourself to sleep. How can words be worse?" It was tough not to show his impatience because he'd promised her parents that he would protect her before they left Pine Ridge and he'd always regarded her as a little cousin. But he needed to make things right with his wife, so Sky should start talking already.

She ducked her head. "Then I'll just tell you. I was in my room, trying to read, and then…the room wasn't there anymore. It was night, and we were in the courtyard. Eldritch were coming at us from all directions, and Korin didn't answer your calls. It was just you and me, fighting for all we were worth, but Raff...you *died*. I saw it happen, the spear that impaled you straight through, pinned you to the ground. I saw the Eldritch who killed you."

Just a bad dream, he started to say, but he couldn't get the words out. The fact that she'd run straight to him, sobbing her heart out, proved it was more. He'd never heard of a Latent seer developing powers this late, but then, the pride mistress at Ash Valley had shifted for the first time at twenty-seven, so he probably shouldn't dismiss what Sky had seen. She was only twenty-two, and possibly the stress of her recent captivity and the situation overall had awoken some dormant power.

"Can you remember anything else? Anything that might help us pinpoint the date?" If she was right, then an attack was coming. Just knowing that might give them the necessary edge.

"Not really. It was dark, and it wasn't today. That's all I'm sure about."

"Close your eyes and try. Every detail could be critical, Sky."

"Then...you believe me," she whispered, sounding shaken.

"I can't afford not to. The stakes are too high. Let's focus and see how you can narrow down the vision."

Too bad Bibi isn't here. She should test Sky and if necessary, take her for training, if she's awakened as a seer.

"It's a clear night...oh, the moon. It's fuller. Five days, maybe as much as a week? I'm not sure, I'm not good at judging that stuff."

It was probably too much to expect that she'd seen a calendar or glanced at the clock during the vision, so the moon might be their best marker. "All right, sketch it for me. Then we can match it and approximate how long we have until the incursion."

Raff got some paper and a pen, but Sky's artistic ability didn't narrow it down much. "Sorry," she said. "I'm no good at this."

"All right, then. Five to seven days. If that's the window, it is. I'll talk to Thalia and we'll start preparing for it." An idea occurred to him then, and he got out his phone and pulled the video warning Ruark Gilbraith had sent to taunt Thalia. "Is this the Eldritch who killed me in your vision?"

Sky shook her head. "No, I've seen him before, but I don't remember his name. He's very stern and austere, scary-faced, red eyes and white hair."

Holy shit. That sounds like Gavriel.

He didn't have a photo and it was unlikely that the Noxblade would allow his image to be captured anyway, so Raff drew the assassin from memory, using red pen to shade in the eyes. When he finished, he showed the portrait to Sky. "Is this the one?"

"I think so. Come to think of it, I'm sure he was here when we first arrived. Bad-tempered, stuck close to Princess Thalia until he left with Magda."

Right, that's confirmation. But why the hell would Gavriel kill me?

Because he loves Thalia? Hates me? Wants me out of the picture? He took a bribe from Gilbraith? A plethora of possibilities rioted in his head, until it ached from the confusion.

"You don't look good."

"Tell me about it. Things just got a lot more complicated."

"Because...?"

"My would-be murderer was Thalia's right hand up until recently. His name is Gavriel, the former head of the Noxblades. He's like a fucking ghost, he knows all Thalia's secrets, and he's familiar with Daruvar's defenses."

"Shit," Sky said.

"My feelings exactly."

"What should we do?"

"We're alone here. Not the best scenario, I admit. I need to tell Thalia right away."

"She may not believe you," Sky mumbled.

"Even so, we have to prepare for the worst." Raff stood then. "You get some rest. If you see anything else, come find me immediately."

It was late when he left the library, hungry as hell, tired and perturbed. He missed the warmth of Pine Ridge, too, especially with all the chilly Eldritch nods. None of the staffers he passed on the way to his room made eye contact, like they thought they'd turn to stone if they cracked a smile. Boundaries were serious business here.

A worker was coming out of the suite with an armful of dirty linens as he approached. Raff smiled at her, and her eyes bulged as she took a hasty step back and bowed so low that she almost dropped the sheets. She flattened herself against the wall when he stepped past her, and he made sure to give her plenty of space because he smelled her fear.

Most of them still think we're animals.

Coupled with the unresolved argument with Thalia and Sky's cryptic, fearsome vision, this had been a completely shit day. The only good came from memorizing Titus's codes, and he'd have to go out into the woods to read any word they left. Fair enough, he was sick of being cooped up inside anyway. Sighing, Raff closed the door behind him.

The bedroom was empty, a fire crackling in the hearth. Dinner had been served in his absence, left to cool on the low table in the sitting area. Not long ago, he'd sat there with his wife leaning on his shoulder, eating and talking and laughing. Funny how easily he could conjure that mental image, but he didn't know what to say when he saw her.

Raff waited for an hour, but Thalia didn't come. Angry all over again, he ate cold food, alone, in great furious bites. He even used the bread to sop up his gravy while glaring at her delicate slices of fruit and cheese. It was beyond him how she could survive on such dainty portions, just another reminder how different they were.

He couldn't bring himself to put her food out to be returned to the kitchen, though. Probably she'd slide in when she thought he was asleep and she might be hungry then, so he collected his dirty plate and glass and set them out while leaving her meal on the table, still covered by gilded mesh dome to keep nibbling pests away. Too early in the year for insects, but he'd bet good money these walls housed scampering rodents.

To show proper penitence, he stretched out on the couch, though he couldn't even lay properly. Hours later, Raff woke with a kink in his neck, cussing and aggravated. And his wife still wasn't back. *Stubborn woman.* He stomped over to the bed and pulled back the covers, stirring a paper that had tumbled half-beneath the bed.

The words scrawled on the page chilled him to the bone.

26.

THALIA AND FERITH drove all night.

Under normal circumstances, they could've stopped at a town or settlement to top up the Rover's energy, but in times like these, it was better to run unseen. People would undoubtedly report strangers passing through, even if they didn't recognize Thalia. While she wasn't famous per se, it wouldn't surprise her if Ruark had put her face on WANTED posters or broadcast her face for bounty-hunting purposes.

When the Rover mini ran out of juice, they left it behind. Knowing where the mines were laid let them travel safely, and the drone guided them away from enemy troop movements. It still could, but progress would be much slower from here on out. They were still a hundred kilometers from their destination and Thalia was weighing the best plan for infiltration.

Luckily, the cold snap had passed, so at least they wouldn't risk freezing to death on the move. Dawn broke in the distance as Thalia pulled a layer of pine needles and fallen branches over their vehicle. If a passerby got curious about the abandoned Rover, it wouldn't end well, especially not deep in Gilbraith territory. If she could shift like the

Animari, it would make things immeasurably easier. Not only would that make it easier to travel unseen, but she could also sniff for mines and IEDs along the route.

No point in wishing for impossible things.

Plus, she didn't want to think about the Animari because once that door was open, she might let Raff in, and he would distract her from this mission. Not an option.

"What does the drone say? Did you find us a good route?"

"Define good," Ferith mumbled.

"Relatively safe. Moving during the day holds some risk, but we can't stretch this out over a week. Too much caution will get us caught, same as not enough."

Ferith cocked her head. "Are you telling me, or yourself? Sounds like you're scared."

"To death," Thalia admitted.

"It would be worrisome if you weren't. This is an all-or-nothing endeavor."

"I know. Thank you for coming with me."

As she began to walk, following the path the drone had identified, Ferith nodded. "I'm the last of the old guard. So many Noxblades died getting the two of us here...there's no way could I stop now, not like Gavriel did."

That sounded like a judgment. "He had personal reasons for not being able to walk with me any farther."

The other woman didn't respond to that, and maybe it didn't matter if Gavriel had been disloyal. She had wished to have him beside her during this mess, which might've been what he wanted—to instill some flicker of regret over his departure—but she'd only wanted his tactical strength, not his emotional support. And that was precisely why she'd cut him loose.

"Stop stating the obvious, and let's go," Ferith said.

They walked for ten kilometers, hard hiking cross country, when they spotted an isolated farmstead. According to
the map, they were well past the border into Gilbraith
territory. There would be no help coming from her own
people, if she and Ferith ran into trouble, but they had to
gamble here.

The Rambler was old, years out of production, and
beaten all to hell. This family probably needed the vehicle to
take their produce to the nearest town. *I'll make it right later.*
Right now, these people were allied with her greatest
enemy, even if that support came only in nominal form.

She had all kinds of contingency plans, but the actual
theft took no effort at all. They didn't even need to hack
anything; Ferith just hit the start button and they took off,
sticking to secondary roads that should take them to
Outwater, the town closest to Braithwaite.

This will all be over soon, one way or another.

Much later, Ferith parked the Rambler in a copse of
trees. They slept for a few hours, and now, as twilight
gathered, they'd walk the last two kilometers to Outwater
and figure out the next stage of the plan. Thalia touched her
hair uneasily, as it was both a beacon in the twilight and an
identifying trait.

Ferith eyed her. "Want me to cut it off?"

Thalia couldn't remember the last time anyone had
taken a blade to her hair, but she stifled the instinctive
protest, a quiver of affronted vanity that she couldn't afford.
"Do it."

"Wish we could've put together a better disguise before
we left Daruvar," the other woman said, as she started
hacking.

She shared that sentiment. "I had no supplies laid in. This…" Thalia stopped talking, aware that Ferith probably knew what she was about to say anyway.

"Isn't how you pictured things playing out," she finished.

No scissors, so the assassin sawed her hair off in a ragged, chin-length bob. Ridiculous to be upset, but as the other woman stuffed her shorn locks into a trash bag that she found in the back of the Rambler, it was hard not to snuffle like a child. Thalia gritted her teeth and turned toward town.

"We can't leave this here. It's evidence."

Ferith hefted the sack with a nod. "Agreed. I'll find somewhere in Outwater to dispose of this."

They were lucky that House Gilbraith hadn't set up checkpoints yet, but then, Ruark must be scrambling for a new plan, since Tirael had failed, and he'd lost his grip on Daruvar. He wouldn't expect a frontal assault—he must know she couldn't field that many soldiers—but Thalia didn't imagine he would expect such a daring strike, either. Unexpected boldness might carry the day.

Coming over the next rise, she spotted the lights of town, bright and beautiful against the backdrop of night. If she didn't know they'd already passed the border, this might have been one of *her* settlements, similar in layout and design. There were no walls, nothing to stop the Golgoth brutes, should they push this far, but before she could worry about an outside enemy, she had to vanquish her internal foes first. She pulled a dark knit cap over the ruins of her hair and set her shoulders.

"This way," she said.

Ferith followed her, surefooted and silent, making

Thalia uncomfortably aware that she was the weaker link in this partnership. Yet she couldn't simply assign the Noxblade to Ruark's death and wait for results. No, to prove her worth, she had to take Ruark's head as she had Tirael's. Only then would the challenges stop, and she could focus on unifying the people and moving forward with progressive policies that would pull their provinces into the modern world.

At the outskirts of town, a ramshackle wooden hostel flashed a VACANCY sign. This wasn't the sort of place that cared if you came on foot, only if you had local currency. While Thalia hovered outside in the shadows, Ferith took care of the rental. On her return, she sighed and shook her head at the sight of Thalia stamping her feet.

"It's cold," she said.

"I'm aware. Here's the room key, wait for me inside. I'm going shopping."

Thalia *intended* to follow instructions, but half a block away, she glimpsed a fire barrel with several thin and sickly people clustered around it. *More proof that Ruark doesn't care about his people.* Her father hadn't either. Thalia intended to change all of this for the better, implement infrastructure to protect the impoverished and infirm. Nobody said anything when she eased into their circle, though they did complain when she dropped the sack into the fire.

The nearest male grabbed at the edge of her jacket. "Are you dimwitted, child? Don't you know how much burning hair reeks?"

"Sorry," she whispered.

An older woman slapped him on the shoulder. "Oh, leave her be. It's fuel anyway, and we all smell a bit already."

"Thank you," she said.

Thalia had studied etiquette for all kinds of occasions; none of them covered a situation like this. It might seem suspicious if she dumped the bag and immediately ran away so she lingered, pretending to warm her hands, and soon the conversation she'd interrupted resumed its course.

"Anyway, be careful of the gray tar coming out of House Manwaring. It's not safe," the homeless man said.

Gray tar? What's that?

"It's not even a decent head rush. Heard it's supposed to make you stronger, more resilient, but the people who take it, they get fearsome strange after a while."

As Thalia parsed that information, she recalled Raff saying that the soldiers from House Manwaring that attacked them after the hunt smelled strange. Off. *Maybe they were using this gray tar?* Perhaps it was developed to make her people better able to stand up to the Animari and Golgoth in combat. That meant the other houses intended to go to war, following Ruark to potential annihilation. A cold chill suffused her.

Deciding she had warmed herself long enough to seem casual, Thalia returned to the hostel, still thinking about what she'd learned. Nobody seemed to be paying attention when she slipped into the grungy closet of a room. She made a point not to look in the mirror or she would have had to face the pale, frightened woman in the mirror.

Not a queen, just a terrified nobody.

By the time Ferith came back, she had herself in hand, calm and stoic once more. The Noxblade dumped her purchases on the bed. "Here's what I could find. Hope it's enough."

Russet hair dye, disposable brown contacts, varied

cosmetics, cheap, thick trousers and a heavy sweater. "I can work with this. I've got an idea."

"That's good, because once you're geared up, I have a lead on someone who supplies provisions to Braithwaite."

THERE WERE NO Noxblades left in Daruvar.

And Raff's wife had gone to *personally* assassinate her political rival. What the fuck was wrong with the Eldritch anyway? He leashed a snarl, chained up his rage, when all he wanted to do was shift and track Thalia in wolf form. Fighting his instincts had never been so fucking tough.

He had only a rudimentary idea about the chain of command since he was supposed to be a damned consort, no actual power, but now suddenly, command of Daruvar's forces had fallen into his lap. Questions about supplies, costs, and when to reorder, well, he knew even less about that shit, and there was a goddamned queue of people outside the strategy room waiting for his word.

Raff cast a helpless glance at Sky. "Can't you help me out? I don't even manage the minutiae at Pine Ridge."

She leveled a sharp look at him. "Maybe it's time you did. Don't look at me, anyway. I scheduled a call with Bibi to try and get a handle on why your wife's former head of the assassin guild might suddenly murder you." Saying that, she got up, opened the door, and sauntered out, which seemed to send the signal that he was available.

Damn it all.

An Eldritch male he recognized as a soldier stepped in as Sky left, executed a deep bow, and remained standing until Raff waved an impatient hand at the seat opposite. "I don't suppose I can stop you from telling me what you want."

"First, I should introduce myself. I'm Commander Olwyn. We met briefly at the wedding, but...well."

Yeah, best not to linger on that memory, Raff thought. He also figured he could be forgiven not remembering names when the event turned into such a horror show.

Olwyn went on, "The princess left instructions that all our forces answer to you in her absence, so I'll be taking my orders from you, sir."

"And what would those be?"

"Sir?"

"What orders do you imagine I have?"

"I'm not paid to imagine things, sir, but I've got a list of issues in hand that demand your immediate attention."

What the hell.

It was the height of poor judgment to leave him in charge of a demesne that he barely understood. Hell, he didn't even know the patrol assignments in Daruvar, and this pasty Eldritch fool had a roster of fires he was supposed to put out? His first impulse was to scramble, just as he had when he was a pup and the teachers produced a complex assignment that made his head hurt. He imagined how sweet the woods would smell and how good it would feel to run, the wind blowing through his fur—

But the stakes were much higher now. Thalia's people would suffer if he refused to take up the slack in her absence, and for whatever reason, she'd trusted him to keep the home fires burning. Raff didn't let himself think about anything else; she was coming back, and he'd *absolutely* have a chance to make things right when she did. If Raff went to the woods, it would only be to gather intel from Titus's people, and after he dealt with Commander Olwyn's emergencies.

"I'm listening," he said, finally quashing the urge to flee.

"First, let's talk about Daruvar. We need to vary our patrol routes, and then we should talk about drone deployment..."

At first, the questions weren't too bad, but then the commander started asking stuff about places Raff had never even been. "Let's discuss options for increasing protection on our settlements. The threat level has risen, and we've skirmished with soldiers from Houses Gilbraith and—"

"Hold up, has this escalated to a full-out civil war?"

Commander Olwyn wore a grave look. "We're at the cusp, sir. If not now, soon, and if we don't have measures in place, civilian casualties could be catastrophic."

"You're telling me that the rest of the houses..." Except for Gilbraith, Raff was blanking on the other names. "Wouldn't hesitate to strike at Thalia like hyenas, nipping away at her, until they take her down?"

"If that's possible," Olwyn said, "if she can't hold what's hers, then she's not fit to rule."

"Fuck. And you call *us* animals," he muttered.

"*I* don't," Olwyn said.

"Fine, come on. Let's map it out."

He spent a full two hours discussing strategy, while well-aware that he wasn't Korin's equal when it came to planning and tactics, but Olwyn nodded with satisfaction once he saw what Raff had in mind. "That should mitigate our lack of walls, though we'll need to dig the mines up once we settle things with House Gilbraith."

"You don't doubt the princess? Even though she's gone off without telling you shit about her schemes and left you with me?"

Olwyn shook his head. "I wasn't even a soldier originally, sir. I started with her from the very beginning, when I worked in the kitchens at Riverwind. She asked me to enlist and to train, to prepare myself for the struggle to come, because she needed loyal men."

"And you did all of that, rose through the ranks, just because she asked?"

The other man raised a brow. "Aren't you doing all of *this*, just because she asked? Besides, it's rather special that she did. How often does a princess take note of someone from the kitchen? I wasn't all that attached to the pot-scrubbing anyway, if you must know the truth."

Raff laughed. "I guess not. If we're done for now, send the next petitioner in."

"Understood. Thanks for your time."

It was nothing short of miraculous what Thalia had accomplished; under house arrest, she'd built a loyal retinue who would fight for her to the last. He could do no less.

A plump woman came in next, her pale hair twisted up in a complicated do, but he could tell by her somber attire that she must be staff. Maybe it wasn't fair, but since they all had pasty skin, fair hair, and light eyes, it was damned hard for Raff to tell most of these Eldritch apart. The fact that they didn't show age in the Animari way only made his life more complicated, and shit was already tough enough.

"How can I help you?" he said in what he hoped was a pleasant tone.

"Well, I'm Madam Isoline, the chatelaine, a fancy way of saying housekeeper, I suppose. I keep Daruvar running, keep the fortress relatively clean and the soldiers fed."

"Gotcha. And...?"

"Funds are running low, sir. We need to tighten our belts, or the princess must sell something to keep the fortress going as it has been, but with tensions as they are right now, finding a buyer for jewelry or property could be…challenging."

"Right, which leaves us cutting expenses. What are my options?"

He wouldn't ask his wolves to come to their aid again. Soldiers were one thing, and the need was dire at the time, but no way in hell would he let Animari civilians deliver provisions in the middle of the Eldritch civil war. Not only would that be dangerous for his people, he also didn't want to give their enemies the chance to hijack the supplies.

"Food," she said softly. "I hate to make this recommendation, sir, but I believe it's time for us to go on rations. The soldiers need the best of what we have left, and the rest of us will…make do."

Raff could picture the kitchen staff eating porridge for days and the severity of the situation registered all over again. "I appreciate your dedication and your sacrifice. Princess Thalia does as well."

"We know, sir, we all do. That's why we're with her—and you—until the end."

27.

THALIA GAZED AT her reflection in awe.

Lileth probably wouldn't even recognize her. The change in coloring made all the difference, and the cheap, bulky clothes added volume to her figure, lending the impression that she could be Animari. Which was vital to their plan.

"What do you think?" Ferith asked.

"It's an impressive transformation. I don't think anyone will look closely at me." She checked the time then. "Too late to make contact with the vendor?"

Ferith nodded. "We should snatch a few hours of sleep and then go to the warehouse near dawn. From what I hear, they deliver supplies early."

"Understood." The room had one bed, and the other woman started to settle on the rickety chair near the window. "We can share," Thalia added.

"I appreciate the offer, but I can keep watch more effectively from here. The security in this place is terrible, or rather should I say, nonexistent."

"It'll keep us out of the cold, so we're better off than many in Outwater."

Ferith cast her a quizzical look, so she elaborated on her brief encounter at the fire barrel, disposing of her hair and the revelation about the gray tar. When she finished, the Noxblade sighed.

"That was unwise. I agree that those people need our help, but we're in no position to deliver it right now. You risked our mission...for what?"

Thalia almost said, *to destroy evidence of who I am,* but that answer didn't feel quite right or completely true. In her disbelief that even Ruark Gilbraith could be so cruel, she'd wanted a closer look at those people, hoping they had some reason other than desperation for huddling around that fire. Closer inspection hadn't comforted her at all. They had all been cold and hungry, lines of pain and deprivation carved into their faces, Eldritch faces that normally showed no age.

"I understand your anger, and I won't take such a foolish risk again. But if anything, I'm more determined to win now. I have to, so that I can redistribute wealth and implement long-needed social programs."

Ferith snorted. "You don't need to convince me. This isn't a campaign stop."

"If an election would work, I'd ask Ruark to let the people decide, but that's never been our way."

"No, such things have always been decided in shadows and blood."

"It's ironic, when you consider it."

"What is?"

"That I'm trying to usher in a kinder, gentler future through the most brutal means."

"Stop waxing philosophical and go to sleep," Ferith snapped.

On a creaky bed with questionably clean linens, Thalia

shouldn't have been able to sleep at all, but she did. Maybe it was Ferith's presence on watch that let her snatch a few hours of rest. Whatever the reason, she woke full of grim resolve. She washed up in cold water and popped in the brown contacts. It was like looking at a stranger's face.

"Ready?" Ferith called softly.

"I am. Is it far to the warehouse?"

"About a kilometer. Do you have something for the necessary bribe?"

Thalia twirled the flower pin in her fingers. Small and pretty, the broach was just valuable enough to tempt someone but not make them question where such a treasure had come from. "Right here. Let's go."

They left the hostel in the hazy predawn light. Mist rose up from the ground, which was still cold, but it was already warmer than it had been, creating pockets of fog. The haze gave the town an eerie, ghostly air, as if they crept along the rim of reality, skating up against other worlds. Ferith's footsteps were supernaturally silent, and Thalia tried to match the assassin's stealth, but she lacked the same years of dedicated training.

None of the businesses they passed were open, and maybe it was strange to be so hungry when all she needed to do was focus on killing Ruark Gilbraith, but she imagined piping hot pastries stuffed with roast vegetables and cheese, hot bowls of soup thick with barley and—

Stop, she scolded herself. *You can eat whatever you want once he's dead.*

"Do you regret marrying the wolf?" Ferith asked suddenly.

"What?" She couldn't be more surprised if the Noxblade had slapped her.

"I just wondered. You left in secret with only a note. It seemed to me you would have included him in your plan, if you truly valued him."

"Regret isn't the right word," she said. "I still think the move was right for our people. We wouldn't have come this far without wolf tech and their martial support."

"But he's not your partner."

Thalia sighed. "Let's stop. I can't believe I have to say this but stay on task."

"Understood, Your Highness. But you're not thinking about your empty stomach anymore, are you?" Ferith grinned.

"That...is true. How did you know?"

"I heard it growling. More than once. But it's a good detail to sell our story. How likely is it that the heir to a great house would starve herself?"

"You make a good point. Is that the warehouse?"

A squat, corrugated metal building sprawled across broken pavement. From the overall look of Outwater, Ruark Gilbraith had given nothing back to the town that supported his estate. Taxes were set by the province ruler, and Thalia suspected he had been robbing these people for years. The roads were a mess, the people were hungry, some were homeless, and almost everyone wore threadbare clothing. Fury raged through her like wildfire.

"Enough," she said through her teeth. "This is enough, there will be no more."

"Easy. Remember your cover story," Ferith cautioned.

At this hour, they were already loading the crates of produce onto vehicles, supplies that Ruark had probably paid only a pittance for, demanding it as tribute, as part of his noble entitlement. Pulling his heart out with her bare hands would be too good for him.

She adjusted her expression to match the story they were selling and stepped hesitantly toward the workers.

"Sir? Could I have a moment of your time?"

The man idling near the front of the Rover did a double take when he saw her, so she guessed her disguise must be effective. "You're a long way from home, miss."

He thinks I'm Animari. Perfect.

"I have no choice," she whispered. "My family won't let me be with the one I love. Even if I die, I have to see him at least once more. Could you help me?"

She got a skeptical look in exchange for her best acting. "What're you saying?"

"He works in the kitchen at Braithwaite. I've tried to get a message in, but it doesn't send, I'm not sure why."

The driver spat. "That Ruark Gilbraith is a paranoid bastard. I'm sure he has jammers, controlling messages in and out. Worried about traitors and spies, they say."

It's assassins he should fear.

"Well, I just want to see Eldred's face one last time. I'll help you unload your boxes in exchange for a ride in. I'll just speak with him for a moment and leave with you. Isn't there a way you can help me?"

"Your family disapproves?" the driver guessed.

"His too."

"They would. But it *does* seem heartless not to let you say farewell. I suppose that's why they sent him to work at Braithwaite? Best way to keep you two apart."

"I know," she said sadly.

"I'd like to help, I would, but I'd be risking more than my job to smuggle you in, sweetheart. Do you understand what I'm saying?"

Thalia widened her eyes, hoping she looked sweet, harmless, guileless. "You need more motivation? Well...I have this. It belonged to my grandmother." She spread her fingers to reveal the flower pin, sparkling in the sun that was trying to rise above the trees. So far it hadn't banished the mist.

The driver smiled and plucked it out of her hand. "We have a deal. Put on a hat and some goggles, ride in back and keep your eyes down. We're leaving in fifteen minutes."

TIME WAS TICKING away, and every moment Raff lost, he wouldn't get back again. Not because he might fuck up and Gavriel might impale him as a result.

His problem was something else entirely. The longer he spent away from Thalia, in bitter, icy silence, the worse he felt. By now he couldn't even breathe for the panic tightening on his heart. He told himself, *she's fine, she's probably fine,* but not knowing, not having her within arms' reach might drive him crazy. Already, he was itchy as fuck, pacing like a caged animal in the cold, echoing chamber that felt so lifeless without her.

She might be facing down Ruark Gilbraith right now. Might be dying on his sword. Fuck, she could be a lifeless skull, just like Tirael, atop Gilbraith's walls. Certain Eldritch customs were just fucking sick; it was absurd they considered the Animari less advanced.

At least we don't poison each other and train our children as assassins.

Sometimes he could believe the allegation that the Eldritch had bred the Golgoth for battle, eons ago, because both peoples were both brutal and terrifying. The Eldritch just hid it better, behind delicate manners and quiet elegance.

Commander Olwyn stopped him in the hall, his eyes full of questions. "I hear you've put the staff on rations. How long can we hold out?"

"I'm not sure. You'd better talk to the chatelaine."

This is all too fucking heavy. He heard his old man then: *"Why are you pretending? You were never good for anything but drinking, fucking up, and running away."*

Sometimes he thought maybe it would be better if his father was dead, because then, maybe he could forgive him. But he'd gone quietly mad instead. Sometimes the old bastard was a half-feral wolf, and sometimes he was a pathetic soul who cried endlessly and asked for Raff's mother. He couldn't even hate somebody like that.

It was getting hard to breathe and Olwyn was still talking. More troop questions, more strategic meetings? No fucking way.

Before he made the conscious decision, he was running, out the door and through the hallway. Though it was dark, he could see perfectly well and navigated the labyrinth of corridors to the courtyard, where he demanded they open the gates. The guards didn't question him, just as well, because he only had a head full of fear and rage, no words to temper his snarls. If they'd thought he was a beast before, his behavior tonight would confirm all their worst doubts.

Better to get out and run, clear his head, and maybe he could get some information from Titus's people. If Raff was lucky, he might even run into some enemies that he could chew to pieces. Outside the gate, he stripped and tucked his clothes beneath a tumble of stone. It wasn't even cold enough to make him shiver, and the night was clear, stars glittering overhead like they had somebody to impress.

He didn't know what shifting felt like to anyone else, but for him, it was a relief, like letting go of the strings that kept him in man-shape. Sometimes Raff thought he was supposed to be a wolf; that was easy and natural. Being a man? Hard as fuck.

In wolf form, he ran, blending into the lengthening shadows. Part of him knew this wasn't responsible. He should stay put, keep being the tower of power that everyone else could lean on, but he could *feel* himself unraveling.

If he took a break, he might be able to wait for her. Calmly, with composure. She had to know none of this shit was his strong point, and she'd just left, like that, leaving behind only a fucking note. As a rule, Raff didn't memorize things he'd read. He couldn't recite poems or sing along with music he heard. But that goodbye letter was etched on his heart.

> *I've gone to kill Ruark Gilbraith. If I succeed, I'll be back.*
> *If not, you're free to do as you wish. Well, you're free*
> *anyway. Please look after Daruvar in my absence and*
> *extricate yourself safely from our territory if I fail. –T*

No salutation, no closing, not even her whole name. He couldn't cry in wolf form, but he could howl, and he did. Not at the moon, but at the torrent of conflicted emotions rioting through him. He hated her, he wanted her back, he wanted to burn something down and hold her tight, all at the same time.

Why the hell does she do everything alone?

It was him; it *had* to be him. He'd been too honest

about his flaws and, so she knew too much to trust him when she needed someone most. These thoughts were killing him, so he cut them out with ruthless dedication and focused on the wind in his fur, the damp earth beneath his paws, and the myriad scents hanging fresh in the early spring air.

His head finally, blissfully empty, he ran down a rabbit and ate it raw. Then he was calm enough to search the trees in the zones Titus had shown him. The first three spots had no new markings, but toward the border, he found trail sign, recently left, too. He recognized the scent as one of the Animari who had met up with Titus at the cabin, but not a person he'd encountered in the flesh.

It had taken him hours to memorize their code while Sky alternately sobbed and slept, but now he could read the word left behind. *Enemy on the move from the east.* That would be Gilbraith's people, maybe coming for Thalia's head. *Just as well she's not here.* Raff didn't think Ruark would lead the assault. Everything he knew about the asshole suggested Gilbraith was a coward.

First, Gilbraith tried to coerce Thalia into marrying him, then he went after her using a secret, hidden half-sibling. *What's the next move?*

Suddenly the idea hit so hard that he practically saw sparks. *Gavriel.* If he returned now, nobody would question it and he'd have access to anything he wanted inside the fortress. The scenario Sky had glimpsed in her vision might come to pass under one circumstance—if that red-eyed bastard betrayed Thalia and came for her on Ruark's payroll, he might easily shift targets when he found only Raff instead. Not out of frustration, but to weaken her support.

If I die, Korin will cut our losses and step out of Eldritch business. Leaving Thalia alone against her enemies.

The rabbit roiled in his stomach. Like a dumbass, he'd run off without telling anyone where he was going. Daruvar was essentially open for the taking, if someone had clearance to get inside. But that was probably just Raff's wild imagination working overtime.

Gavriel loved Thalia. That devotion had been clear to pretty much everyone at the conclave.

Yeah, and watch how fast a twisted love goes bad. Loving someone who didn't love you back? It could drive you to desperate, unforgivable acts.

Dread gave him wings as he raced back to the fortress, half expecting to find it in flames when he crested the steep hill. It all seemed quiet enough when he crept up to the walls, but caution never hurt. Silently, he shifted and dressed, out of the guards' sight, before signaling at the gate for entry. They shone a light down and watched for a good two minutes to make sure his arrival wasn't a trap.

"I'm alone," he snapped as the heavy iron doors finally ground open. "Has anyone else come tonight?"

"Just Gavriel and Magda," the sentry replied.

Shit. It's started. And I don't even know what chain of events I need to stop.

28.

"**I** HAVE TO go alone," Thalia said.

Ferith clenched her fists and paced, eyeing her like she wanted to protest. Finally, she answered, "Did you even *try* to make up a story that included both of us?"

She shook her head. "This was the most believable, and one person seems harmless enough. If I added you to the mix, how would I explain it? You're not even in disguise."

"True." The Noxblade let out a long, exasperated breath, but her eyes were dark with worry. "If anything happens to you—"

"Then I wasn't meant to lead. Don't hesitate to swear fealty to whomever emerges on top in the grapple for the throne."

A sudden slap rocked Thalia back on her heels, and she gaped at Ferith, tasting the blood now trickling from her mouth from where her inner lip split against her teeth. She touched her mouth in silent shock, but there was more startlement to come.

Ferith glared at her. "If you go in with that mindset, you *will* fail, and you *will* die. We came to win, your highness. I'll do my best to get in on my own and back you up, but if I can't, your brain and your blade will carry the day. Do you understand?"

Her eyes teared up, not from the pain. Nobody had ever cared enough to slap her before. Not even Lileth. *Ferith...Ferith is my friend.* She'd never had one before, at least not so that she was certain. It was all distance and protocol and etiquette, endless years of it.

She blinked away signs of weakness and nodded.

"Yes," Thalia said.

She didn't waste her breath on any last words. Whatever it took, she'd get this done and meet up with Ferith afterward. Raff, too. She felt strong enough for that confrontation as well. Without a single look back, she hurried toward the vegetable truck and found the vendor waiting at the back.

He hesitated, studied her split lip and then said, "Was that one of your boyfriend's relatives?"

Ah, he saw that.

Thalia lowered her head, pretending to be too cowed for eye contact. "Yes. She didn't even want me to say goodbye to Eldred."

"She didn't have to hit you," he muttered. "Well, get in back and keep quiet. If they inspect the goods, let me do the talking."

"All right. Thank you."

Raff would laugh at her impression of a meek Animari female, mostly since she'd never met anyone who fit that profile, but her people didn't have much experience with them, so this was the best way to elicit sympathy. She hopped into the cargo area and the doors closed. Two or three men got in the front, and the vehicle juddered into motion.

Good thing they didn't search me for weapons. If we pass through security, things could go sideways quick.

Most wars were won on the battlefield, but this one would be fought in secret, and it would be over in seconds. *I will prevail. I must.* But now that she was alone and moving forward with no way back, fear settled into the open spaces, the shadows and the doubts she'd hidden in her heart. Tirael's words haunted her.

You're not better. Not more royal or more worthy. You're just luckier.

Well, if that was true, let it continue to be so. A little chill prickled across her skin, then—a possibility so improbable that it had never occurred to her, not until this moment. She thought back to all her near misses, the times she should've died, and might have, if not for some unlikely twist of fate or a quirk of—

Luck. That's my gift.

Her whole life, she'd thought she didn't have one, but it was just so quiet and subtle that she'd missed it. Until now.

It was only a hypothesis, but if she was right, the gift of good fortune would be why even the most improbable plans broke in her favor. *Now that I know, I can factor for it.* There also remained the potential that she was completely wrong, and that if she tried to call on it to make Ruark Gilbraith die, she would be bitterly, brutally disappointed. At the worst possible moment. On the other hand, using her gift consciously would burn a lot more of her life than tapping it accidentally, as she had been doing.

It doesn't matter. Even if I only live as long as the Animari, I can still accomplish a lot. If I defeat Ruark Gilbraith.

Her mind made up, she closed her eyes and tried to activate her gift. She'd always avoided discussions of the subject, she had no idea how other people went about using their abilities. For all Thalia knew, it might be different for everyone. Nothing popped in her mind, no sparks flickered from her fingers, so she had no idea if her luck was active when the vehicle stopped.

She couldn't see where they were, but they had paused once while she was trying to activate her luck, and she'd heard the grind of heavy gates being opened. *We must be somewhere inside Braithwaite by now.* Like she had been instructed, she stayed quiet despite the movement outside.

Booted feet moved around the perimeter, and she heard voices, the low rumble of laughter, but she couldn't make out what was being said. Tension brought her shoulders nearly up to her ears, and she tried to make herself smaller, as if she could will herself invisible. *Heh, if I could do that, I wouldn't have needed to get help from a provisioner.*

The back doors popped open and soldiers dressed un-mistakably in Gilbraith colors stared at her with icy eyes. Then they leveled their weapons on her. "Come out."

"Sir?"

"Step out of the vehicle. Now."

Fight or comply?

She had only a split second to decide, then the vegetable dealer stepped into view. "It's all right. I told them you're my new helper. They just need to do a routine scan, that's all. As long as you're not smuggling anything into the house, you'll be fine."

Thalia strangled the hysterical impulse to laugh. *Like weapons or poison?* She didn't want to kill the man who had been kind enough to get her this far, but if a fight started here, he would sound the alarm and tell the other guards what she looked like, if she left him alive. *I've got to buy some time.*

"Sorry, I'm just a bit nervous," she whispered.

Thalia inched forward, making it look like she feared their weapons, when in fact, she could've taken them away in three moves. Two more to kill both guards. But she wasn't ready to reveal herself yet. Not unless this encounter went bad.

"Here she comes," the vendor said.

When she emerged from the stack of crates, she watched the guards' tension level ratchet down. Physically, she didn't appear to pose much of a threat. They couldn't see her bracers or her hidden twin blades. The minute they started searching, though—

Stop it. Bring on the luck.

She focused hard, reaching, and then she heard it, a soft whispering chime in her left ear. Maybe it didn't mean anything, but she relaxed a trifle as she dropped from the truck onto the loose gravel of the drive. No paved roads inside his compound? Ruark really was a cheap bastard. She mustered a faint smile for the sentries and the vendor clasped her shoulder.

"No worries, this is business as usual. We'll be on our way in two minutes."

"Take off your glasses, miss. We'll start with a retinal scan."

Oh, fuck, Thalia thought.

And something to west exploded.

Six hours earlier

RAFF EYED GAVRIEL, but so far, the Noxblade hadn't produced the spear from Sky's vision. At the moment, he was pacing, fists clenched, after hearing that Thalia had gone with Ferith on what might be an impossible mission. He'd punched Raff in the face over letting her go alone— fair, so he'd taken the hit—but when Gavriel came at him again, Raff sidestepped and slapped the asshole in the back of the head.

"Enough. We have to decide how to proceed."

He still didn't know if he could trust Gavriel, as the treachery scenario still burned bright in the back of his head as one possibility, and he hadn't gotten the chance to talk to Mags privately yet. She might know if Gavriel had turned; she would have noticed any sketchy behavior or clandestine meetings. Picking up on that shit was her job in Ash Valley.

Most of him wanted to say, 'fuck it' and rush to Thalia's aid, but a small portion couldn't desert Daruvar when she'd left the place—and her people—under his protection. He also couldn't see leaving the fortress with Gavriel, given what Sky had foreseen. Maybe that made him a superstitious fool, but he had to plan his course carefully and pick the path that didn't end in tragedy.

I need the best of both worlds.

"Let's have your brilliant plan," Gavriel demanded.

Once, Raff would've made a joke about how that wasn't his wheelhouse, but right now, Thalia needed his best, so he dug deep, and it wasn't even that hard, when he reached for it. Without answering, he spun and strode toward the strategy room. Gavriel was still yapping at him, but Raff tuned him out as he reprogrammed the drones currently patrolling nearby. They'd all be back at base within half an hour.

The Noxblade grabbed his shoulder just as Magda came in. Her hair was freshly braided, and once Raff would have paid her a compliment or flirted a little, but those days were done. This task was too important to delay.

"Leave him alone, he's trying to help your princess." When Gavriel didn't let go, Mags grabbed his arm and twisted. "Do we have to fight...again?"

Gavriel glared at her and uncoiled his fingers. "Don't test me."

"Why, do you like it or something?"

"Get out of my way or get a fucking room," Raff snapped.

He pushed past them and ran for the stockpile his people had laid in before they left. Food would have been nice for the hungry workers in the kitchen, but instead, he had crates of munitions. If Thalia succeeded at Braithwaite, if Raff's idea proved helpful at all, the scarcity of supplies would cease to be an issue after today.

All or nothing.

The other two followed him, and the group picked up Commander Olwyn along the way. "Do you know how to arm and load the drones?" he asked.

Mags nodded, but the Eldritch men offered blank looks. Raff sighed. "I'll teach Olwyn. Mags, you show Gavriel the ropes. We need these in the air as soon as possible."

"You're striking at Braithwaite," she guessed.

"Damn right I am. I'll drop payloads on the fences. I don't know exactly where Thalia is, but if she's already inside, the distraction will draw forces away, and if she's trying to get in, a breach in their defenses can only help her."

"You're planning to bombard a location where—" Gavriel clamped his teeth on the words, looking as if he meant to chew them and spit them out. "What an idiotic idea!"

"It's the best I can do from here," Raff said. "She left Daruvar in my care, but I'll be damned if I leave her without backup. I can program the drones to scan for her, and if she's nearby, I'll abort the strike."

"Do it," Mags urged. "I agree with your assessment, and it seems unlikely that she can take out Ruark Gilbraith with only one Noxblade at her side."

Thalia and Ferith, against a small army. He got cold chills just thinking about it, and he let out a snarl, nearly losing control of the fear and rage that made him want to go wolf and start running. *No, can't do that again.*

With their help, Raff armed the drones with explosive shells. Good thing that the heavy weapons the Golgoth favored hadn't reached Eldritch territory yet. One CTAK could've brought down the walls at Daruvar and turned the tide for Gilbraith, but the bulk of Tycho's forces were scattered, the majority concentrated in bear country, which was Callum's problem, not his.

"All right, new flight pattern laid in. I'll monitor remotely from the strategy room. Payloads will deploy in five and a half hours."

NOBODY HAD STIRRED from the room, even when the chatelaine brought tea. There was nothing extra to be had in the larder, so Raff downed the herbal mess with a grimace and tried not to think about how hungry he was. If he was better at planning, he would've hunted down more than a rabbit. Still, the hot liquid did fill up his stomach a little. Magda caught his eye and made a face in sympathy.

"You don't like it?" Gavriel asked, but he was talking to

Mags.

"It tastes like wet weeds."

Raff agreed, but he wouldn't say so as Madam Isoline was gathering the dirty dishes. He'd never noticed this about Mags before, but she didn't much care about people's feelings. The housekeeper had doubtless done her best with limited supplies.

"Tact can be charming. You should read up on it," he said to Mags.

She laughed. "Fuck that. Honesty is the best policy. That way nobody can ever claim they didn't know what I'm about."

"I'm sorry," the chatelaine said quietly. "Will there be anything else?"

"No, thank you." Raff gentled his tone.

Huh. Thalia's people feel like mine. When did that happen? But there was no denying that he had the same urge to protect the Eldritch, just like they were members of his own pack. In fact, he was about ready to fight Magda over her rudeness; he squashed that urge with effort.

Commander Olwyn cleared his throat, likely noting the awkward atmosphere. "Are the drones on target?"

He stood, heading over to the screen to check, though he'd inspected their progress not more recently. "ETA ten minutes now. Too soon to scan for the princess specifically, but I'm not showing any humanoid life signs to the west."

"That will be perfect as a distraction," the commander said.

Mags nodded. "Let's hope she's found a way inside."

With a sibilant curse, Gavriel lunged to his feet and started to pace. He didn't look any paler than usual because his skin was like steamed fish already, but his blood-red eyes blazed murder, and his hair whipped around like his anger gave it electricity. Raff pretended not to notice that wrath; it wouldn't help if they fought but waiting sucked.

Come back to me, he thought. *I have a lot left to say.*

"I tried calling her," Gavriel said then. "But her phone is off."

Raff smirked. "If that surprises you, then you're dumber than you look."

"She's smart to run silent. There's always a way to pick up on electronic chatter. Coming in quick and quiet offers the best chance for success," Mags noted.

He hated how impersonal she sounded, like Thalia's life didn't matter. As his temper flared, the symbols on the screen reached their target, one by one, and flared red, indicating multiple successful strikes. "It's done. Only time will tell if we made a difference."

Gavriel grabbed him by the shirt front. "If she falls to Gilbraith, if you let her die, I'll kill you. I hope you know that."

Suddenly what Sky had seen made sense, only it wasn't what he'd feared. Vengeance, not treachery.

Raff only nodded. "My life is in your hands."

29.

T HALIA RAN.

She didn't have much time, after slipping away outside the kitchens. Instead of searching for the fictitious Eldred, she had to hunt down Ruark Gilbraith and kill him. Maybe she had Ferith to thank for the distraction, but whatever the case, she still had a job to do. Braithwaite was in utter chaos, thanks to the explosions still booming to the west.

Mentally she reviewed the plans she'd memorized and tried to guess where Gilbraith would be. A strong leader might be at the front, directing his troops, but since he'd never once attacked her in person, that seemed unlikely. *No, he'll be hiding somewhere in case the danger is severe.* Workers ran past her, fleeing from various parts of the house, which was old and built of pale stone, too many windows to be considered secure.

A soldier stopped her, as she headed for Ruark's private quarters. "Who—"

Thalia ended it there with a twist of a poison blade. The guard gurgled and fell; she hurried away from the body. No time to waste. Now the clock was ticking. With people running everywhere, they'd know the enemy had gotten inside but covering her tracks wasn't worth it. The survivors would all swear fealty, no matter what she did here.

Thalia kept her head down, and though she got a few looks, due to her Animari disguise, nobody cared enough to chase her down. Deeper into the wing set aside for Ruark and his cronies, she saw fewer and fewer people. It seemed like many of his followers were scrambling to loot the place and save themselves in case this was a full-scale invasion.

Timing it carefully, she waited out a couple of guards who seemed to be on alert and patrolling the wing, but most of them had gone to investigate the bombardment. *Lucky me.* The explosions finally stopped, which meant she didn't have long. Ruark's officers would knock the lower ranks back into place soon enough.

They won't get the chance.

On her way through, Thalia heard fighting in other parts of the house. *Ferith must have found a way in.* Her own progress was burning luck—and life—each moment she ran unchallenged, but it was worth it. Once she found Ruark, she might never need to use her gift again. A flicker of a feeling led her to turn right, and toward the end of the corridor, she glimpsed a squad of six fully armed Noxblades. All their weapons would be poisoned, and they were on high alert.

Ruark is behind the door they're guarding.

Taking a deep breath, she stilled just around the corner to assess what she could use to turn the situation to her advantage. The six needed to die quick and quiet or Ruark would be ready to fight the second she walked in, and she might need the element of surprise to guarantee a win. Pushing her luck too far might kill her. Literally.

And I don't want to keel over from blazing out here. I want a life. With Raff.

That certainty leveled her out, so that her heart stopped hammering in her ears and she surveyed the scene with a second stolen glance. Lights overhead. A shot from her bracers might short them out, a gamble worth taking. Before she could overthink, Thalia wheeled out into the open and sent a streak of lightning zinging into the light strip overhead. The lights dropped, as she'd hoped, and she fired twice more, then sent a glass vial spinning at them. That was one of Ferith's favorites, a smoke toxin that would melt their lungs and leave them vomiting blood, but it would take a while before she could pass safely to kill Ruark.

One of the Noxblades stumbled toward her, slashing with clumsy hands. It was hard to be a graceful, elegant dealer of death when your eyes were oozing blood. She backed away as the emergency lights built into the walls flickered on. The red strobes lent the dying assassin a surreal air. He lunged at her and hit the wall as she danced away. Really, she should just shoot him, but it was more fun to watch him slide down the wall, leaving bloody handprints. The rest of them stayed in the poison cloud, choking and dying in such a painful way that Ferith might have even winced.

"Darien?" A male voice called from behind the door. "What's happening out there?"

Darien must be dead, she figured.

She didn't answer. It would be funny if Ruark stumbled into her poison trap, but she should've known he wasn't brave enough. In the end, she killed two more patrols while waiting out the cloud. The rest of her poisons all required contact or ingestion, as it was dangerous to carry too many of those vials. If you ever put a foot wrong, it was an easy yet excruciating way to die.

She tossed a meter strip to make sure the air was good and when the test paper came back yellow, she rushed to the door, stepping over the bodies. The door was locked, but she found the keys on a Noxblade's body, the one who had gotten closest to her. Probably Darien. Silently, she unlocked the door, using all her strength to shove aside the furniture Ruark was trying to hide behind.

Thalia rolled into the room and came up on one knee. Ruark's knife slammed into the wall just above her head. She fired once with her bracer. Not a kill shot, but current strong enough to leave him twitching on the floor. Without hesitation, she rushed at him and didn't say a single word as she slit his throat. He tried to gargle at her, but it was probably bullshit anyway, so she put her foot on his face until he quieted.

That's for Lileth.

"I win," she said. "I guess it's my lucky day."

Closing her eyes, she focused until she heard the chime in her left ear again. No need to push her luck further. The next step was fucking gruesome, but she still sawed through his neck to take his head. It would go on a spike next to Tirael's, right after she let everyone know the war was over.

I hope I never have to do this again.

Boldly, she strode from Ruark's room to find that ten guards had gathered outside. They hesitated until Thalia lifted the bloody trophy for their inspection. If they wanted to fight, she'd oblige. Her bracers were at half, and she was used to the strobe of the lights, now. She waited one heartbeat, two.

Then they dropped to their knees and bowed their heads. "Long live the queen!"

It was impossible to tell who started it, but soon they were all chanting. She let that go on for a moment, then said, "Where's the comm room? I need to send a message on all channels, all frequencies."

"This way," said a slight woman with dark gold hair.

Warily she followed in case it was a trap, but as their group moved through Braithwaite, they gathered others, none of whom seemed inclined to challenge her while she was toting Ruark's severed head.

Raff was right. We are rather monstrous.

And she wanted to change that. Taking the silver throne would be a fresh start.

"Here we are, Your Majesty."

"I'm not crowned yet."

"You will be," the woman said.

Thalia hoped that was true, but it wasn't the time to rest on her laurels. "Get me on the air," she ordered.

The closest technician scrambled, fiddling with the equipment and then he handed her the headset. "Audio only, I'm afraid."

"Good enough. The rest of you can bear witness." She plopped Ruark's head onto the nearest table and the Eldritch lowered his eyes in respect. "Play the following message on repeat for the next hour."

"Understood."

She donned the headset and spoke calmly. "This is Thalia Talfayen. House Gilbraith has fallen to me, and their lands are mine. I claim, by right of conquest, the silver throne. You have three days to send emissaries to Daruvar to pledge fealty, or you will share this traitor's fate. That is all."

HOURS AFTER THE drone strike on Braithwaite, Commander Olwyn woke Raff with an urgent shake. "You need to hear this."

Still groggy from dozing off in his chair, he processed the words slowly, followed by a wave of relief so profound that he might have fallen over, if he wasn't already sitting. "She did it."

Gavriel's shoulders slumped and he closed his eyes, lowering his head in a moment of silence. "Looks like you get to live, beast."

"I'm grateful," Raff said.

He couldn't even bring himself to bare his teeth at the Noxblade since he knew Gavriel had served Thalia well, and she couldn't have come to this point without him. Sky was curled up on the floor, asleep at Raff's feet in wolf form, and he considered waking her to share the good news, but since she'd been operating with some level of apprehensive dread ever since her first vision, he let her rest.

Mags came up next to Gavriel and set her hand on his shoulder. To Raff's astonishment, the Noxblade not only let her touch him, but he also appeared to take some comfort in the gesture. Tension slipped from his body in the few seconds they were in contact. *Interesting.*

From all around the keep, the sounds of celebration echoed in the night. Music and exuberant shouts suggested that the rest of Daruvar had heard the message as well, and while food might be in short supply, they were probably tapping the casks that had been in the wine cellar for heaven knew how long. Never in his life had Raff been the one to shut down a party, and he wasn't about to start now.

He eased to his feet and avoided waking Sky, still managing to dream on despite the ruckus. Commander Olwyn was cracking open a decanter of good whiskey, pouring shots for Gavriel and Magda, but Raff shook his head. Without making his excuses, he left the strategy room at last, feeling like he'd aged a hundred years in these hours.

The drones would be returning soon, and he set the first one to scan for Thalia. She should be back soon. He paced the walls until he couldn't feel his feet, then he went to the kitchen to get some more of the tea Mags had disparaged. The housekeeper beamed at his request, her blue eyes bright, and filled a thermos to the brim.

Didn't want that much, but...

"Thank you."

"It's my pleasure, Prince Raff."

He almost dropped the steel cylinder in surprise. "What did you call me?"

"It's your title, now that you're married to the queen. Well, she will be at any rate. I expect we'll have the fealty pledges and the coronation soon. More properly, it's Prince Consort, I suppose, but that's such a mouthful. You don't mind the short form of address?"

"Er, no," he said.

Until then, it hadn't really sunk in—what her victory meant. *I'm married to the fucking Eldritch queen.* Korin would laugh her ass off.

"Will there be anything else?"

"Get in touch with your usual supplier. We can't have people going hungry longer than they need to."

"I will," she said. "And...thank you."

He scraped a hand over his beard, suddenly self-conscious. "For what?"

"Thinking of us, of course. Old Lord Talfayen never stepped foot in a kitchen, and he lived well over five hundred years."

Mumbling a response he hoped made sense, Raff made his escape and drank all his tea in solitude. It felt like he had been waiting for Thalia for a thousand years.

At dawn, she finally came, in a vehicle painted in Gilbraith colors. When she stepped out into the courtyard, Raff went to her at a run, ignoring the dirt and the bloodstains. He picked her up and twirled her. In his arms, she felt warm and perfect, but he was afraid that maybe he couldn't hold onto her because she might melt into seafoam or shimmer into a sunbeam that disappeared when he blinked.

"I'm taking her," he said to Ferith, currently climbing out of the Rover.

"Please do."

Thalia didn't fight as he carried her bridal-style toward their quarters. "We need to talk," she said.

In a way, that was worse than kicking and screaming. Those words weighed as much as four huge stones, but he kept moving. Past the cheering throng, onward to the dim corridor that led to their room. The fire in the hearth was nearly burned down, just ashes from tending it the night before.

"About what?"

"Our future."

Frantically, he tried to remember exactly what the fucking contract said. Now that she'd secured her crown, did that she mean she wanted him to go? *I'm supposed to stay for three months, I think.* Hell, he didn't even know what he'd done wrong—that she'd leave with such an ice-cold note.

Raff folded his arms across his chest, knowing he looked defensive, but he was starting to get pissed. No greeting, no apology? *She's the one who left.*

"Go ahead," he said.

"I want to strike the no-fidelity clause from our agreement."

That startled him so much he almost fell over, and he clutched the wall in a vain attempt to recover the composure he was trying to project. "What?"

"I've thought about it, and I'm an only child. I can't help that. It means I'm completely opposed to sharing."

"Sharing...*me*?"

"That's what I said," she snapped.

"Do you think I'm sleeping around or something?"

She lifted her pointed chin, and that look was pure adorable spite. "I don't know what's going on with you and Sky, and I don't care. It stops now. I'm claiming you."

What the—oh.

Realization filtered down slowly, and he put the pieces together of what she must have seen—and how wrong her conclusions had been. Amusement and tenderness vied for dominance, and he savored both those feelings, because her aggravation meant she cared. A lot. That note hadn't been cold. She'd written it while she was pissed as hell.

Damn, I love this woman.

"Like a tract of land?" he suggested.

"Exactly. I'm planting my flag."

"What about the agreement?"

"We'll renegotiate."

"What if we just burn it and be together? We'll be here when we need to be, and in Pine Ridge when that's right."

"I want to meet your father," she said softly. "And Catrin, of course."

"You'll hate him. He's awful. He'll probably insult you. A lot."

Thalia smiled. "I can take it. If you hadn't noticed, I'm

pretty damn tough."

"That you are. You're also brilliant, beyond lovely, and you've become every bright star in the night sky of my life."

He moved to pull her into his arms, but she stopped him with a look. "Really? You actually said that?"

"Too much?"

The sparkle in her eyes said she thought he was charming but would die before admitting that she liked his flavor of cheese. "Just a bit."

"Then how about…I love you. And…please don't walk out on me again."

"Better."

There was a lot more to say, but Raff wanted to fuck. She smelled like blood and violence, and it shouldn't have been so hot. "Looks like you saw some action. Are you hurt?"

"Nothing major. I'll be fine."

"Anything you want to say before I put your mouth to better use?" That was so filthy he couldn't believe he'd said it, but her eyes glittered even more with sheer, delicious lust.

"Mm, just this."

He listened as she explained that she had been wrong about her gift—that it was luck after all. She told him everything that he'd missed and how she'd activated her power, and that the bombing saved her at exactly the right moment. Possible, he supposed, but it might be coincidence, too.

Raff cocked his head. "How can you be sure?"

"Because," Thalia whispered. "I married you."

Since he remembered saying that to her before, it was the perfect answer.

30.

THALIA TRIED TO lead Raff toward the bathroom, but he pulled back on her arm, so she spun into his arms. It was a slick move, practiced, but she wouldn't think about all the times he must've used it to perfect the maneuver. Instead, she'd focus on how well she fit against him and how delicious he smelled, soap and clean air with just a hint of wood smoke.

"Keep looking at me like that and I'll forget what I needed to say," Raff warned.

"I'm listening."

"I'm guessing you saw me comforting Sky and took off in a snit. Without letting me explain. That shit stops now. We're going to have a relationship built on mutual trust and excellent communication."

"Such lofty aspirations," she teased.

"I'm serious, woman."

She couldn't believe that she even liked hearing *that* from him. "Such a wonder when I have it on excellent authority that you rarely are."

"Well, I'm dead set on this...and you." While she watched, he searched until he found their marriage contract and fed it to the dying fire, page by page. "Now that's done, you should understand that Sky is like family, a pup who comes to me when she's scared."

"Something happened?" Thalia asked.

"Seems like the stress awakened her as a seer. She had a vision where…" He hesitated, but Thalia motioned him on. Grimly he continued, "Where you failed, and I died. Gavriel executed me for letting it happen and…I do believe it was a true glimpse of one possible, very dark future."

"Why do you think that?" Her people didn't have shamans or prophets like that, but since he wasn't arguing about her gift of luck, she wouldn't question the accuracy a wolf seer's vision. Still, she wanted to hear his response.

"Because I might well have let it happen," Raff said softly.

"If I failed, you mean. You're saying that you'd have let Gavriel kill you? That you'd die without me."

Why didn't I trust him? She might have still made the decision to go alone, but she wouldn't have been so cold about it. Wrapping her arms about his waist, she hugged Raff tightly, silently vowing never to let him go.

He stood silent.

"Never mind, you don't have to answer."

Clearing his throat, he lifted her and carried her toward the bathroom; Thalia looped her arms around his neck. The hot water probably wouldn't last long enough for them to have exhausting shower sex, but at least she could scrub away the road grime and dried blood. He turned the old-fashioned handle and stripped her down while they waited for the hot water to circulate through the elongated, ancient pipes.

"What's with your hair?" Raff ran his fingers through

the short bob and sniffed. "Smells like chemicals."

"The dye will rinse out. Growing it again will take some time."

"I've got plenty," he said, backing her into the stone shower stall with his body.

With the door shut, it was crowded, but Thalia loved the way it felt, slipping against his strong, wet body. Raff washed her first, and she didn't think he was trying to be seductive, but his hands on her felt so good that she wanted more. Teasing, he lingered on her belly, and she marveled that he always remembered the little details.

She braced her hands on his chest and closed her eyes, splaying her thighs a little more, but he didn't touch her there. No, he was brisk in washing everywhere else, including meticulous attention to scrubbing away the color from her hair. By the time he finished, the water was lukewarm, and he nudged her toward the door.

"I'll finish up quickly. Wait for me in bed."

Outside the steamy bathroom, their chamber was chilly enough to raise goose bumps on her damp, bare skin. Sometimes she swore the stones held an age of extra chill and that inside the fortress, it was colder than the spring day allowed. She dove under the covers and burrowed in. Her wet hair would probably be a mess later, but she didn't care.

Only her eyes and the top of her head were visible when Raff came out a couple of minutes later. The pale towel wrapped around his hips contrasted deliciously with the brown of his skin, and she wanted to lick up the water beading on his chest. She followed him with her eyes, until he came to her.

"You're like ice," she chided.

"Warm me up?"

He wasn't asking for an apology, but she owed him one nonetheless. "I'm sorry I got angry about what you said regarding Eldritch children. I've had a chance to think about it, and you're right. Some of our customs *are* terrible. That's one of the first changes I'll make."

"No more Noxblades?" Raff asked in evident surprise.

"There will be updates to the training timetable anyway and we'll wait until the candidates are old enough to consent."

"Beautiful *and* wise," he whispered, nuzzling at her ear.

Thalia turned her face toward his mouth like a flower seeking the sun, and she melted when his lips parted so she could taste him. The kiss went nuclear so fast; he was *hungry,* in a way he never had been before. His lips told of need and want, and each stroke of his tongue gliding deeper into her mouth filled her with the heady rush of desire.

Raff was already hard, and she smiled as she pulled back, remembering that awkward first time that never quite took off. Now she never needed to wonder if he wanted her; he didn't try to hide it. He pulled her on top of him, yielding dominance with a little growl of invitation.

"You've claimed me. Will you savor your prize?"

Grinning, she shook her head. "Would you be offended if I had you hard and fast?"

"Not this time. Feels like it's been forever since I touched you."

Still, she reveled in straddling him, feeling the slide of his hard cock against her ass as she dug her nails into his hairy chest. He hissed a breath, a curse, then lifted his hips. It would've been cruel to tease either of them further when she'd already gotten so turned on in the shower, even if he hadn't meant it as foreplay. Thalia rose up, held his shaft still, and sank down with a luxurious sound. He jerked and arched, before getting a hold of himself. From his expression, she might be torturing him instead of preparing for a wild ride.

"Good?"

"Fuck," he said.

Could've been a curse or a request—either way, Thalia started to move, her eyes slipping half closed at the delicious tension rising in her lower belly. Hot friction, the quick rise and fall of her hips. Impossible to be anything but selfish, moving so that her pleasure spiked higher and higher, but from the way he twisted and moaned beneath her, it was feeling great for him too. She caressed his chest, his shoulders, ran her fingers through his hair and touched his lower lip to feel the soft gulps of breath he couldn't hold.

"You're so hot," he whispered. "Burning me up. I should've beat one out in the bathroom first. Last longer."

"I'm glad you didn't. It means you couldn't wait and that you had to have me."

"Fucking true," Raff grunted.

She could watch his face all day, the way his head fell back when she dropped down, the way his mouth opened on a silent groan when she swiveled her hips and clamped down. Raff raised his knees and started to move under her, pumping upward in quick, short strokes. He cupped her hips in his hands, pulling her against him harder.

Suddenly, he tensed, his abs quivering. "Stop now. I can't..." A deep groan swallowed the rest of his sentence.

"It's good. Come with me."

"But—"

"If we make a baby, we do. Just come."

THALIA'S EYES SHONE like magic, like silver, in the shadow of their bedcovers. Raff surrendered to her then. She pinned his hands against the bed and rode him faster, until he couldn't hold it. Orgasm broke over him in relentless waves, up from his lower back, tightening his testicles and he shuddered with each hot spasm. She was already so wet and his come only added to the slick deliciousness of it all. Vaguely, he was aware that she hadn't quite gotten there yet, but he was too spent to do more than hold her when she slipped off his softening cock and rode his thigh to a wet, messy climax.

Fuck, she's beautiful.

Afterward, she leaned down to kiss him deeply and curl up against his chest. His whole body smelled like her, and he had zero inclination to take another shower. Her hair felt like soft down against his fingers, and he missed the long spill of it, but some sacrifices were worth it. Thalia doubtless felt the same.

"That's the first time," she said.

"What?"

"That you came inside me. Before, you were so careful."

Raff stroked her back. "With good reason."

"Just think," she murmured dreamily. "You might have just planted our babe. What would he look like? Would he have a gift or be able to shift? Or both?"

Shit, when she talked like that, he could imagine it too, though he'd never much cared about extending his father's bloodline. Now, though, he was picturing Thalia ripe with child, her belly round, breasts plump, and it was uncomfortably arousing. Suddenly, he couldn't stop envisioning how she'd taste and smell; the hormones would alter her body.

"You're getting me stirred up again."

"Already?"

Thalia touched his slippery cock like he might be joking, and yeah, it was already halfway there. He groaned and closed his eyes. "Devil woman."

"I guess you like the idea of me having your baby."

"It wasn't on my to-do list until you mentioned it," he snapped.

"Well, I'm willing. Just don't be too disappointed if I can't or if it takes a while."

He grinned. "I'll live with putting in the work, no matter the outcome."

She smiled back, eyes bright as twin stars.

Maybe Raff would have gone for round two, if someone hadn't knocked firmly on the door. Ferith called, "You have guests!"

"What the hell? Who?" Thalia pitched her voice to carry.

"Emissaries from Houses Manwaring and Vesavis. I believe they're here to pledge their loyalty and sign peace accords. And from early drone sightings, I think we'll have someone from House Gilbraith here within a couple of hours."

"Holy shit," she said.

Raff nudged her toward the edge of the bed. "Matters of state require your attention, it seems. And I'm not going anywhere without you. Promise."

Hurriedly she rose and dressed, taking him at his word. At the door, she paused. "I love you. I suspect you already know, but—"

"I do know," he said tenderly. "Go be regal."

Lounging in bed didn't seem like the right move, so he

took a quick, cold shower to settle his libido, then dressed in the suit he'd worn for their wedding service. Since then, there had been attacks, conspiracies, and funerals, but they had weathered everything together. He had every intention of being a damn good prince consort, whatever the hell that entailed.

Gavriel met him on the way to the courtyard. For once, though, the Noxblade didn't look furious, only somber. "We're preparing for her coronation. Will you program the drones to make sure there are no unpleasant surprises?"

"With pleasure."

That task kept him busy for a bit, and by the time he got to the courtyard, decorations were already being hung. The chatelaine hurried about, snapping terse orders, and crates of supplies came in by the truckload. It made sense that there would be a celebration after her official ascension to the throne.

I'm married to the queen of the Eldritch.

This time, the thought didn't startle him at all, and he resolved to step up his game in every possible way. Thalia would never lack anything due to Raff slacking off.

"You look determined," a familiar voice said.

He turned to find Korin, just arriving along with a slew of other familiar faces: Callum, the bear clan leader, Dom and Pru from Ash Valley, a pretty, red-haired woman who kept staring at Callum. After a minute, he placed her as Pru's cousin, Joss. A few minutes later, the Golgoth Prince arrived with his queen, the cat shifter, Sheyla. Maybe he should've predicted that people would turn out en masse for such an important occasion, but he still couldn't quite quell the flicker of surprise.

Still, he tried to cover. "Welcome to Daruvar. It will be

a while until the festivities start, but I can offer refreshments until then."

"We can," Thalia corrected.

She was magnificent in a silver gown with her hair standing up in spikes that somehow managed to be both elegant and fierce. Her eyes were outlined in purple, her mouth the deepest rose, and he felt like dragging her to bed all over again.

Thankfully, he resisted that urge.

"The queen cometh," Alastor quipped in the ironic tone that irritated Raff.

"Everyone's here now." Thalia didn't walk so much as glide, as if each of her steps was cushioned by air, and he loved her so much, it was tough to breathe. "There's no need to delay."

Since the staff was still scrambling to set the last pieces in place, they might disagree, but Raff wasn't about to steal her thunder. When she greeted each guest with a warm smile and a handshake, he followed her down the makeshift reception line like he knew what the hell he was doing.

I just have to smile and not fuck this up. Simple.

He'd never figure out how she'd organized all of this so fast, but sometime later, he took his seat with everyone else. This was Eldritch business; the rest of them were present as witnesses and guests. A bishop in a crimson robe presided over the occasion, intoning a deeply spiritual prayer in ancient Eldritch, then the eerie human-pipe-singing began.

Finally, Thalia took the stage in slow, measured steps, bowing her head so the bishop could place a simple silver crown on her head. The corona sparkled in the early spring sun, catching the engraved flower and ivy pattern. Though it had been polished, Raff could tell the crown was incredibly old, long stored in some deep, dark vault.

She turned to the envoys from the great houses then. "Do you pledge to me?"

"With our hearts and lands, we are your true and loyal men," they vowed.

"It is done," the bishop said. "Behold your queen, Thalia of the Silver Throne, first of her name. Long may she reign!"

Cheers went up from the courtyard, the ramparts, everywhere their people had gathered. Later, there would be wine and feasting, but Raff could not tear his eyes away as Thalia came to him amid a flurry of dried herbs and flower petals, where she'd had him waiting at the edge of the red carpet.

"This is your Prince Consort. His word is like mine. His heart is one with mine. Love and follow him as I do. We are united in purpose, and that is to drive Tycho's forces from all our lands, Animari and Eldritch alike. We will have peace. We will have freedom."

Raff believed her, as they all did, but only *he* had the right to sweep the queen into his arms and kiss the crap out of her. He'd do that later, when the pomp and circumstance were done. No question, he already had both peace and freedom, because she loved him. For now, he played the elegant gentleman, took her hand and kissed it, bowed deftly to the jubilant crowd.

As for the rest of them, they could damn well find their own happy endings.

Author's Note

I'm so thrilled that you read *The Wolf Lord* and hope you're eager for more in the Ars Numina world. *The Wolf Lord* is the third book in a projected six-book series, as follows:

The Leopard King
The Demon Prince
The Wolf Lord
The Shadow Warrior
The War Priest
The Jaguar Knight

Would you like to know when the next book will be available and/or keep up with exciting news? Visit my website at *www.annaguirre.com/contact* and sign up for my newsletter. If you're interested, follow me on Twitter at *twitter.com/msannaguirre*, or "like" my Facebook fan page at *facebook.com/ann.aguirre* for excerpts, contests, and fun swag.

Reviews are essential for indie writers and they help other readers, so please consider writing one. Your love for my work can move mountains, and I so appreciate your effort.

Finally, as ever, thanks for your time and your support.

CPSIA information can be obtained
at www.ICGtesting.com
Printed in the USA
BVHW041927270519
549367BV00012B/383/P